TO WHOM
EVIL IS DONE

KENNETH ALDER

TO WHOM
EVIL IS DONE

Author's Notes

The characters in this novel are products of imagination. The exception is Saddam Hussein former President of Iraq. The views and values of my characters are certainly not my personal views and values. The viewpoints are ones I feel might be held by extremist characters. Militant Fundamentalist Islam is a major threat to the civilized world. This is an existential threat we ignore at our peril.

The existence of biological warfare is well known. Most major governments of the world have worked and are still working with these dangerous pathogens. The creation of bio- weapons is a danger to humanity. Such destructive weaponry reflects a clear and present threat to each of us. Sadly, events in this story could happen and soon.

CHAPTER ONE

Baghdad, Iraq

Al Mariah Bomb Shelter

August 3, 2003

Iraq/United States War

It began in the midst of dust and darkness. Darkness nearly beyond comprehension. This darkness, far more than the absence of light, came as the darkness of a tomb that held the silence of death. And in truth, Death was here.

Death claimed this place as her own.

Yet she felt puzzled. Death cast her eyes through tons of shattered concrete and twisted bars. Here were hundreds of bodies of those who had every reason to live. Death smiled, she was the end of all hopes, all dreams, and all reason.

Strangely one lived. Death drew toward the solitary beating heart. A girl with olive skin and black hair lay trapped within massive blocks of shattered concrete, the only survivor out of 467 people. Darkness was no handicap. Death gazed upon the face of this young girl whose radiant dark eyes showed terror.

Then Death pulled back. *What was this?* Death felt anger replace the girl's terror. Anger transformed into tremendous raging hate. Upon the forge of hate the sword of revenge formed.

Death pondered. Seldom had death seen such hate. This was interesting, and not the time to collect this beautiful girl. Death smiled and withdrew into the void.

~ ~ ~

January 6, 1990

Evening

Baghdad

Fifteen Years Earlier

"Her name will be A'isha," said the soft-spoken street merchant known only as Ibd, his voice firm and decisive. He was small with dark features, known as a modest, kind man, with many friends, but no enemies. Active in the faith he remained generous to the poor. Ibd pushed a food cart through the market streets of Baghdad. His opinion as to the correct name for the newborn girl had never varied throughout the evening. His lifelong neighbors were in serious disagreement.

"Ibd, you must be reasonable. Allah has shown his disfavor by giving you a sixth daughter. You are vain to choose the name A'isha."

"A'isha was the favorite wife of the Prophet Mohammed himself. She fought by his side and after his death she became a judge of the people." This observation caused several other neighbors to nod their heads in agreement.

The baby's strong cries reminded each listener that another life had been granted and a name was a serious matter.

"Please," replied the tired father. "Let us wait for the Imam to arrive. He will give his opinion and I swear to Allah I will abide by his decision." "For now, I must see my wife." This quiet statement silenced the men. No one would leave. The naming of this child was a major issue for Ibd and for his neighbors.

Friends would be part of life's major decisions. The Imam was a high servant of Islam and upon his judgment the issue would be settled. A word from the Imam could bar the gates of paradise. To be in his presence was an honor. Ibd rose, grateful for his friends' counsel. They were strong fibers which gave him strength to endure the bitter world.

Ibd knelt next to his wife. "Miri, my love, thank Allah you have survived," said Ibd to the exhausted woman who lay upon a simple cot, the pain she'd endured etched on her fine-featured face.

She asked "How is the rest of the family? My labor was long."

"Do not be concerned, my love. They are safe."

Her eyes searched the face of her husband. "It was Allah's will to grant us another daughter."

Ibd answered with certainty. "Do not regret the birth of this child. She will be important to Allah. I've heard voices in my sleep."

His wife smiled. Ibd was a kind, modest husband . . . a good man in a world which cared little or nothing for the poor. This girl child would be the sixth offspring. The baby already demanded her milk.

The baby had adult eyes. The impression was unnerving. Miri asked the midwife if anything was wrong with the baby. Sadness sounded in the midwife's voice when she spoke.

"Knowledge does not always bring peace to the heart. I have known several like this child, each born to the sword. This girl has a destiny." With these words the old midwife departed.

~ ~ ~

Ibd did not pretend to understand her cryptic words. He was a simple man and his wife a modest woman. He prayed this child would be pleasing to Allah . . . was somehow special.

He had his faith, his foundation. He addressed Miri in soft tones. "Who are we to know the will of Allah? We will submit to his will."

Miri heard the knock on their door. "It must be the Imam." Ibd ran and opened the main door and greeted his honored guest. "May Allah bless you."

The Imam addressed the gathered assembly. "Greetings to each of you. May Allah bless you during the present hour and upon the hour of your death." The Imam appeared brimming with health. His voice was strong. His eyes were steady. "Peace be upon you, Ibd. Let us seek the will of the Lord."

Ibd covered the points of contention held by each of his neighbors. He explained his dreams and his own certainty. The Imam listened. He knew how the powerful considered such simple men to be trash of the earth. Yet simple men had spread the words of the Prophet across the civilized world.

But his heart troubled him. He too had strange dreams. Could this be the child to defend Islam from the onslaught of the hated infidels?

The Imam felt a strange power in their midst coming from the adjoining room. Now was his time to speak.

The Imam began. "The name of each child is important to Allah. The name of A'isha is most unusual and is not a name to bestowed lightly. It is difficult to know the will of Allah in these matters. Let each man pray."

The Imam asked Allah to be among them. The prayers continued for nearly an hour. Then the Imam halted the prayers. He asked for the child to be brought among them. Ibd walked into the bedroom where he took the child from Miri's arms. He wrapped his daughter in a torn blanket and carried her into the waiting assembly.

The Imam felt new energy in the room. His heart raced. Was it possible this child could be the one for whom the believers prayed? Could a girl-child repel the infidels? He had to control himself. "Ibd, would you please hand the child to me?"

Ibd passed the child to the old cleric. The Imam carefully examined her. Yes, he thought, there is power in this child. The baby gazed steadily upon the Imam who felt her force. The child appeared to be evaluating him. She trapped him in her gaze. Then the child smiled at him. He felt the presence and peace of Allah. He had no doubt as to his judgment. He handed the child to Ibd. The Imam waited for his return.

The Imam addressed the assembled men. "The name of this child shall be A'isha. I must warn each of you. None will speak of this evening to anyone." With this somber statement the Imam rose and left Ibd and Miri's dwelling.

The world would never forget their infant's name. A'isha.

CHAPTER TWO

Fifteen years later, A'isha lay buried under tons of shattered concrete. All she could remember was a blinding flash and a thudding explosion. The Amiriyah Shelter where she lay had been reduced to a grave for hundreds of innocent civilians.

The Amiriyah Shelter, well known by the local population, was a designated shelter. Two large bombs had pierced through the eight-foot reinforced ceiling. In a split second all lay dead except A'isha.

A'isha opened her eyes in utter darkness. Was this a horrible nightmare? She remembered listening to her father telling her mother to be brave. Now there was only silence. She realized her fate: alive but entombed in rubble.

A'isha listened for signs of life. The moments passed like heavy tears of eternity. All were dead. She wanted to drift away. Why was she alive when those she loved had died?

Is this not the eternal question for survivors? It is not for mortals to know why some live and some die. Why do some surrender while others resist? Why do some lie down, and others rise up? Perhaps it is fate and nothing more.

Fury pushed aside fear in A'isha.

August 19, 2003

The military onslaught caught no one in Baghdad by surprise, Western military power being common knowledge to the Iraqi citizenry. Yet when the hammer fell, it struck an incredible blow resulting in vast devastation in minutes. Enemy sorties by the hundreds dominated the skies.

Baghdad residents heard huge explosions from every sector. Striking bombs sounded like rolling thunder. Not a bridge remained standing. Only powerful generators kept essential public facilities operating. The innocent, whose only crime was being born in the wrong country at the wrong time, died.

Thousands of survivors moved tons of debris in the slim hope that Allah had spared friends and loved ones. Perhaps Allah might care . . . perhaps not. The bombs hadn't discriminated but struck without regard to age or class.

Medical personnel couldn't cope, with barely time to separate the living from the dead. All facilities exhausted their medical supplies. Doctors operated without anesthesia.

"Dr. Showkit, this man is hemorrhaging. His leg is crushed," said a female aide.

Dr. Showkit, a wiry man, remained calm no matter the circumstances. His dark eyes were kind and intelligent behind wire-rim glasses that gave him an intellectual look.

Despite that calm demeanor, he felt he was working in hell. He'd been on duty for 61 hours. The patient's mangled leg's prognosis, of course, could only be hopeless.

"Apply a tourniquet quickly and prepare to amputate the limb," The young aide returned with the grim tools in her hands.

"Dr. Showkit, is there no other way?" She had turned pale.

"Under the present circumstances this is our only means of saving as many as possible," he replied. He'd read that wars kill far more civilians than military personnel, and today seemed like supporting evidence.

This was his first exposure to war. Its reality repulsed him. There was no glory and certainly no romance. Like all middle-class workers, he had no influence with his government, nor did he want it.

In normal times Dr. Showkit practiced psychiatry. Today keeping people alive was more critical than concern with their mental states. "Bring the patient into the operating room."

Dr. Showkit said in a low tone. "Help hold our patient while I remove the leg." He turned to the aide holding the handsaw. Be brave. All is in the hands of Allah."

The patient gripped a wooden dowel in his teeth while twisting in agony. In thirty seconds, the deed was done.

Dr. Showkit spoke to the patient after the operation. "Forgive me, brother. Allah sees all and will not forget your suffering."

~ ~ ~

Military High Command

August 25, 2003

Baghdad is an ancient city with many secrets. Few areas of earth carry more history than lands that embrace the Tigris and Euphrates Rivers where ambitious men thought to their sorrow it would prove easier to plunder than produce. Their armies disappeared under its desert sands. War has been a constant feature of this accessible place. This contest still raged in 2003.

Few world leaders rose to power from beginnings as low as Saddam Hussein's, an illegitimate child in a culture that does not take cultural violations lightly. He began life on April 28, 1937, in the village of al-Ouga about a one-hour drive north of Baghdad. His biological father died before the child's birth.

Saddam's uncle Khairallah Talfah, an Iraqi army officer, raised him. Saddam grew up in the Tekarte area with a growing reputation for brilliance and cruelty. In primitive tribal countries such attributes often precede leadership.

At twenty-two he joined "The Party of Arab Renewal" known as the Ba'ath Party. Saddam took a leading role in the assassination attempt against Iraqi strongman General Kassem in 1959. This attempt failed. Saddam, although wounded in this effort, escaped prison, and fled to Syria.

From Syria, he went to Egypt in 1962. Saddam returned to Iraq after his old enemy Kassem was deposed and executed in a public square in 1968. Saddam began his climb of the Ba'ath party's rungs of power.

On May 16, 1979, Saddam spearheaded the poisoning of President al-Bakr. By age 43 Saddam Hussein assumed control over Iraq.

Saddam Hussein's hulking figure sat alone brooding in the dark shadows of a bunker. Only the red glow of a cigarette would have revealed his presence had anyone been there to look. Saddam sat calculating his odds of survival.

Saddam believed he ruled by nature's cruel demands. Survival of the fittest justified his behavior. Saddam had no pretenses to morality. The desert knows nothing of mercy. Saddam had no religious beliefs. He maintained the illusion of Muslim piety. Islam had its uses. Islamists seemed unusually interested in war, plunder, and the enslavement of women.

Saddam realized he could not survive by military means. He had to find a compelling reason for his enemies to let him live. In a dark hour in that hidden bunker Saddam devised a rescue plan. No stranger to life and death gambles, Saddam knew his revenge against the West would come later.

He played his last card as he prepared his message to the West. It only took one word to cause the West to recall their armies of overwhelming might. The word was *Jihad*, Holy War against unbelievers. *Jihad* allowed Saddam to survive and to plot revenge against the United States of America.

CHAPTER THREE

Washington, D.C.

September 7, 2003

In a small office in a gray building a man sat and pondered. Caucasian, slight of build, age 32, this young CIA agent seldom attracted attention. Yet his intense blue eyes might have been perusing a distant shore.

Jackson analyzed military actions past, present, and future. He'd been assigned to focus on the heated Middle East some years ago. He held a PhD in World History and International Politics from Columbia University in New York. When the CIA offered him employment he accepted. Within two years he became fluent in Arabic to read from primary sources without needing translations.

Jackson served the CIA well. His success rate of predicting trouble was so high colleagues joked about his being clairvoyant. The Company hired a personal assistant to run his errands and installed a shower in Jackson's office.

Office parties and the occasional dinners with colleagues formed his social life. He liked to walk along the Potomac River alone. Walking helped him think.

His reports became legendary. Socially awkward, he curried no favors. Blunt, clear, and objective, Jackson became the leading authority on the Middle East and its fevered religion.

He had no illusions that his own government's political leaders could be dangerous. U.S. leaders operated on the profit motive. If a player stood to gain more than he stood to lose the player moved aggressively.

The Middle East wasn't so simple. The shooting war with Iraq was over. To politicians and military, it had been a satisfying war. "Desert Storm" had been perfect with low casualties. This raised government spirits while it put the Vietnam failure to rest.

Jackson believed any celebration was premature. Costs might not all be in.

United States leaders were culturally blind, assuming the other player wanted land, resources, or money. It was assumed that the other player used logic while seeking power, felt fear, and had doubts.

Above all, the assumption that the other player wanted to live seemed to be a given for all humanity, just as our country believed. Hence, the basic assumption prevailed that the other player was exactly like us. Jackson knew this to be wrong. History had known players who wanted nothing Americans held so dear. These were the dangerous ones.

In Islamic countries many had no interest in prolonging their lives. The normal threats of financial loss, prison, or death did not faze these believers. Many Islamic people looked forward to dying. Fundamental believers of Islam were a grave danger. This was hard for Americans to understand. Islam is infatuated with martyrdom.

The United States Government often used Muslim fanaticism for its own cynical purposes. In 1979 the United States used Muslim fighters as cannon fodder in the harsh terrain of Afghanistan.

The United States pumped tens of millions of dollars in weapons and supplies to the rag-tag "Holy Warriors". These believers would fight incredibly hard to repel the Soviet "infidels."

The Muslims drove the Russians out of Afghanistan by 1989. This was the first major defeat of a Soviet Army since 1917. The United States was ecstatic.

Jackson knew weapons alone couldn't have defeated the Russians. It was the ragged Mujahedeen who brought the Soviet behemoth to the ground. The belief that Allah had provided their victory also carried danger, instilling the idea that they must conquer the world.

Thousands of Arab fighters returned to their home countries with few skills beyond fighting. These fighters worked toward extreme Islamic governments in their countries. These hardened men had no qualms about using guns and bombs.

These incredible warriors had inflicted more damage on the Soviet Union than anyone noticed. Jackson stated the Soviet Union was mortally wounded and would fall into ashes within a decade. Few agreed. When the Soviet Union did fall in 1989 Jackson received a raise.

Jackson saw the Middle East as an organic whole. Action that hurt one part of the Middle East affected the entire Arab world. The United States secretly encouraged Saddam to invade Iran in 1980.

Iran had over three times the land mass of Iraq and four times the population. To the United States it was a win-win situation. Or so it seemed.

The theory behind all this was that Sadden was truly a secular ruler. Deeper United States policy was to encourage Muslim States to kill each other. Thus, the States of Iran and Iraq would be divided against each other and mutually weakened. The United States loved to use such policy.

The Iraq/Iran war lasted for 95 months. Iraq and Iran each had lost about 200,000 fighting men. The war ended a nearly perfect draw. However, 400,000 fighting age Muslims were killed. Combined civilian losses were around 500,000. Both Iran and Iraq were seriously weakened. The old game of divide and conquer still worked.

The United States hoped to reduce Saddam to another Middle East kinglet. Saddam would be reduced to playing with his harem and toys. The United States claimed to be owed the net income of Iraq for years to come. There were smug smiles in the White House.

The Western bean counters forgot that they were facing a man who had killed many men eye to eye. In an instant the tables were turned completely. Saddam now had the money from the West, a massive, trained army, and still held complete power in Iraq. He also controlled the second largest oil reserves in the world. With a smile Saddam felt he was debt free.

Saddam began to rebuild his country with materials and expertise from Europe rather than the United States. This left the United States holding a sizeable empty bag. Iraq was added to the list of Evil States that were not in the United States' pocket. The United

States, outraged at being pushed out of Iraq, would do anything to destroy Saddam Hussein.

Jackson felt something new growing, some horror, an extraordinary evil had invaded humanity. A person of incredible force was stalking the United States. He could not rest until he had discovered its identity. Had Death begun stalking the entire world? As darkness fell over the Potomac River, Jackson remained at his desk . . . thinking.

December 3, 2003

Saddam Hussein survived the Gulf war by the thinnest of margins. His beloved military machine had been shredded; his domestic economy reduced to ruins.

Thousands of Iraqis were without medical treatment. Starvation served Death. Iraq's infrastructure had turned to rubble. Millions lived at risk because of a lack of public sanitation.

Saddam lived in controlled fury. UN economic sanctions were forming against Iraq. The weak, the poor, and the children, so called 'collateral damage' would die in hundreds of thousands. Sanctions never affect the elite or the military.

Saddam fumed. The United States bombed Iraq for over 45 days and nights and would kill humans in any numbers to get at him and Iraq's oil. He stood alone between the United States and that treasure. He viewed everyone and everything in Iraq as his property. In his controlled fury Saddam determined to achieve revenge.

Saddam's survival had been a close thing. The United States had recently lost Iran to Islam's aggressive militant edge. He'd pointed out to the West that if he was overthrown then Iran would take power. This would change the balance of power in the Middle East. A new authority would rise with hatred of the United States.

Iran wanted the Western powers out of the Middle East. A new Shiite government in former Iraq would work relentlessly to overthrow Saudi Arabia whose fall would endanger Western civilization.

CHAPTER FOUR

Saddam encouraged the United States to use him as a ploy to build ever more powerful military bases in Saudi Arabia thus leaving the United States stronger in the Middle East. The United States corporations could use him as the Middle East's boogie man, thereby feeding their military industrial interests. In turn, these gave generous support to likeminded politicians. Saddam bought time but the United States would never rest until his death.

Saddam drew on his cigarette with cool appreciation. His days were numbered, his enemies powerful. He might live another ten years, but all things end. His enemies would kill him sooner or later.

He had no fear of death and no regrets. He'd had many women in more varieties and ways than he remembered. That was good for a man. Saddam had no idea how many people died because of his directives, surely tens of thousands.

Those who stood in his way had to die. It was the real law of power. He had tortured many of his enemies himself because enemies deserved their fate.

The most important thing was to leave life even. He wanted to owe nothing to another with none to owe him unpaid debts. Revenge was the duty of any man of honor, to depart avenged of all wrongs.

~ ~ ~

The United States topped his list, arrogant whore forever preaching peace and freedom while selling the world billions of dollars in armaments that killed tens of millions. The so-called friend of democracy supported the most vicious police states in the world. Never once had the United States suggested that Saudi Arabia adopt democracy. America preached peace while holding the world hostage with her nuclear arsenal of 7000 weapons.

He seethed. Perhaps he should leave the United States a gift to remember? He was a small-time killer compared to the great United States of America. Could he think of a way to kill enough Americans to even the score?

The history of the world does not record the exact time that Saddam reached his final decision. It may have been that very day. It may have been during the forty-two days that Baghdad had been under round the clock bombings. Saddam vowed that the world would never forget his name.

Another name never to be forgotten belonged to a fifteen-year-old girl: A'isha.

~ ~ ~

Dr. Showkit studied the blue sky for perhaps the last time in his life. His secretary had called him out of his hospital ward. A Commander of the Republican Guard had ordered Showkit to his hospital office. There was never any question of delay or evasion.

Showkit and others knew that to resist Saddam in any way meant death for self and all his extended family, a penalty exacted many times.

After the doctor entered his office, a beefy soldier searched him and checked his medical identification. Showkit asked no questions. No one would answer. After the soldier escorted and placed him in the waiting sedan he blindfolded Dr. Showkit who pushed down fear as they traveled smoothly making many turns. He lost his sense of time before the vehicle stopped, and silent escorts guided him into a cool building.

Once a soldier removed the blindfold Dr. Showkit peered at his surroundings: a small windowless room. The air conditioning hummed as the doctor stood.

Many were seized from their homes and offices by the government, never to be seen again. Still, he could think of nothing that he had said or done that could have landed him here.

The truth or falsity of any charge was irrelevant. If suspected of wrongdoing you were killed. He knew he may have been called for professional reasons. He'd given a psychiatric opinion in various situations. However, he'd never been handled like this. Scared, he trembled.

A short, bespectacled man in uniform entered and gestured the doctor to sit down. Dr. Showkit could feel his interrogator's-controlled energy before the man commenced.

"Dr. Showkit, it is good of you to come on such short notice. I am a member of the State Security Department. I assure you that no harm will come to you. These are dangerous days for Iraq. They demand greater security and greater protection for the assets of our country. You are one of these national assets. The State of Iraq requires your professional help."

The doctor hoped his relief wasn't so obvious as to cause a loss of dignity. "May I ask why I am called upon?"

"I do not know the exact matter. My task is to ask you if you are willing to work on a project of the highest military significance. I am commanded to say that the importance of this enterprise is of the highest national level. You would have access to the full resources of our government. If materials or resources are needed that our nation cannot provide, then the full international purchasing power of Iraq will be yours to draw upon. Do you have questions, Dr. Showkit?"

Dr. Showkit answered, "I am happy to serve my country and its government in any way I can. I will do my best to fulfill the State's requirements."

The unnamed official said, "I am pleased you accept the assignment. The task will be given to you by a higher ranking official. Thank you again for your cooperation." The small man rose and Showkit, blindfolded again, was escorted to a bigger chamber.

Blindfold removed, Dr. Showkit looked about him. He sensed he was below the earth's surface. An imposing bench rose like a throne, a single door directly behind it. He had a sense of being observed. Dr. Showkit regained some confidence. He was here to do a job, therefore unlikely to be killed.

The door opened and a big man stepped through. His eyes were wary, but with an aura of authority. This was no mere military officer or busy bureaucrat. The man took his seat and perused Dr. Showkit with the coldest eyes Showkit had ever seen. He met the eyes of a psychopath who projected the potential of death.

Saddam Hessian spoke, "Doctor, do you know who I am?"

"You are Saddam Hussein, President of Iraq and leader of our country," the Doctor replied.

"Correct," Saddam replied, "I have called you here on an important matter. It is sensitive and will be known to no one beyond you and me for some time. You will explain any problems concerning the mission directly to me. It is a matter of the highest national and personal importance. You are to speak to no-one about any part of this mission. The slightest leak will cost you the ultimate penalty. Do you understand?"

"Yes Mr. President, I understand and will serve you and my country. May I know what is the goal? I will do my best to perform the task and to keep you abreast with reports."

Saddam paused, then began, "This is a one-way door, Dr. Showkit. Once you know the mission you will be committed to it with no turning back."

Showkit had no choice. No one denied Saddam and lived. The Doctor also found himself becoming professionally interested in the project.

The idea of a truly big project fascinated him. This project must be of incredible importance if the President of the entire country was directly overseeing it. "Mr. President, I am willing to go through the door."

"So be it," replied Saddam. Saddam's eyes shone with anticipation. "The goal is to find and train a single commando to infiltrate the United States and cause massive damage to our enemy. The commitment and training of this commando must be of the highest order. The mission must be performed flawlessly. The commando's goal is to destroy a nation."

"There is a no chance that the commando will live. The selection and training of such a person is your mission. We will kill more people in one strike than the world has ever known. Never again will a Western power invade Iraqi lands. Do you understand the goals?" asked Saddam.

Dr. Showkit was stunned into silence. He thought quickly. Saddam appeared to be in full control of his mental processes. Saddam would go forward with or without his professional help. To protest was out of the question. The only result of such an action would be his execution.

Besides, the challenge intrigued Showkit, a man of science. "Mr. President, it is a challenge to train such a soldier. Few soldiers must plan and make personal decisions. Few operate individually. It will be difficult to find and train someone for the mission you describe. The lone commando would not have the benefit of group support. She/he must be responsible for all decisions. To be solely responsible for the deaths of millions is a tremendous psychological burden."

"To perform the mission with the certain knowledge of an impending martyr's death takes unshakable commitment. Nature has programmed us to survive," said Dr. Showkit.

Saddam took in the details, his eyes turned flat and cold, the eyes of a cobra.

Saddam asked, "Are you afraid of me Dr. Showkit?"

"Yes, Mr. President," answered the doctor.

"Good. Fear is an excellent motivator. I have no desire to kill you. This matter is much more important than either of our lives."

"This mission is necessary for me, the Iraqi people, and all Arab peoples. A day of reckoning is due America. Too many of our people have been killed, and the West in her arrogance feels nothing. The West has technology we lack. The United States is overconfident, a dangerous flaw.

"Arabs understand that certain acts must be paid in blood. Nothing else will suffice. Not gold, not gems, not silver, and not even oil which the West confuses with power. Power does not grow out of technology."

"Power grows from the center of a man's will. It was not technology that changed me from a raggedy village bastard into the ruler of Iraq. It was my will and the courage to use it."

"What I require from you is one person prepared to enter the United States within three years able to operate alone for up to three more years. That person must kill on command or when certain events come to pass. This operative must want to die to fulfill the mission. You'll have unlimited resources at your fingertips. If you succeed you will be rewarded with riches and your life."

"If you fail, I will kill you and your family. Using your professional knowledge, tell me what type of individual you must find for this task."

"Mr. President, the mind must be malleable. This requires a person under the age of sixteen. I would suggest a young girl. Girls are mentally more mature for their given age and yet their minds are still accessible. Women can be more dedicated, fearless, and committed to a cause then men."

"From an operational standpoint, women are less likely to be suspected of military activities. This commando should be an extremely religious woman. This allows her to shift the responsibility for her mission onto Allah. It is important that she be of the Shiite branch of Islam with its strong martyr tradition.

"The trainee must believe the mission is ordained by Allah.

Our commando must view the United States as a deadly threat to Islam. Allah must be her only source of emotional bonding. Death must be seen as a reunion with Allah and thus life on earth is not desirable. Death must be viewed as merely stepping through a door. The trainee must be drenched in hate."

"She must have no attachment to the world of the living. Every action must be in preparation for her mission. The trainee must never know comfort. She must see the world as total evil, its non-Muslims unworthy to live."

"One requirement overshadows everything—she must despise the United States. She must have a level of psychopathic rage that erases her humanity. She must be a force of Allah. She must see herself as an avenging angel in a human form. She sees herself as Allah's flame to torch the earth."

"Hate this deep requires a mind that is permanently warped. To kill for the sake of Allah must be her sole purpose. Although clinically insane this person must be capable of being trained and guided. She must be a psychopath but capable of being controlled. Psychopaths are not created; they are result of trauma beyond all human understanding. Only Allah could create and direct such a person."

"She must be a tool of the Almighty. If such a woman exists—then this is Allah's will—for nothing mere mortals can do without his help could create such a raw force." Dr. Showkit fell into silence.

Saddam gave the order. "Find me this angel of death and let us place the sword into her hands." Doctor Showkit bowed his head. When he gained the strength to look up, Saddam was gone.

CHAPTER FIVE

Baghdad Iraq

D r. Showkit sat at his desk. Much of Baghdad still existed without essential services. What water was available might not be potable.

As always, disease arrived close behind war's dark shadow. Both young and old fell ill, dying by the thousands, many suffering from diseases associated with malnutrition. After all, the United States coalition had flown over 100,000 sorties over Iraq and dropped over 100,000 tons of explosives. The outcome was predictable and well planned.

Dr. Showkit had to find the candidate for Saddam's project code named "The Sword." If he had any needs, he gave a sealed letter to an assigned aide and the list was filled without delay.

For security reasons Dr. Showkit had to ask for all ages and both sexes even though his target group was females between thirteen and sixteen. No one could suspect anything more than State record keeping.

There were over 20,000 children in Baghdad alone suffering from mental trauma. Schizophrenia diagnoses appeared unusually pronounced and age of onset much lower than normal. All the symptoms of war: flashbacks, sleep disturbance, extreme depression, social alienation, and severe anxiety descended without mercy upon the victims. Many of the worst cases withdrew from human contact. Suicide skyrocketed among all ages. Medicines were unavailable. Patients died for lack of medical care.

The search for Saddam's commando was not going well. To this date there were over 3000 females in the targeted group. He studied hundreds of faces and hundreds of records. The human carnage of war was a crushing sight that reappeared in his dreams.

For most, the situation was grim. The teenagers' gaunt faces showed deep mental distress. Nearly all were strongly affected by fear and had no wish to be exposed to personal danger ever again.

Fear was incompatible with his mission requirements. The candidate had to be without fear to perform her duties in the military mission. The elusive emotion the Doctor was searching for was rage. The rage had to be psychotic and this madness had to be the foundation of the candidate's very being. The only constant emotion must be the desire for revenge. The only goal must be a consuming desire to destroy. As a man whose life revolved around giving health and healing, he dared not think too hard about what that rage might cause.

Dr. Showkit had time. Finding the right person would prove the key to success. He leaned back in his chair, closed his eyes, and concentrated on how to find someone at an early age that had the mature traits of a dedicated adult. She would have to be capable of independent action and possess extraordinary ruthlessness. Yet she must be so unbalanced that revenge was her only purpose in life. Perplexing.

Dr. Showkit double-checked his figures. Out of 3000 possible candidates, he reviewed and rejected 1627 patients. So far none met Saddam's requirements. That left around 1400 more to examine. He was not optimistic.

The candidate had to be sane enough to function yet insane enough to kill millions of people—including herself. What had he overlooked in his analysis? His subject had to be extremely devout. Religion was well understood to give many individuals the moral strength to die without fear. He had to do better—much better. The solitary Doctor ran his fingers through his thinning gray hair.

Who could have predicted that the result of his solitary concentration would change the world? Is there a reason that the mind often supplies what the human will seeks? Who can know?

A sudden insight struck Abu Showkit, M.D. He'd made a mistake. This Sword of Allah would not be found among those victims whose minds had failed. This living flame of Allah's wrath was not among the mentally crushed and broken. He had overlooked his own requirements.

Ideally the candidate had to be the sole survivor of military attack. Ideally the candidate had to have no living relatives. Ideally she had to be a Shiite girl younger than sixteen. This made the girl an orphan. A young girl with no surviving family would be sent to an orphanage. He could not suppress that certainty.

~ ~ ~

August 3, 2003

A'isha lay barely conscious when she heard voices above her. She was buried in this tomb of dust and darkness. Small, broken pieces of memory surfaced.

In her extremity she thought she heard her mother talking to her. At other times it seemed she could hear her father praying. Suddenly a flash of blinding light—then silence.

The truth hit her with crystal clarity. There had been a bomb. All she knew and everyone she loved were dead. She tried to feel every inch of her entrapment. During her feeling and groping she'd felt part of a human body. By running her shaking fingers over the body, she could tell it was part of a human torso with the head attached.

In horror, she ran her trembling hands over its features. The face seemed smooth . . . delicate. The right side of the upper skull was crushed into a mass of clotting blood and broken bone.

Her fingers recoiled as she touched the sticky blood and the ragged edges of the skull. Some force inside of A'isha forced her to continue her exploration. Her fingers traced down the sides of the victim's face and throat. Then she traced gently down the corpse's neck. The skin was soft. She touched something cool, and A'isha drew her fingers back.

A'isha forced herself to return her fingertips to that soft skin. She touched something smooth and metallic. A flexible necklace.

Her fingers trembled as they felt it. She'd touched a delicate Muslim medallion: a small crescent moon with two miniature swords, one sword on each side of the waning moon. Then there was that shattering moment when truth, pain, and agony melted into one appalling moment—it was her mother. A'isha had given her mother that medallion for her birthday.

A'isha began to scream. The loss of her mother, her father, and her sisters caused such searing pain that the sounds were inhuman. She continued screaming until she lost her voice. Then she wept. She wept for all the innocent people in her world dead at the Western invaders' hands. She wept until there were no more tears. A'isha would never weep again.

Then rage swelled. She clawed at the dirt and the concrete of her tomb in her rage, and she swore to Allah that she would kill everyone responsible for these murders. In her rage and loathing she clawed at her confines until her nails were broken and blood trickled down her delicate fingers.

In her exhaustion, her face sank to the damp, sticky, earth which carried an acrid smell. Her face rested on soil drenched with her mother's blood. A'isha was too weak to move. The feel and smell of her mother's blood sank into her. A'isha wished she could weep but her tears were gone. She wanted to rise but her strength had vanished. Too weak to make another sound, she craved escape from this suffocating tomb. It seemed she had been within this womb of death for eternity.

Then her thoughts suddenly disconnected. She saw visions of flashing lights and she heard sounds of mystical beauty. She envisioned a shimmering throne covered with dancing colors. She saw an image made of moving flames. The image was unclear: it was a Being—a Force—an awful power. She raised her hands to cover her face.

A gentle voice said, "Weep not my little one—for the innocent of all worlds reside with me. Your parents and loved ones are with me."

"All life belongs to me. Wipe your mother's blood from your face for you have been chosen to deliver my justice. You will punish those who feel that the power to kill bestows the right to murder. You will punish those who in their material comfort have forgotten the world's suffering poor."

"War is the ultimate evil and those who wage war in aggression or for gain must pay a high price. Lift your eyes upon me—you are my little one: I give you a gift—the Sword of God. I place it in your heart. Use this sword to slay those in the West who in their lust and frantic accumulation have forgotten me. I will send a message to the powerful nations of the West who in their arrogance spread death and oppression and calls the result—Peace."

"Slay them by the millions and tens of millions. Perhaps some will repent and turn to me. The innocent of the world will be avenged. I will be with you always. My discernment will be in your mind. You are my Angel—my Angel of Death."

A'isha felt sharp pain from a blade entering her heart, but the blade melted, and she felt ultimate peace. She swooned and fell into a deep sleep.

She did not wake up until she felt strong human arms pulling her from the rubble. Her rescuer was struck by her physical beauty as he carried her to the medical station.

She said to him "Save me, my friend—for I will avenge us all." Her rescuer remembered her words until he died. He never forgot A'isha.

CHAPTER SIX

August 13, 2003

Muhammad Iqbal made his way through the Al-Najat orphanage's crowded corridors. Muhammad was the director of this nightmare along the Tigris River. It was a half-way house to death. There were no medical supplies, little food, and seemingly no one in the entire world cared about these sad-eyed wards.

He felt like a ruined general walking across a body-littered battlefield. War's devastation spread before him. Helpless and hungry, many children were crippled in body and mind. Muhammad thought that he'd seen all the suffering of the world. That was before the Gulf War.

All in the name of justice and their accursed lust for oil the United States imposed sanctions upon the Iraqi people, a starvation blockade. Did the West believe that Saddam would go hungry because Iraqi children died of starvation? The elite of any country stay rich and well fed. No, this was a planned genocide against Muslims. Muhammad prayed that the leaders of the United States would burn in hell fueled by the oil after which they lusted. Where was their famed humanity?

Iraqi women in rags were abandoning their children at the orphanage and fleeing in tears. They had no means by which to feed their children. He reminded himself Allah was not blind. Allah saw all things.

One must be patient and wait for Allah. Muhammad had to hold back unmanly tears. He must set a strong example for the children.

Their eyes followed him as he walked past hundreds of dirty cots. The children seldom made a sound. They seemed to sense there was nothing to be done for them. Yet the empty eyes haunted Muhammad as the children gazed after his every step. Often he would stop to say a few words to them. Invariably the children spoke little and yet were so polite.

Hundreds of them had died in his wards without making a sound, as if not wanting to disturb anyone. Their tiny bodies, lacking shrouds or coffins, were buried in a mass trench. A few hasty prayers, a few shovels of dirt, completed the deed. The hope of the Iraqi people died. An entire generation of children murdered.

A child might ask Muhammad to pray for him or her. The last child who had asked for prayers had afterward thanked Muhammad and gently slipped away.

"*How much can a human take?*" he wondered. Muhammad begged for food from any State, private, or international source. The Iraqi State gave little assistance, and the international community didn't care.

Muhammad did his best to feed his children with almost nothing. Sometimes he managed to bring a truckload of wormy flour that could be made into a watery gruel. Sometimes some rice made it through the labyrinth of officials by an act of Allah. Common people might bring a cart of rotten lettuce or a few raw potatoes to offer the children. Surely, Allah would reward their sacrifice. How would this horror end?

Did the governments of the world not realize that suffering and starvation are wombs of war? That many who survived this hell would later pick up a rifle? *And who could blame them?* Muhammad thought to himself. Was it any wonder that the East would learn to hate the West? As he looked around he saw hundreds of children who had every reason to seek revenge.

Hopeless people have nothing left to do but fight. The cots seemed to recede into an endless distance, but Muhammad knew that he was just exhausted. His perception was weakening.

The human predators came daily to stalk the orphanage. The Iraqi government sought any boy who appeared old enough to hold a gun. A youth of ten was not too young to fill the ranks of a military decimated by the West. Muhammad hated to see the boys swept up into the flesh-eating monster, war. But what could he do?

In the military the boy would receive food and some chance of survival. What madness it was that men did to each other! Here in the orphanage a boy had no long-term hope.

There were no normal adoptions. Older boys with some physical or mental problem were taken as slave labor in shops or on farms. At least they had some chance to live.

Older girls presented their own problems. Almost no man could afford one as a legitimate wife. Girls as young as nine were eligible for marriage, but there were few suitors.

Then there was the flesh market. The most attractive girls would be taken as sexual slaves. Again, Muhammad had no choice. There was no demand for normal labor. Iraq was in a state of siege. There remained only basic survival.

Muhammad felt he must save the children if possible. However, many of his wards could barely walk. How was he to save them? Was the world so heartless that they had to die? He knew the answer. Yes.

Muhammad noted one of his assistants bringing in an older girl. The assistant seemed to be saying something to her and pointed to a cot. The girl shook her head and walked to a far corner. Tall, wearing dark peasant garb, she took care to keep her face in shadow. Her movements showed surprising strength and purpose.

She was unlike the cowed victims. She knelt in the corner and arranged her cloak, then lowered her head in prayer. A frightening aura surrounded her. Something in the room had changed.

There was a dangerous tension coming from the shrouded girl in the corner. Muhammad motioned his assistant to join him in the hallway. "Hamza, tell me about this new patient," Muhammad said. Hamza was a trusted assistant and had been a Godsend to Muhammad for over four years.

A handsome young man of 24, he had a genius for scrounging food for the orphanage. Everyone liked him. His friendly personality was a great part of his assets. Many children were alive because of Hamza's genius.

"Sir, this girl was the sole survivor of the Amiriyah Shelter. Nearly 500 people died, including her entire family. She lay without food or water for three days. The workers found her unconscious in close confinement with her mother's rotting body. Only Allah could know the hell she went through."

"Her name is A'isha. She seldom speaks. She suffered some days before the doctors could see her. The triage doctor stated that she was traumatized. She had no one so I brought her here," the earnest young man said.

Muhammad had to press with a question. "Hamza, is there something more? She seems unusual. Do you find her attractive?" Muhammad asked.

"Sir, she is incredibly beautiful. "Hamza paused.

"Hamza, the flowers of Allah are meant to be appreciated. There is something else, is there not?" Muhammad pressed.

"Yes. She frightens me. I feel she is dangerous. If I were to touch her I fear I would die. When she looks at me her eyes are as cold as night in the desert. It's as though she can read my thoughts. There is a power in her. I've never seen anything like it."

"My mother told me of witches when I was a child. I always laughed at her. I am not laughing now."

Muhammad took the information in thoughtfully. He was in the presence of a mystery.

It would pay to go slowly. "I will bring her food for the next few days. Let her have time to recover from her agony. You have done well. Be at ease and laugh again." Muhammad advised. Hamza walked away. The girl in the corner never moved.

Days passed. During his rounds Muhammad took notice of A'isha. He made a point of being the person who took her a small bowl of food daily. He tried to draw her out with brief salutations.

"Peace be with you, A'isha," he'd say as he set the bowl of pathetic liquid beside her. A'isha never responded. There was a distance between the world and A'isha that even the orphanage director, Muhammad, could not cross.

The sense of tension in the air remained. However, A'isha did not always remain in her corner. When there were no adults, A'isha moved around the room. Muhammad learned this information from the children themselves. At first Muhammad was fearful that A'isha might harm the smaller children. Thankfully, that fear was ungrounded.

Without exception each child would say how much A'isha had made everyone smile. Such contact raised their spirits. Apparently an encouraging word, a touch or a smile from A'isha gave the starving children a little more strength.

On the ninth day when Muhammad said, "Peace to you A'isha," he heard a low melodic voice say, "And to you, Muhammad." A'isha's response raised his spirits for the rest of the day.

However, Muhammad was concerned about her beauty, afraid the human predators would find her. She moved with the grace and poise of royalty. Yet a frightening sense of danger followed her. She kept her face nearly always in shadow. When her eyes were visible they appeared distant as if she was looking for someone to arrive who would come from far away. When she looked directly at him it seemed she read his mind. Muhammad sensed that A'isha could kill in a second and feel nothing. This mystery deepened on a fateful Thursday in the third week of her stay.

A member of the upper class came to Mohammad's office. Muhammad loathed this known dealer in the sex trade. Just under the surface of daily life in all Muslim countries there is a slave market primarily of females.

This dealer said he'd heard of a beautiful girl known as A'isha. Muhammad, desperate to save her, explained A'isha was unbalanced, not suitable for any purpose. She was mad and possibly dangerous. The sex dealer only boasted of his ability to cure any intransigence by the whip.

Muhammad prayed that Allah could stop this evil man while they walked into A'isha's ward. With a sinking heart Muhammad took the man over to the silent shrouded figure in the corner. A'isha was seated leaning against the wall, her arms on her knees, her head tilted downward.

The dealer stood directly in front of A'isha, and he addressed her sharply. "Look at me woman and let me examine your face!" A'isha did not say a word and moved not a muscle. Muhammad's heart raced. The air became still and heavy with crackling energy. Perhaps the dealer felt the pressure as well. His voice rose. "Speak to me woman, or I shall buy you like a cow and beat you like a dog."

Slowly A'isha lifted her head and pushed her shroud back so that her face and her eyes were clear. Her eyes smoldered with hate and focused deep into the eyes of the transfixed sex dealer. A voice slowly crawled out of her throat, and it was a deep hard voice that dripped with malice. It was not the voice of a human. It was a voice from hell.

"You filthy swine, never again will you touch the little children. Never again will you deal in your despicable trade. Listen to my words. This very day you will die."

A'isha began to emit horrifying laughter. The sound rose higher and higher. Frightful, the sound seemed to come from a place of pure evil. The dealer turned pale and stumbled backward toward the ward door. A stain spread across the front of his trousers. He could not take his eyes off A'isha. Finally, he turned to run, and the hideous laughter followed him in his flight down the hall. Her words were loud, sharp, and clear.

"Run you pig, today you die," Then A'isha slowly covered her face with her shroud and lowered her head in silence. Muhammad was finally able to break away from her hold upon his person. He rapidly went to his office to pray. He prayed for two hours, and the sweat poured off his body. He had never been so frightened.

Muhammad received word that evening that the sex dealer had died before the sun went down in an automobile accident. A'isha didn't move for over two days. During that time, she never touched her food.

CHAPTER SEVEN

As the days passed A'isha walked among the children even when Muhammad visited the ward. A mysterious figure, she seemed nearly invisible in her encompassing cloak. She seemed to move without a sound. Her voice was nearly impossible to hear as she went from one child to another. On the rare occasions that Muhammad could hear her voice it sounded beautiful.

The children adored her. Often she would hold a frightened child against her body. The effect on the child was electric; the child would be at peace instantly. Many times, A'isha would comfort dying children. A'isha often told them, "Fear not my little one, neither Allah nor I will forget you."

On another occasion Muhammad heard A'isha tell a dying girl, "Rest and I will join you when it is my time." This was all troubling. A'isha gave the impression there was nothing she could not foretell. A dark violent destiny surrounded her.

Time and again, A'isha would accompany the tiny bodies to the trench that served as the grave for these innocent ones. The very air around her person seemed to vibrate with rage. It seemed that a bolt of lightning would strike any person who said a word to A'isha during these moments. It was as if there was a magnetic field about her that no adult could invade without her permission. A'isha ate little or nothing at all, worrisome to Muhammad.

Many times, Muhammad would watch A'isha take her own meager portion to a starving child. Often the child did not have the strength to hold a spoon. It moved him to watch this silent, dangerous woman coaxing the dying child to eat. There was a vast chasm between A'isha and the world. A'isha drew strength from a source that was completely unknown.

A'isha had been at the orphanage nine weeks when she sought out Muhammad in his office. A'isha hadn't come to him for any reason. It was rare that she spoke to him at all. His gaze had been upon his papers, and it was not until he felt a presence that he looked up, startled. It was A'isha, silent as a tall, regal apparition.

Her voice was steady, showing no emotion. "Muhammad, I will be leaving you and the children in a few days. A man will be coming for me. I have been waiting for him and soon he will find me."

Muhammad was stunned by the statement. He knew nothing of this, and her statement was unsettling.

"A'isha, how can you be sure? I did not know that you had any relatives. Have you received any communication from someone you know?"

"Muhammad you are a good man. In truth, you are far too good for this savage world. I have no one. I can only tell you that my time is near." A'isha left the room as quietly as she had arrived. He could not escape the certainty that the world had made a major shift.

November 3, 2003

Dr. Showkit pressed his search for the right candidate for Saddam's mission. For a commando to enter the United States, remain undetected possibly for months or years, and then carry out a sophisticated military strike demanded a rare individual. For that same mortal to sacrifice her own life to fulfill the mission required someone of exceptional dedication.

The person Dr. Showkit sought must nurse deep, pathological hatred against the United States. Such people existed. He felt confident he could find her. His candidate would be found in an orphanage.

The sheer number of war orphans worked against him. There were now dozens of small orphanages rather than the three or four state institutions of former days.

As he walked through such orphanages he saw appalling suffering. Most of the children were starving, many were badly injured, and all of them alone in the world. Thousands of children had died and thousands more would follow. Someday the United States would feel the suffering that the Arab world had known for years.

Dr. Showkit pressed on with his search. With each passing day he was more confident that his search would end successfully. He was being pulled closer to the object of his search by the hour. It was an odd and unscientific sensation. Dr. Showkit felt himself being drawn closer and faster with each passing day.

Today he was to search in the Al-Najat orphanage in southern Baghdad. His records showed that the orphanage director to be Muhammad Iqbal. The orphanage consisted of a sordid set of low buildings along the Tigris River. The estimated population was nearly 3000 children. What it must be like to be responsible for that many unwanted orphans!

As Dr. Showkit walked through the door of the main building he was overwhelmed. Not a breath of air moved. Several children shared each cot and dozens more lay on dirty blankets along the walls. The flies crawled over every tiny body like maggots on a rotting corpse.

The wards were quiet. The children did not have the strength to protest their suffering. Many children were near death. A large man with a full dark beard and sad, expressive eyes stepped out of a tiny office.

"I am Muhammad Iqbal, director in charge here. Who are you and in what way may I help you?"

"I am Dr. Showkit with the Mental Health Department of the State Services."

"I see," Muhammad said. "Have you come because of my repeated requests for food and medical supplies? This orphanage is in desperate condition. Is there anything that you can do for us?"

"I may be able to help you, but I am here today to gather information on the number of clients that you might have that are suffering from mental problems," answered Dr. Showkit.

"Please come into my office," replied Muhammad. The office held a small desk and two chairs. "There is nothing that I can offer you to drink or to eat. Our needs are far beyond my ability to fulfill them. I hope you can understand."

"I am humbled that you can do anything for these children. The Iraqi State is struggling to meet its obligations. I am only one man, and my duties are limited. What can you tell me about your patients?" asked Dr. Showkit.

Muhammad rubbed his eyes in weariness. Dr. Showkit could see this man was overwhelmed with sorrow. "We have 3000 children in these run-down buildings. Every child is malnourished because of a lack of food. Around 30 children per day are buried in a simple trench behind these buildings. They are dying of starvation, of numerous diseases, and some of their wounds."

~ ~ ~

"We do not have simple aspirin or basic antiseptics. We have no food except what can be obtained by charity. Approximately fifty new children are left on our grounds every day. Hundreds of thousands of children will die in Iraq in the coming years."

"Nearly one third of these children suffer from some type of mental condition. My medical records are incomplete. The ones that are here are the nameless, the helpless, and the forgotten. Many of these children are too young to speak their names."

Dr. Showkit said, "The State is poorly equipped to handle young mental patients. What is the number of possible mental cases that are over the age of 13?"

Muhammad regained composure, "Forgive me, I am dying of sorrow. I am being crushed. There are around 150 patients who would be in that age group. Over 100 of those patients would be girls."

"Muhammad, we did not make the world. We can only do our best. Can you to lead me through your wards?"

"Come with me. Perhaps you can save one or two," said Muhammad. "It will be as Allah wills."

"As Allah wills," replied Dr. Showkit.

The situation was worse than Muhammad had described. There was extreme hunger as well as diseases. Many of the patients were comatose or nearly so. Dr. Showkit wrote patients' names within the age brackets that Dr. Showkit had requested. Showkit concealed the quick evaluation he was performing in his mind.

CHAPTER EIGHT

They entered Ward Six. At first, it seemed like any of the other wards: unbearable heat and a mass of helpless children who seemed to extend forever. Nevertheless, Dr. Showkit felt a quickening of his senses.

He felt something in the ambiance but didn't pause in making assessments. Muhammad continued his slow walk through these crowded aisles of humanitarian disaster. Dr. Showkit felt sorry for the children, but also a growing anticipation. Someone was watching him. He knew it.

Dr. Showkit saw a girl leaning against a fly specked wall. He felt himself being drawn as if by invisible fingers to her. She wore plain dark peasant clothes; a black hood was pushed back from her head. Her face was beautiful. Dr. Showkit froze in his steps.

The girl's intense, luminous eyes studied him, her eyes beckoning. The girl retained beauty even with her physical frame gaunt and angular. Her black hair reflected random bits of light. Her light olive skin had a slight radiance. Her personage conveyed strength and purpose. She seemed to send out a sense of power, so absent in every other ward.

Muhammad witnessed the tension between Dr. Showkit and A'isha. "Dr. Showkit," he whispered, "you must come with me to my office. We will discuss the young girl you see against the wall. Her name is A'isha. She is something of a puzzle when she isn't showing her mysterious and discomfiting strengths. There are things that you should know. Please, come with me."

For a moment Dr. Showkit didn't hear Muhammad. A'isha smiled in a cold controlled manner. Then she covered her head with her hood and her face disappeared. Only then did Dr. Showkit allow Muhammad to lead him to the tiny office.

The two men sat looking at each other in silence, one a man of science, the other a devout man of great compassion.

Dr. Showkit broke the silence. "Tell me what you know about this girl. She possesses something remarkable. I have never experienced such intensity and power in any individual. But I think the strength may be fueled by a searing hatred."

Mohammad drew breath and spoke. "A'isha is 15 years old. She was the sole survivor of the Amiriyah Shelter. Nearly five hundred civilians perished in the massive bombing attack.

All her family members and neighbors were slaughtered. She was discovered barely alive three days after the attack next to her rotting mother. Something related to that horrible experience has altered this girl beyond my mortal understanding. She speaks only to children and rarely to me."

"Her effect on children is positive. Her relationship with adults can only be described as threatening. She appears to have a good sense of the future. There is a hidden purpose in her heart that she has never confided in me."

"She speaks to the children with a voice so soft I seldom hear. Occasionally I can hear her whispering parts of the Koran as she sits shrouded against the wall. She accompanies the body of every child who dies. She never sheds tears. Nevertheless, I feel her rage, terrible in its depth of passion. Something terrible lives in that girl."

Dr. Showkit absorbed this information. He tried to control his rising hopes. "Please be patient with me Muhammad, I must ask you questions. I need answers to the best of your knowledge. Does the girl have any friends? Does she ever appear to hallucinate? Has she ever appeared to suffer anxiety attacks? Does she wake distressed or even screaming?"

Muhammad thought on these questions, "A'isha does not give the slightest evidence of having any friends or human attachments. She has been here for over nine weeks, and I've never seen anything but perfect personal control. No weeping, no evident dreams, and no signs of anxiety. She shows no personal weakness of any kind. The only emotion that I have sensed is fury. She seems to have some type of personal rage she does not discuss."

"I have an unnerving sense that she can read my mind. Perhaps she has some type of highly developed awareness. A'isha seems to have a sense of destiny, as if she is moving toward a great event. One gets the impression that somehow A'isha will affect the world. It is strange."

"Do you think she could kill another human?" Dr. Showkit asked. Muhammad did not need to think long, "I have no doubt that

A'isha could kill another human being. I am only giving you my impression. I have no professional training."

Dr. Showkit thought, "*Yet you would have been a great mental health analyst, my kindhearted man. It is a mercy of Allah that you do not know that you have described the rarest of assassins—a psychopath who is a totally rational mass killer.*"

Dr. Showkit decided to interview A'isha. Was she malleable? Could he sharpen her sword of hate? Would she allow herself to be directed at the enemy? Was A'isha a warrior who would shade even the great Saladin? Could this girl be "The Sword of Allah" for whom Saddam searched?

"It is possible this girl would respond to treatment in a specialized hospital. I would like to talk to her. If she is willing, do you have any objections Muhammad?"

"None, it is up to Allah" answered Muhammad. Dr. Showkit pondered an awesome truth—it was totally up to Allah.

Dr. Showkit walked to Ward Six with Muhammad. A'isha still sat where they'd left her. Her hood covered her inclined head. As they approached A'isha removed her cloak, exposing her face to Muhammad and Dr. Showkit.

Her eyes held mystery. Showkit might have been looking into a deep lake. The girl projected strength and patience. She had the look of one accustomed to waiting.

Muhammad broke the silence. "A'isha, this is Doctor Showkit. He wishes to have a few words with you."

She spoke in a deliberate cadence. "I've been expecting you, Dr. Showkit. I waited for you to find me. I trust we'll serve each other." Her eyes studied his.

"A'isha, I don't believe we have met. Perhaps you confuse me with someone else."

Her eyes hardened. "Many people are confused. I am not among them. I have a great thing to accomplish. You can help me."

The girl seemed to communicate easily if she so desired, her speech understandable. He pressed, "A'isha, can you tell me something of your childhood and of your parents?"

A'isha's eyes became cold. "Childhood was my time of innocence. I am not a child anymore. My parents are dead, murdered by the infidels of the West." A'isha's voice took on a sharp edge.

"Many have died, A'isha; it is the price of war," Doctor Showkit answered. *Now* was *the moment of truth.* Did A'isha accept the losses of war with resignation or with anger? Did she hate enough to kill on a massive scale? The eyes darkened and the flames in their depths began to rise.

"Do not play with me, Doctor. You need me; and for now, I need you. You have the material and the education I need. Do not be so sure of your childish skills that came from schoolbooks. I have been raised on the words of Allah—and Allah controls everything."

~   ~   ~

"I also have skills and as you are aware—they are rare. You have some questions. I will give you answers. You have doubts and I will give you certitude. Look at me, study my face and decide whether I am the warrior you seek."

Dr. Showkit looked at her. Her eyes engaged him. He felt her strength. He felt that he was falling from a great height, his body spinning. He kept falling toward a distant dot on an immense blue blanket. Closer and closer he fell. The dot became larger and larger.

He kept falling toward earth. He discerned the shape of continents and recognized the land masses of North and South America. He felt no fear . . . could do nothing but observe. Objects became clearer. He saw cities, their tall buildings approaching at amazing speed.

He recognized a monument in a harbor. He continued to fall above New York City. He'd been there before. He kept falling toward the Stature of Liberty.

Yet something was wrong. Nothing moved in the great city. Dots resolved into larger dots and smaller dots, larger dots into automobiles and the smaller dots into people. He saw thousands of cars and tens of thousands of people. Yet nothing moved.

The dead lay everywhere, spreading into hundreds of thousands. The people were motionless. All ages and genders were dead, children scattered like tiny leaves among the adults, all motionless.

Here was Death in all its heinous majesty. All the bodies lay silent—equal—and dead, displaying the great democracy of the grave. Wealth, class, race, and former power meant nothing. A light wind blew loose pieces of litter across the ground. Fallen women's skirts fluttered over legs that had received and given pleasure.

Hats rolled and tumbled. Many of these men once had great expectations of wealth and comfort. The dead all joined the eternal river of the forgotten. The city was silent.

Without warning he saw image after image of city after city. Boston, Atlanta, Houston, San Diego, Los Angeles, San Francisco, and Seattle. All the same: dead bodies—bodies by the millions. Nothing moved in the cities except windblown trash.

He felt massive movement again. His vision swept across the great prairies and vast farmlands of North America. Here were signs of life. Tiny groups of life looked like a handful of shipwrecked sailors cast upon lonely islands. The islands of humanity were few and the ocean of Death vast.

~ ~ ~

The haunting truth hit him. The United States no longer existed as a great power. Gone were the arrogance and the wealth. Gone was the conquering giant that strove across the earth. Gone the power that killed at will and subjugated the weak. Gone—all gone. Nearly all this great land was gripped by—death—by silence—the desolation complete.

The outline of a face startled Showkit. Gradually the image of a beautiful woman appeared. Her long hair was dark, her eyes a cool liquid. A'isha. She spoke softly. "Believe in me my friend—trust me —help me prepare myself. Train me in the name of Allah. What you have seen is possible with your help. I am the Sword of God. Help me sharpen. I will avenge us all!" After those words Dr. Showkit returned to the world he knew.

CHAPTER NINE

D r. Showkit had no idea how long he'd been transfixed. It must have been only moments because Muhammad did not appear to be unduly alarmed. "What a gift this girl has," No-where in ponderous academic literature had he ever read about such a case. His search ended here. He had found Saddam's Sword of Allah.

"A'isha, would you consider moving to another place to learn new skills? We will work well together. Forgive me for my doubts. It's difficult to find one's true path in this life. I am only a weak believer. I stand in awe of your faith and your power. Will you come with me?"

She tossed her head and for a moment looked like a challenging teenager. "Only you hesitated. I've held no doubts." A'isha stood. "Let us begin. I understand the road we must take is long." A'isha turned to Muhammad and spoke softly, "Allah will bless you, Muhammad, and will receive you in due time. I shall be there to meet you."

Dr. Showkit and A'isha walked down the dusty halls that smelled of human waste and out of the Al-Najat orphanage toward a waiting car.

"The sun will set soon, A'isha," the doctor said.

"Yes, in Allah's time the sun will set on our enemies, too." A'isha replied in a flat tone. The teen was gone. With that she draped her head with her cloak and kept silent.

To Muhammad, watching the car roll away, A'isha's coming and her departure with Dr. Showkit was a great mystery. He felt sad, a sort of heart sickness that he couldn't understand. A'isha would live and kindly Muhammad couldn't understand why that thought could make him so ill at ease.

A'isha was unusual and perhaps Allah did have a purpose for her. He could remember her words, "A man will come for me. I've been waiting for him." Today that man had arrived.

Muhammad began to pray. When he rose from his prayers he noticed that it was a rising full moon. He could not remember seeing such a color. Like a huge sphere of blood.

~ ~ ~

December 4, 2003

Jackson continued his search and analysis with growing concern. The Gulf War had been a huge confidence builder for the United States. Its military branches were flush with the pride of victory. Jackson perceived their arrogance as dangerous.

Muslim fighters in Afghanistan wanted an Islamic world government. Muslims' hatred of the West was as fierce as their hatred of the Soviets.

Once again U.S. cultural values blinded its leaders. Washington thought of the Muslims as cultural hillbillies. The image of Mujahedeen warriors charging with swords against Western military machinery was ludicrous. However, the Muslims were deadly serious in their dream of a unified Islamic world.

Islamic martyrdom still existed. Islamic fundamentalism was on the march. Yet someone more dangerous thrived. What Jackson did not know was the name of one Shiite girl in Iraq.

A'isha.

December 7, 2003

Few people in Dur noticed the old man praying in a tiny Mosque in a poor neighborhood. Its other worshippers were of the laboring classes.

In his seventies, he dressed in common peasant clothing. This old man was from Kazakhstan in Central Asia. In earlier days, that area had been under the iron rod of the Soviet Union.

In fact, Abdrahman Alibekov whom most called Yazid, "the Quiet One" had lived all his life in the Soviet Union. His only companion was Allah. Otherwise, Yazid seldom spoke and avoided the excesses of communism. In that brutal system he'd learned the value of the coin of silence.

Yazid had been a lifelong secret Shiite Muslim. In the Soviet Union, he'd only had a hidden Koran.

For Asians it was unusual to get ahead in the Soviet system. His grandfather had been a ruthless communist who executed enough citizens to impress even a killer of Stalin's caliber.

This opened many doors and Yazid benefited from his cold-eyed grandfather's talent, indeed appetite, for murder. Yazid studied hard as a youth and his academic skills did attract attention. Gifted in the sciences, he graduated at the top of his class from the Komsk Army Medical Institute.

He became a military doctor, albeit one who cared little for human life, but whose deepest interests were microbiology and infectious diseases. Attentive superiors noticed and they transferred and promoted him.

The Soviet strategists saw the limitations of nuclear weapons. This weapon had a return address that invited mass retaliation. Dark Slavic minds turned to the study of biological weapons. In time, biological agents proved cheap and deadly. Yazid became part of a vast biological weapons system known as Biopreparat. Biopreparat would become the largest bio-weapons industry in the world.

Yazid met few obstacles in his career. Quiet and competent he posed no threat to his superiors. His simple habit of doing any job well kept them lulled. He felt content with work.

The secret of his contentment? Islam. His parents had been secret Muslims since their youth. His family was Shiites who have often been in a minority position in Muslim culture. Shiites used a practice called "taqiya". Taqiya meant to conceal one's true beliefs in a hostile environment. These habits of deception served Yazid well.

~ ~ ~

The background of biological weapons is well known. Archers of ancient armies dipped their arrows in manure and rotting bodies to increase their deadliness. The Romans catapulted infected bodies over enemy walls. Rotting carcasses poisoned water sources.

During the French and Indian wars, the English gave native peoples blankets infected with smallpox. In World War II, Japan spread the plague over China. The resulting deaths of the Chinese were in the hundreds of thousands. The past is prologue.

All major powers experiment with the great killers: polio, influenza, cholera, plague, tuberculosis, smallpox, and typhus. They invested hundreds of millions of dollars in refining anthrax, botulism, and others. And so, it goes...

The first Soviet facility for biological warfare research was the Leningrad Military Academy. In 1930 the first efforts were attempts to cultivate typhus. By the mid-1930s much research moved to Solovetsky Island, a cold, barren prison camp in Siberia for political prisoners. At Solovestsky Island diseases such as Q fever, glanders, and melioidosis were applied to helpless, dying prisoners all in the name of research.

Everything was classified. Prestigious scientific organizations stood at the heart of Soviet research: the Institute of Protein, The Institute of Molecular Biology, The Institute of Biochemistry, and the Institute of Bioorganic Chemistry among many others. The ancient cities of Russia were all involved: Minsk, Leningrad, Moscow, Volgograd, and Sverdlovsk.

Yazid worked for long years to meet and overcome challenges to biological attack. Temperature and weather conditions mattered. Viruses lose effectiveness in bright sunlight. Rain, snow, and cold wind currents also had an effect. Such physical problems were a challenge to one like Yazid. But with time and effort Yazid and his colleagues surmounted most of these problems.

However, Russia wasn't the only place where science was making deadly leaps forward. In July 1973 two scientists in California succeeded in splicing genes from a South African toad into the DNA of E.coli. This was the first result of the new theory of gene splicing. It was now possible to cross biological barriers between species.

~ ~ ~

This created utterly new forms of life. Such a feat was as revolutionary as splitting the atom. This affected scientists everywhere. Making a Super Killer became real. The new creation would be beyond any known cure.

Scientists called this new biological weapon a chimera, a mythical monster that had the head of a lion, body of a goat, and the tail of a snake. The new science would allow two or more diseases to be combined.

The hybrid was much more dangerous than its parents divided. New biological creations could be blended into any number of genetic combinations. Each could take months or even years to decode. The attacked population would not have time to discover the genetic key. No defense existed.

~ ~ ~

Developed countries could be overwhelmed in just days. Health care workers would be infected first. Within three days almost all doctors, nurses, and medical staff would be dying. Social panic would strain State and Federal law enforcement agencies beyond the breaking point. A complete social breakdown was possible. The attacked country would not have any means of self-defense or be clear who to counter-attack since the disease would not have a return address.

The new science was difficult to sell to the military. Old soldiers live in the past, expecting future wars to be fought like previous ones. Most warriors who fought with tanks couldn't conceive of a virus as a major weapon. A few military leaders did see the future. Viruses were cheap, silent, and invisible. No amount of armor could resist them. Yazid believed mankind without Allah would not survive. Humanity could survive only under a Muslim theocracy. The full blessings of Islamic religion would bring international accord. He cared only because it was his purpose to serve Allah.

When the Soviet Union fell on December 26,1991, Yazid slipped away with ease. His Asian features, native central Asian background, and Muslim faith made him invisible. He dressed and acted like a poor peasant. His repeated explanation for crossing borders, his desire to return to family members, went unchallenged.

In Iraq Yazid found his destiny.

CHAPTER TEN

December 8, 2003

At sunrise Dr. Showkit had already been studying for over two hours, not unusual because in the desert all activity is governed by the blistering sun. His office was in an unremarkable villa on the outskirts of Ramadi, fifty miles west of Baghdad. Ramadi was a combination of rural living with close access to Baghdad's resources.

A'isha's accommodations were Spartan. She lacked any amenities, sleeping on a rough wooden bunk without a mattress, several worn blankets, and a three-legged stool.

Dr. Showkit intended to control every element in A'isha's environment, to train her mind and body to survive adversity. Hard conditions make hard people. To mass murder in the tens of millions took a psychotic killer that could remain focused. It would take intense training to bring that candidate to a point of perfection.

A'isha had been at Ramadi for two weeks. Dr. Showkit encouraged her to pursue prayer. She obeyed without comment or complaint. A good sign.

The trainee willingly followed orders with silent patience. She seemed to grasp everything around her with that spiritual strength.

Her diet was simple: dates, bread, and a few bits of goat meat. For liquid A'isha had water. Showkit sensed A'isha was fully aware of his manipulation.

He hadn't discussed the mission with her yet. A cool serenity made it seem as if she knew her life would be short. Did she hold unusual reserves? Nothing bothered her. She prayed and meditated for hours. His newly discovered womanly commando showed great patience and self-discipline.

He looked over his notes finding it obvious there was no one size fits all when it came to psychopath profile. Psychopaths came from all walks of life. Most experts agreed psychopaths were the most dangerous to society. A religious psychopath was less common. A religious psychopath allowed the killer to leave all responsibility to God. In a sense, God performed the acts of mass killing.

Dr. Showkit felt confident A'isha was the right selection.

Strangely, however, international professional literature did not include revenge as a primary motivator. The West was insensitive to tribal Arab cultures. In tribal cultures a person's honor or the honor of their family might be the most valuable possession the family possesses. Attacks demanded revenge.

The time to talk to A'isha was at hand. He rose from his desk and put his files away.

December 9, 2003

A'isha sat against the outer wall of the grounds of her new quarters. This outer wall formed part of a large courtyard enclosed by a low stone fence. It contained a small garden with a fountain of flowing water. A listener heard the blessed liquid running over the small rocks, a beautiful sound. The sloping ground gave her an unimpeded view toward the East. A'isha could watch stars fade as the glow of the sun climbed to meet the horizon.

A'isha had often viewed the sunrise from her tiny family home in Baghdad where she watched her father prepare his cart for the customers.

Baghdad was part village, part city, part past, and part present. A'isha remembered it as home. She often accompanied her father on his daily labors.

In Baghdad people bargained over the price of everything. It was part of the joy of living that adults would spend a half hour debating the merits of a particular piece of fruit. In the end, a fair price would be paid. It was natural. It was home.

All that changed when bombs destroyed so much. Her parents were dead. Her innocent sisters were dead. Her friends and neighbors had also been destroyed. There was no reason this had to happen. Her parents had never harmed anyone. Her neighbors were simple people with normal frailties. Nor could A'isha imagine better people than her parents.

In her tiny home in Baghdad, she had learned the Islamic profession of faith— "the Shahadah." "Ashhadu an la ilaha illa Llah, wa ashhadu anna Muhammad rasulu Llah." These were the first words spoken in her ears as a newborn: "I testify that there is no God but Allah, and I testify that Muhammad is his Prophet."

She would carry the words in her heart up to her last seconds of life. A'isha thought of her peaceful father as she awaited the rising sun. She'd studied the words of the Prophet and explored her conscience.

Had not the West invaded her country? Had the West not attacked as aggressors? Were simple civilians and children murdered? The answer was simple—the West had violated the most sacred commands of the Koran. In the vanishing darkness she imagined the sun as the coming wrath of Allah.

As sure as Allah lived she would avenge the deaths of her family and all the innocents. She'd have her revenge on the hated United States who came with its planes and bombs. Did these unbelievers think they could kill whomever they wanted at no price? A'isha knew Allah would guide her hand.

Allah had been with her in the bomb-shattered building during her hours of thirst and agony. Allah had comforted her and protected her in the darkness of her three-day horror. Allah was with the dying children at the orphanage. He strengthened her as she accompanied their bodies to their graves, innocents dead before they had a chance to live.

A'isha was only a weapon in Allah's hands. She hadn't forgotten her vision. Allah had called her his "little one" and said He would be with her always. Allah made her "the Sword of God". Allah commanded her to slay the murdering unbelievers in untold millions. This she would do.

She'd been given power and could see many things that were hidden from her when she was a child. She had new abilities of concentration previously unrealized.

She must wait for the hour Allah had selected for her revenge. There would be no mercy.

Allah would guide her. She had to be patient. She sat motionless until the sun cleared the horizon. In time it would rise on her day of revenge. She only had to be patient.

~ ~ ~

December 11, 2003

Dr. Showkit sat lost in his plans. Today he'd talk to A'isha. He would have to feel his way in this dangerous endeavor.

He found her seated, leaning against the stone wall of her quarters. She'd been watching the sun rise, both radiated power. An aura of violence hovered around her.

When the doctor came within a few feet of her he had the strangest feeling he was about to speak to an inanimate object.

A'isha spoke first. "Good morning, Doctor. You've decided today to discuss serious matters with me. You've waited nearly two weeks to see if I am tractable and patient. Tell me Doctor, have you assured yourself of my suitability for this project?"

He nodded. "Yes A'isha. This is a good day to talk. Please come with me to my office where we'll have privacy."

In response she followed him and stood in front of his desk. "Please, be seated," the doctor said. "Our goal is difficult. We will work together. The direct approach is best to broach our team effort."

"I've been selected by the Iraqi government to find an agent to carry out a massive military strike against the United States on its own soil. The mission is complex and the person who fulfills it must be able to work alone for long periods of time. It would be correct to call this person a soldier for Allah."

"At a certain time or upon specific conditions, this Iraqi soldier must initiate a massive strike that will destroy the United States. American deaths will be in historic numbers, ruinous to America. Also, the Iraqi agent will not survive her mission."

"A'isha, you have suffered losses as have many Iraqi people. The Arab world has endured domination by the Western countries for too long. A'isha, I ask you directly—are you the one we seek?"

It is strange how at certain times a decision or an action can balance the lives of millions of people on the edge of a knife blade. The past, the present, and the future seemed to merge for a moment—and wait. To Showkit, the world held its breath, waiting for the response of a fifteen-year-old Muslim girl.

Showkit's office seemed to darken. The girl remained silent and motionless. Her eyes caught his attention. They seemed to smolder. Patterns of light and darkness shifted rapidly across her face. Those eyes were a window into hell.

A'isha spoke with the hiss of a viper, "I will kill them all. Give me the sword and I shall slay them. I will slay them by the millions and the tens of millions. In the name of Allah, it shall be done. Then, I will return to Allah. I am his Sword."

Dr. Showkit froze, terrified. What horror was this? Finally, he regained composure. "A'isha, yes, you are the Sword of Allah. I will help prepare you and train you. It will be you and Allah who strike the blow. You will avenge the Arab peoples. Leave me now—we will begin tomorrow."

~ ~ ~

Alone again, Showkit pondered what he had experienced; despite his scientific learning, this was a mystery from Allah. The professional classification for A'isha was a psychopathic killer. She was clearly traumatized by the three days and three nights confined with her mother's corpse in the building's rubble. Her only goal now was revenge for the deaths of her family and all the innocent Iraqi's murdered in the Gulf War. She was consumed by hate and she would have her revenge. There was nothing he could do to prevent this deadly mission. He had many family members in Baghdad. Did he have the right to place them on meat hooks to die slowly? He prayed. The Sword of God was being formed. He received only silence.

~ ~ ~

December 20, 2003

Yazid always took meticulous care in preparation for the Salat, the prayer for intercession. All devout Muslims made this prayer five times a day. Yazid intended to be acceptable to Allah. This was a good time for reflection both on who he was and how he could help make the entire world Muslim. For decades Yazid had studied the art and science of biologic weapons.

The production of the bio-product was simple for those who were knowledgeable in the basic science.

The virus must be activated, stabilized, hardened, and then reduced to the correct size by a milling process. Dispensing the virus particles involved random wind currents moving the invisible mist for miles. Russia had achieved lethal effectiveness up to 50 miles.

Yazid had also worked in Koltsovo, Siberia. The secret name for this facility: "Vector". By 1988 "Vector" had the capacity to produce 25 tons of deadly pathogens per year. This was more than enough to kill every human on earth.

He smiled considering the wisdom of Allah. Large cities would be vulnerable. After an attack, foodstuffs would be consumed in 48 hours. A few days without electricity would render food in refrigerators spoiled and deadly. What a complex organism a city is! Everything must work perfectly for the organism to live. Commerce would be disrupted, and the lack of normal human interaction would bring the most modern city to chaos in hours. The breakdown of civil authority and police protection would be swift.

The supply of water and electricity would fail because both items are maintenance intensive. Every home would be thrown into darkness. Violence and looting would begin.

Flash Fire would kill all age groups. Diseases that kill the young and old often leave the prime producing class intact. However, Flash Fire would kill everyone equally with no regard to age, sex, social or financial class. Flash Fire was truly democratic in its killing. The problem solvers would also die.

CHAPTER ELEVEN

Yazid escaped the Soviet Union through Central Asia via ancient smuggling routes. Using them he could go to Iran, Afghanistan, or Iraq.

After the U.S. bombings, Saddam, Yazid figured, must be hungering to avenge his losses. Yazid had learned from watching his grandfather, that power grew in violence and innovation.

He labored for several difficult months to gain access to Saddam, so insulated by security rings. Yazid, also security minded from childhood, did not seek to meet Saddam himself.

Yazid needed Saddam's money and power to realize his own striving and activate his ambitious plan to serve Allah. The dictator, of course, always sought new weapons, weapons unknown to his enemies.

The years spent in the Soviet system had taught Yazid the value of patience and of secrecy. He began courting the Iraqi dictator by sending a letter to a well-known Iraqi scientist. He explained his expertise in biological warfare but did not identify himself. The letter explained that he intended to produce biological weapons to strengthen Iraq and the cause of Islam. He preferred working alone in a laboratory with no assistants.

Yazid advised the surprised scientist to bypass the chain of command to ensure utmost security. His letter's recipient had no choice but to follow Yazid's instructions. Saddam was famous for testing officials to assess their loyalty to him.

The scientific information in the unsigned letter showed the writer to be no crank. The local scientist recognized that the writer was well versed in virology and genetic engineering.

Yazid succeeded in conveying his message to Saddam by using the main tool that opened doors to the dictator: absolute fear of Saddam himself.

The slow dance between Saddam and Yazid went on for months, each aware of how spies flood bureaucracies. Step by careful step the dancers drew closer. Yazid wrote of his desire to create a bio-strike against the United States.

Saddam and Yazid established a relationship where only two people stood between Saddam and Yazid. This "two-link" chain is one of the hardest security methods for governments to penetrate. The first link was a member of Saddam's own family, the second a common Iraqi soldier.

The communication system was the essence of simplicity. Saddam would give a sealed message to the first link who would meet the second at different locations. The second link would meet Yazid at different places.

Saddam would have the second link murdered after the young soldier delivered the message. The second link ended as a permanent cut-out whose knowledge died with him.

The executed soldier's family was told their son had been lost in the service of his country, and would receive a liberal financial compensation for losing him. Saddam was as fair as his survival allowed. He didn't think of the possibility of a weeping fiancé, or of the broken-hearted father.

Together Saddam and Yazid would change the world.

~   ~   ~

December 24, 2003

It had been over a year since Jackson felt his first pangs of unease. Jackson admitted to skeptical superiors he found no evidence. Yet, something stirred, a growing evil lurked closer. Jackson caught occasional sensations of it moving ever nearer by the day. Someone or something with true destructive power grew in a void of spiritual emptiness. He sighed.

Perhaps he would find the invisible predator tomorrow.

~   ~   ~

January 2, 2004

A'isha sat on a rocky outcropping in the Iraqi desert, a remote section of the Anbar Province two hundred miles west of Baghdad. This night wheeling constellations made time visible above her. Four cold hours must pass before the sun could lift free over the horizon bringing scorching heat. Her only protection from the elements during the previous days were the ragged robes she pulled around her. By day she loosened those hoping for moving air. A'isha hadn't eaten for nine days. This trial was to last ten days to teach A'isha the blessing of eternity. The desert destroyed the weak and fearful.

Anything would be better than the bodily torment and mental onslaught of the desert.

The weight of isolation threatened to crush her. Perhaps she would swirl into nothingness inside a stinging whirlwind. Many a strong man had lost sanity in the sheer loneliness of barren wastes, the desert indifferent to humanity. She could be like that. Indifferent to others, serving only Allah. Forever. She sucked at the trickle of blood from ripping at her nails. Something moist for her dry, scabby lips. Was peaceful eternity what came after she consumed herself?

Her newest trainer, Najib, a shriveled old man of the desert, traced his family through Bedu tribes who roamed the Middle East deserts since time before measure. He'd followed the ancient life of a smuggler until an Iraqi military helicopter pilot saw him slipping down a desert wadi just before sunset in the desert.

The helicopter crew took the opportunity to kill this human vermin for sport, first firing a burst behind him to make him run. The old man did not run. He pulled an ancient .303 British bolt action rifle from under his robes and coolly killed the pilot with a single shot through his head at 215 meters.

The frantic copilot attempted to gain control of the listing machine when the old man sent a fatal shot though his chest. The helicopter spun to the ground where it exploded in a brilliant fireball. Unfortunately for Najib there was another. This hunting machine crew was both wary and lucky as the alert gunner on the Russian Hind spotted the fleeing smuggler. A quick burst from him brought Najib down.

When the crew landed, it found no survivors of the first helicopter. The old man lay face down with a bullet hole through his back. They assumed him dead and carelessly rolled him over to inspect the body. With a viper's speed Najib drove his knife into one man's throat and then ripped into the stomach of a second. A shot from the crew chief ended Najib's actions.

Furious, the crew wanted to finish Najib on the spot but obeyed the radio order to bring him to the base. The base commander wanted to know about the old man who destroyed an expensive helicopter with an obsolete rifle.

Unfortunately for Najib, the crew was not to be denied their revenge. They beat him in the desert and guards beat him daily in the excrement-lined cell in a Baghdad prison. Najib received no food, no water, or medical treatment. He never spoke to his torturers, and his threshold of endurable pain remained remarkable. After five days of torture Najib would have died on the sixth in silence except that Allah saved him.

Headquarters had been seeking a man of the desert who impressed his captors by his strength. This unspeaking old man who'd survived two bullet wounds was selected and taken to a hospital. The attendants found it incredible that this filthy, wounded old man still lived. Yet, in only days Najib began to heal. His recovery and resilience astonished the staff.

The old man was under guard around the clock. Dr. Showkit observed Najib and persuaded him to speak. Showkit convinced Najib that cooperation would be the sole key to his continued survival. Najib must teach a young person to survive in the desert and endure great pain. Wary, Najib agreed on two conditions: he asked for his old Enfield rifle and his homemade knife as each held deep meaning for him. The Enfield rifle had been given to him by his father when Najib was a boy. The knife was even more personal. Dr. Showkit delivered them himself to the distrustful old smuggler in his hospital room.

The two men walked out side by side. Hospital staff exchanged relieved glances to see their dangerous patient's departure. Dr. Showkit's relief lay in having found another fitting piece in his puzzle of destruction.

Najib met A'isha at midmorning. Dr. Showkit took him toward the dark cloaked figure seated beside a bubbling fountain in a peaceful garden. Najib paused, sensing danger.

Dr. Showkit whispered, "She is what you feel."

The girl slipped the hood from her head and turned soft dark eyes toward Najib. Those eyes conveyed a mysterious strength. They pulled him toward her. A slow smile bloomed across her face. "Be at peace old man. I've been waiting for you, a lion of the endless desert with much to teach me. Men could not kill you although they tried. You've killed many."

Najib felt an instant affection for this girl. In truth, he had killed many men. The smuggler's world proved dark and violent. Even worse, the few people he had loved in his youth were also dead.

Najib's voice managed to sound both soft and gruff. "Yes child, I shall carry memories of those I killed to my grave."

"Well said, my old fighter. I, too, must kill with you to train me. I, too, have memories to carry to my grave." There was a feeling of gentle fingers probing his past. "Tell me, old man, when your wife betrayed you, did you enjoy killing her and her lover?"

Najib fought to control himself. How could this girl know such a thing that happened long years ago. No one alive knew the tragic details of that hour.

Najib had been young and full of youthful passion. He loved his wife to the point of adoration. Her betrayal had killed them all: she herself, her clandestine lover and Najib. Because of that horrible night Najib lost all love and trust in humanity. He had turned his face to the desert and shunned all bonds and cruelties of civilization. He became a barbarian.

A'isha telegraphed sympathy. She said, "Don't be troubled, old man. Death surrounds us. Killing the man gave you pleasure, did it not? That is understandable. Yet your wife was a different matter. The knife you plunged in her heart destroyed you. The knife you carry at your waist took both their lives and warped your own."

"Be at peace, Najib, your wife paid for her folly. She waits for you beyond Death's gates. You will be reunited and find your lost joy. As Allah has forgiven you, you must train me to serve Allah. My road is long, and my task strains my ability. Strengthen me. I serve as a sword of Allah and will one day meet you and your wife in the gardens of paradise."

Stunned, Najib wondered how this child knew both his name and past. Then Allah touched his heart and Najib began to weep.

Dr. Showkit stood amazed. Here was a man Saddam's torturers couldn't break, yet he wept before A'isha and extended his old man's rough hand to her. A'isha rose with dignity and gently grasped his fingers. Najib kissed her hand and composed himself. "Child, you are a messenger of Allah. Your enemies are my enemies. I will train you, and I thank you for the comfort you have given me."

A'isha said, "The world will remember this hour and Allah will give us strength."

This would prove true. At the end of her life, after the final hours, after the dead had fallen, after the tears had been shed, her words came true.

A world in shambles remembered.

Najib was alone at his camp. He had to test A'isha mentally and physically. His test demanded ten days of suffering alone in the desert with little water and no food. Najib had told A'isha that her mind must seek shelter from the desert by retreating deep within her own soul.

"The mind," he told her, "Has to be trained to separate from the bondage of flesh and blood. The ordinary human body is not life's commander. The mind must rule over flesh. To succumb to pain and discomfort is to die. The mind must live alone and the agony of a body dying in the desert must be ignored. To conquer the body is to conquer the world."

A'isha thought about his words as she endured all that the desert demanded. Najib filled her small canteen with a meager amount of water once a day. No words passed between them. Najib could tell immediately how well A'isha was holding up.

He loved the child but had orders to train her without allowance for her youth. Her strength astonished him. He pushed her beyond reason, yet she endured. He did not yet know her mission. He only knew that she was part of Allah's plan.

During the trial by desert, A'isha showed herself to be a true force. The only question: would she live? If she could live until dawn the ten-day ordeal would be over. Her condition appeared dire. By the sixth day most men would have died. She herself was on the cusp of the grave.

By the ninth day, she'd lived three days beyond hope or reason or anything Najib had ever witnessed. The daytime heat and the nighttime cold had each been unusually brutal. Nevertheless, the ten-day trial remained mandatory. The desert made no exception for love, hope, or age. Once the test began A'isha was committed to Allah. Allah held the fire of any desert day in his hand. Allah sent the cold wind that swept through colorless desert nights. Najib prayed. Time crept on.

Such thoughts were not in A'isha's mind where a battle raged between will and body. A'isha's suffering astonished her, but she had to gain strength for the task Allah set before her. Unafraid of death, she feared only failure. Still, Allah felt far from her at this hour.

Allah planned to scourge her to prepare for her ultimate test. She must ready herself to die. Only in the desert could one truly learn that death is desirable release. Only after enduring hours of eviscerating heat could she understand death as a blessing. The desert night with its hours of crippling cold assured her that death was far better than another endless night in the desert.

After she sat nearly motionless for nine days and nights did eternity became understandable. Only when she'd fasted for nine days, and nine nights did she truly long for the promised fruits and comforts of paradise.

A'isha learned what the ancients had known: God speaks with greatest clarity to those in solitude.

A'isha didn't know the desert is the source of all strong monotheist religions. Moses of the Jewish faith received his clearest messages from God within the desert wastes of the Sinai.

Jesus, son of a carpenter brought his gentler vision after his rigorous testing of 40 days in the wilderness. Muhammad received his aggressive visions from the silent depths of a remote desert cave. For centuries, the desert has burned the dross and the superficiality of daily life from selected individuals destined to change the world.

No thoughts of fame or recognition propelled A'isha in her hours of endurance. She fought constant temptation to drink the entire day's supply of water in a few frantic moments. During the day hell meant reality; a wall of flame burned from a hundred directions; the landscape altered to a shimmering expanse of floating images.

In her exhaustion, A'isha saw images of pools of cool water surrounded by date trees. She watched small groups of people resting with their camels beside crystalline brooks or vast lakes of sparkling clarity. To the dying girl, the cool lakes seemed but a few hundred meters away.

A'isha heard friendly voices of the tribesmen calling her to join them on the shores. The kind voices pleaded with her to come and rest in the shade of the tall date trees. The source of temptation was the dark prince Iblis whose followers are demons known as "jinn."

During each night cold penetrated her shivering skin until its icy fingers clutched her soul. Bitter cold winds swept the weak from the desert entering like knife blades through her black and blistered skin. The moon spread its pale flickering light bringing imagined dangers. Imagined images of horrible creeping creatures stalking her flickered on the dune's edges.

Imagination created fears growing to towering dimensions, and inspired panic. Najib had warned her against the dangers of panic. Running brought death. The desert provided no room for fear. Najib had warned her that only one path leads to life: complete mental self-control.

Fatalism of the desert born is simple: one cannot flee death; one can only accept fate with courage. For those who are going through the trial of fire it is hard to remember, hard to hear reason's low whisper when the mind screams in agony.

A'isha had to find strength to endure.

CHAPTER TWELVE

A great strength of the Islamic people is their willingness to leave matters of life and death in Allah's hands.

Such thoughts were beyond the emaciated girl who'd lost all sense of days, hours, or minutes during her ordeal. She knew only light or dark, heat or cold, and the torture of her personal famine. She yearned for death. When she tried to pray her cracked, ridged lips, thick tongue and mouth felt paralyzed.

She saw images of herself as a little girl running into Mira's arms. Among rippled sand currents she thought she made out a sister who teased her by pulling her black hair.

Then came that memory of a blinding flash of light followed by darkness.

A'isha smelled her mother's blood and the pain of that memory exceeded even this pain of present torture. She remembered running her fingers over Mira's crushed skull. She remembered her humble father's prayers. A'isha could feel a tiny flame of hate return, hatred of America, and she nursed that flame. Someday, with Allah's help she would raise the flame to scorching holocaust.

She thought of her enemies laughing in the comfort of homes in their faraway land, assuming they could kill innocent Arab civilians so casually. Arab dead, including her parents and family, cried out from the ground. "Avenge us," they shrieked out to her.

A'isha's weakened body yearned for death, but not her mind. She wanted to live only until the right moment, to live so she could die for the purpose that was her reason to have been born and named, for the privilege, for the joy of revenge.

A'isha swam against currents of berserk madness. She gathered her thoughts to resist death. Each breath inhaled meant triumph because it meant service to Allah.

She continued to see the image of a distant flame. Despite pain and suffering, she felt herself becoming a fury who swept through narrowing halls. She felt herself rushing upward through swirling air and enveloping darkness, a skeletal wraith from depths of hell.

Her only purpose was to reach the burning object. Her spirit soared towards the flames on that flickering object. They danced higher, so, so high. She strained to reach the object. She would die to do that.

She flew until her mind revealed the object as a flaming sword, a sword of destiny with a blade of silver and fire. *The Sword of Allah.*

When she touched the weapon's hilt her mind burst into a light that illuminated everything around her. She grasped it with hands reborn with newfound strength. She felt a surge of glorious power flow down the blade and into her.

She whispered exultant words. "I shall avenge us all."

Najib heard A'isha's whisper as he took her in his arms. Dawn had broken ending the girl's ordeal of the forge.

~ ~ ~

January 13, 2004

At midmorning in Ramidie Dr. Showkit sat at his desk across from Najib. A'isha's desert ordeal had nearly killed her. She was recovering on intravenous liquids to re-hydrate. It would take three weeks for her to regain her normal weight. It had been a close thing with her life. Nevertheless, A'isha had to be tested to the maximum.

If Saddam's mission failed the consequences would be fatal for both trainers and their families. "Najib, how did A'isha respond to her desert trials? Did she ever complain or show erratic behavior? Did you detect weakness of any kind?"

Najib answered, "A'isha survived conditions which would have killed any man I've known. She has power I 've never seen. She never uttered a word until her ordeal's completion. Then she whispered, "I shall avenge us all." Her words carried intense conviction.

Revenge is her absolute goal. A'isha appears to be a beautiful girl, but she is a force, a deadly force in Allah's hands. No human being should have survived that ten-day ordeal."

"Najib, A'isha has a fateful mission. We must test her to the extreme. Remember she is not ours. She belongs only to Allah. Our task is to push A'isha beyond normal levels of human endurance."

"This mission is of gravest import to Arabs and our holy Muslim faith, not to mention to Saddam Hussein. We must not fail A'isha. We must provide everything she needs. Anything less than total victory would mean our lives as well as our families We must not fail."

Najib replied, "A'isha is a star in the firmament, distant, beautiful, yet so cold. Only Allah possesses her. I can train her. With Allah's help we will succeed,"

Dr. Showkit pondered. Lighter training should happen next. Certainly, A'isha needed physical rest after the desert trial.

"Najib, you have done well. A'isha must be trained and tested at every step."

After the old man left, Dr. Showkit remained at his desk, thinking of the harm this fifteen-year-old girl would ultimately release against the Western world. She would become death in human form. Was this truly a proper mission for him, a man who had promised to "First do no harm?" In his opinion A'isha should be in treatment. He and the Iraqi state was using this damaged girl for evil means. He prayed for forgiveness.

~ ~ ~

January 17, 2004

Over time Yazid, the Baltic featured old man of science formed a relationship with Saddam who provided Yazid funds and property. His underground laboratory stored the latest technology. It was located beneath a bakery which had trucks coming and going in the normal course of its business. This allowed supplies to be delivered without calling undue attention to itself and there was little reason for anyone to suspect it was more serious than any small business.

The underground laboratory consisted of three 40-foot rooms connected in linear fashion. Each had a protocol for usage. Double door air locks separated each room.

Yazid used the standard Soviet risk system for containing dangerous biological substances. Every inch of every room sprayed with an epoxy that completely sealed them. No pathogen of any kind could escape the building through cracks. The epoxy also made the rooms and walls smooth and easy to sterilize.

An array of spraying nozzles lined every ceiling and wall. Advanced biological sensors provided detection of any breakdown in room atmosphere. If that appeared, the safety systems would turn on automatically, sterilization nearly instantly.

In Zone one the operator wore a standard lab jacket with no special protection other than standard safety rules. Zone Two, designated "hot," contained large amounts of unprocessed pathogens.

Centrifuges concentrated the pathogen to its final form in Zone Three. Here drying and milling machines reduced deadly products to the correct size to remain air suspended and able to drift dozens of miles.

The centrifuges proved dangerous because the spinning devices had a high rim speed. If a glass vial broke it would spread the deadly pathogen through the room. In zone three important hot boxes with rubber sleeves allowed him to work with substances too dangerous to exist outside their enclosed containers. This was a world of latent death.

As the "hottest" zone it required "space suits" of heavy rubber, bubble helmets, and large gloves. Even walking in the Zone Three facility was a slow and laborious practice. The stress of working around such pathogens was high. One slip, one accident, or even one unforeseen circumstance would mean a horrible death. Even worse, the pathogens might escape into the population. Still, Yazid remained aware that fatal accidents could happen.

Supplies and equipment were available throughout the world. Any microbiology lab could be used to make biological weapons. There were electron microscopes from Japan, test tubes and ovens from France, centrifuges from Germany and England, electrical components from Canada, and micro-milling machines from Switzerland.

A satisfied Yazid walked through the small laboratory he'd created. He'd been planning every inch for forty years.

Any facility that makes farm fertilizer, vaccines, or pesticides can produce extremely dangerous viruses. Money can buy anything, and cash can buy silence and end paper trails leaving governments helpless to prevent such transactions.

Commercial arteries had become a maze of legitimate and illegitimate companies. Saddam's long arm reached into the darkest commercial corners. Cash is the underworld's only acceptable currency.

The more desired the merchandise, the more certain it would be found and delivered. Demand will create supply.

Yazid had lived for Allah for over six decades, always in complete trust that his God would protect him.

Yazid didn't care about his own earthly fate, only that Islam advance worldwide. Without Allah, the mighty Soviet Union had been like a great oak tree, strong and massive on the outside, but as to that godless tree, the inner core was rotted. In the end, the smallest social storms had brought it crashing to the ground.

Islam would not conquer humankind only by the sword. Allah, blessed be his name, had commanded the procreation of large families. Through sheer numbers Islam could overwhelm any democracy in time. However, Yazid had no patience to wait for the slow victory of demographics. He wanted to see the United States destroyed in his lifetime.

Yazid had no warmth to give a woman or children. He devoted himself to Allah through science. Soon, he believed, an Islamic dictator would take power thanks to his pathogen. He knew nothing could defend against biological weapons. Human soldiers would be obsolete since toxic viruses could kill as surely as a rifle bullet.

A mere five pound can of the right toxin could kill every man, woman or child in a city populated by millions. Death could travel through mail and any of thousands of commercial routes daily. The new killers were not deterred by armor plate or the high morale of specially trained soldiers. The instant a soldier breathed or touched the toxin a cruel death followed.

Typically, high fevers drove the sufferer insane. Brain cells literally melted away. Every orifice in the body shed blood or blood mixed with feces. Human tissue would liquefy, the stench created nearly unbearable.

Everything the sufferer touched would be infectious. Every drop of blood, sweat, or bodily waste conveyed a death warrant when touched by a healthy person. Each victim became a carrier. Human to human contact would spread through populations like wildfire.

CHAPTER THIRTEEN

Yazid had worked for years to genetically merge Smallpox, Marburg, and Ebola into one super deadly virus. Most of his coworkers declared it impossible. But after years of refinement, scientific research had produced strains of smallpox far more lethal than nature's original efforts. This meant solid progress.

Marburg was something new. Transported to Germany via a green monkey, its victims all died in gruesome agony. Marburg liquefied human tissue. The patients went insane as brain cells melted away. Before they died, every pore leaked fatal amounts of blood.

Then there was Ebola, named after the Ebola River, where it originated. It shared some characteristics with Marburg. The mortality rate of Marburg or Ebola were both almost 97%.

Yazid observed how constant mutations are the ceaseless creations of nature's drive to maintain life from the smallest bit to the most massive creatures. A new life form may supplant another, and, of course, may not be benign.

His solitary quest for the super virus had taken thousands of hours. It was no simple thing to create the Holy Grail of biological weapons. Smallpox, Ebola, and Marburg were all viruses. He believed there had to be a common thread running through the entire virus family. There must be a cipher to unlock the secret.

He never forgot the night he broke the code after labouring with the same DNA elements for so many years. The twisted helix of DNA, that long alphabet entranced him. The thousands of DNA bits were a madding jumbled maze of gibberish, an elaborate code of incredible complexity.

He'd said his evening prayers to Allah and recommitted his life to Islam; then something strange happened. He decided to invert the order of several DNA snippets. This time a miracle resulted. The recombination came alive, and all the diverse parts of the pathogen worked in harmony. He cultured and cross tested it against common antibiotics.

The new virus became even stronger in the presence of common antibiotics, seeming to explode with terrible, unexpected virulence in their presence. Yazid stood in awe of what he was seeing. He fell to his knees in thanksgiving. He wept at the mercy and the grace of Allah who gave him such an incredible discovery.

He knew that there would be many hurdles to cross before his final attack, but Allah had given him the weapon he needed. Equally important Yazid also discovered a myelin toxin that had the unusual ability to act as a precise biological time piece. It was possible to control how long the virus could live. A scientist could eliminate a target population with a deadly pathogen set to burn out after a programmed period.

Yazid named his creation "Flash Fire." Flash Fire would go through a targeted population as driven flames through a forest of dead trees. This new life form would squelch any hope of America's survival. Its citizenry wouldn't have time to create an effective vaccination.

To Yazid the separation of Church and State was an American blasphemy. It allowed Satan to exist unchallenged. Under Islam Allah's words were never defamed. Now surviving humankind would not be deluded by false religions. Submissive women would make loving homes and raise worthy children. A world not divided by wealth, power, or race. All would be equal before Allah and war would be banished.

Yazid would happily kill every infidel to obtain peace in a world ruled by Allah. Yazid cherished the old dream of a golden age with no war, pain, or want. He dreamed of a world of eternal youth with the daily joy of walking with Allah. He didn't consider that people have always sought a land of milk and honey: Nirvana, Heaven, Zion, Valhalla, Shangri-la or the Elysian-fields. There were many others.

For Yazid the penalty for defaming or leaving Islam must be death. Unbelievers have no right to live, worship, or hope in another path to an elusive heaven. The world was not large enough for both Islam and other beliefs. For Shiite Yazid, those others must perish.

~ ~ ~

The old scientist stood in his underground laboratory before a stainless-steel counter. A special box with rubber sleeves allowed him to work safely with pathogens.

Inside that hot box container was another small one, sealed and of stainless steel. When Yazid escaped the Soviet Union he carried four flasks representing nearly 40 years of intense experimentation. The endless work in the Soviet Union finally paid off. Each vial contained eight ounces of the dehydrated Flash Fire virus. Thirty-two ounces represented his entire life work. The hot box before him contained sterilized syringes and very fine needles as well as fresh chicken eggs. Viruses must grow in living subjects.

The technique involved injecting microscopic amounts of dehydrated virus in chicken eggs, then sealing them with paraffin. The monster would grow and feed on its living host: the lowly chicken egg.

Then it would replicate itself until it engulfed the host. The eggs were punctured, then stripped of their viral mass. Flash Fire would demand more and more food. In return it would multiply into trillions of malignant particles, a killer capable of destroying every human being on earth.

A virus created by a man who felt that he was called to save the world from itself,

Flash Fire now existed, and life would never be the same.

Yazid had no knowledge of A'isha. Not a member of the academic, financial, or political elite, she would show that many dangerous people have no army, no academic learning, but carry a firm immovable belief.

January 23, 2004

Washington, D.C.

Jackson still searched for the ogre hovering on the edges of his intuition, a monster still invisible to his colleagues. He felt certain it posed a grave threat to the U.S. and the world beyond. Someone lurked in darkness. Jackson could feel that someone growing in strength and power. He'd been in this business too long to doubt his own premonitions.

The political elite were awakening to threats like ISIS whose goal was to export fundamental Islam to the entire Middle East. ISIS recruited from the hopeless, hate filled, and desperate. Destruction approached Jackson mused. The most dangerous threat can approach from one who operates alone, when plans and secrets lurk in just one mind.

What if a leader financed someone not being "run" by home country intelligence services? Layers of informers would be by-passed. What if the agent wasn't trained through normal channels? Jackson decided to treat these possibilities as reality.

This threat posed challenges. A lone agent, one with no record, a person who'd never joined a political or extremist group would be hard to discover or identify.

This could be the profile of the stranger who haunted him. It seemed likely the killer would have religious motivation. Unfortunately, these tended to be people with heartfelt grievances against the United States. They numbered in the thousands in the Middle East.

Western values were creeping into Muslim countries. Devout Muslims observed western values entering to destroy the values of Islamic culture hundreds of years old. The Koran demands death for such an offense.

He felt certain the unknown being stalking the world was a Muslim woman, a woman loaded with hatred. Jackson got up from his desk and stood next to the many books that lined the walls of his office.

It was time to go home.

January 27, 2004

Dr. Showkit had not rushed his training or evaluation of A'isha. He had to be sure she met all psychological requirements. The girl still perplexed him. On rare occasions he saw a tiny trace of the protected child still in her. At other times she was the most mature of women.

At times, A'isha used the inexplicable power of clairvoyance. She was intelligent, yet her thinking was simple with everything either black or white as was very common in psychopaths. Her twisted world accepted nothing gray. You were either with or against Allah. She trusted no one although proved malleable with her trainers.

A textbook case of isolation, she'd remain by herself for hours in one place. She possessed an uncanny ability to sense all movements around her. She sensed danger before a clear threat appeared.

Unfailing in her attention to training, she'd shown no signs of a weakening in her desire for revenge. If anything, the arduous training brought more hatred of Westerners. If not for the West, her loved ones would still be with her.

She absorbed lessons and answered questions correctly and succinctly. She never socialized in idle conversation. Her life consisted of her mission, vengeance her only purpose. Her anger did not come in flashes but stayed a slow deep burn. She seldom talked about her purpose; she believed her day would come. When it did Dr. Showkit had no doubt, the world would cringe and shrink.

January 28, 2004

A'isha leaned against her quarter's outer wall shunning the comfort of sleep. Dawn would break in a few hours, her favourite time.

A'isha found the thousand small night sounds comforting. She sought strength in solitude. She mourned in the darkness for her lost family. The injustice of their deaths fuelled her fierce avenging hatred and turned her to hard thoughts.

"Allah are you here with me this night?" A'isha asked.

A deep voice spoke. "Yes, little one. I am here and will always be with you."

A'isha said. "Allah, I miss my family so much the pain is nearly unbearable."

"I know your pain is great, my little one. I also know that your strength will carry you to complete your purpose. Some few people are destined to alter the world. You are one of those few. Your well-earned days of rest will come. You will know love and peace. Your family and friends are with me and are at peace."

"You are the sword I will use to remind the mighty that the poor and helpless belong to me. Their bodies are not to be used to pave the road to empire. Many nations have craved empire, spending fortunes in blood and money to achieve this goal. Their ambitions consume them. An ancient book says, The title of empire will pass from nation to nation. And it will."

You are my weapon to humble the West whose goals have exceeded the length of their arms. They will taste the bitter fruit of defeat. The great West will be brought down by a child who is the sword of Allah."

"Allah, I have only myself. How will I obtain the skills to accomplish this mission?" A'isha murmured.

"Fear not. I am the one who gathers the winds. I control the ocean waves. I cradle the moon in my hands. I created mountains and the eagles that mount their heights. I know each star by name. Nothing succeeds if I oppose it. Nothing fails if I will it."

"I am always with you, even till the final second of victory."

CHAPTER FOURTEEN

February 24, 2004

Baghdad, Iraq

D r. Showkit waited at an unknown location to see Saddam. A'isha had progressed. Her language and cultural training were scheduled to begin. Dr. Showkit wanted to be sure she could manage all operational details.

A side door opened. Saddam Hussein entered and took his seat behind a large desk. As before, Dr. Showkit feared him. This powerful man could and would kill anyone at any time he chose.

"As we agreed, it is now time for you to bring me up to date on our project. Is the candidate doing well and what is the schedule?" asked Saddam.

"The candidate is doing well. Her progress is straightforward. She shows no sign of wavering in her resolve to avenge her country. We are on schedule with her training," answered the Doctor.

"Your requests for funding have been modest. Are you sure you have the tools on hand to bring the candidate to the highest level of efficiency?" Saddam asked.

"Monetary needs at this point have been low with the candidate still in her mental training stages. To test a mind only requires adversity."

"So far you have asked for little and have accomplished a great deal. What do you require at this point?" Saddam asked.

"A'isha needs a mentor in cultural training, language, and sexual skills. A woman between 24 and 30 years of age; very attractive and sexually sophisticated, ideally an American Muslim born and raised in the United States."

"This American must be college educated and speak both Arabic and American English of the Midwest variety. It would be ideal if the mentor has rededicated herself to Islam because of a religious experience. The mentor must have solid reasons for hating the United States. The mentor will become an onsite trainer."

Saddam nodded, "Within a month a woman will come to your door and say, 'I may be the new mentor.' Take her in and evaluate her. If you are not satisfied with her, I will send another. We can find the right mentor."

"Another question. Your potential lone agent is an orphan, is she not?" asked Saddam.

"Yes, she lost all her family and friends during the bombing campaign," Showkit answered.

"How do you rate her? How strong is her will? How strong is her hate?" pressed Saddam.

"She has strengths beyond normal mortals. She is eager to avenge both her family and Iraq. She is the sword that we seek, more than I'd hoped for," said Dr. Showkit.

"Is she beautiful?" asked the dictator.

"Yes, but her beauty is matched by her dangerousness. She will never be normal. Her mental force is mysterious. A'isha is neither a lover nor a playmate. She is murderous and lives only to destroy the United States."

"At times she has a mysterious ability to read other's thoughts. My professional opinions are based on extensive observation," said Dr. Showkit,

"She sounds interesting. I will meet her before she leaves on her mission."

Showkit nearly winced. "As you wish, Mr. President, all in this land belongs to you. However, this mission is delicate as you know. We'll do well to keep it from complications."

Saddam snorted. "I have many women for my pleasures. I won't compromise the mission for such a simple thing as sex. She sounds interesting as a person. Meeting her President might strengthen her resolve and impress upon her the importance of her mission."

"Possibly such a meeting would be productive. That decision is in your hands."

"So be it, expect your female mentor soon," said Saddam as he stood and left the room.

~ ~ ~

February 27, 2004

Her American name was Kay Johish, but her original name had been Zaynab Bint Jahish. Born in United States as a middle-class Arab, she learned about the conflict between Jews and Arabs as a child.

However, she'd grown up with her family in Lincoln, Nebraska, a Midwest university city. This safe town proved a good place to grow up.

The Americanizing of her birth name was intended to make the social process more comfortable. Now at age twenty-seven she had chosen English as a second language as her field of study. She became a teacher.

Although she had spent many years in America's heartland her father remained obsessed by the hopeless despair in Palestinian refugee camps.

In Palestine, her father had prospered as a merchant. He was an out-going person loved by everyone. He believed in education and had gone to night classes to earn a degree in bank economics. He spoke English, French, and Arabic

Palestine had been beautiful with a wide diversity of social classes. But during the Jewish War the Jahish family walked 37 miles at gun point to one of the numerous refugee areas little more than concentration camps. Their home, their property, and even their personal effects were confiscated by Israel.

Thanks to her father's education they were eventually able to move to America where the father of the family fell back on degree in economics and obtained a good job with a large bank.

He had experienced little trouble getting into the United States. All countries welcome people with a good education, a good police record, and have the extra money to get started.

The family adjusted well to the new country. The Midwest was friendly, and no one seemed to mind that the Jahish family was Muslim.

The family spoke Arabic at home while English was the language of school and social activities. Kay was bright, beautiful, and social. Her classmates accepted her as a normal American girl. She grew into a tall woman whose long black hair had an appealing sheen.

A charming conversationalist, she had the ability to make anyone feel comfortable. She did well in all her subjects. She had no shortage of boyfriends. By the time she was a sophomore in High School, like several of her friends, she'd become sexually active.

She enjoyed the control sex gave her over young men. Watching her drift away from the lifestyle of a devout Muslim, her parents worried.

Nasir, her older brother provided her an anchor. Despite drifting apart in approaches to life they remained close siblings. Nasir was a devout Muslim and tried everything to return his headstrong sister to Islam.

Her parents were frantic about their daughter. Kay loved her parents, but they seemed so boring compared to a nonstop series of parties, sex, and drugs.

Nasir and his sister talked, frankly. Nasir spoke of the serious duties of religious life and Kay tended to talk about having fun. However, the bond between the brother and sister remained close and strong. Nasir told his sister that Allah had a purpose for her life and in time she would find it. Kay maintained that God had better things to do then be concerned about a girl who wanted just parties and sex. Nasir insisted that he had been having dreams showing Kay as a reformed Muslim assigned by Allah to play a major role for Islam.

Declaring his words too creepy for a free spirit like herself, Kay let the good times roll.

Nasir, a political activist, spoke to as many groups as possible to discuss the complex relationship of the Arab/Jewish conflict in Palestine. His speeches drew attention from the Jewish community. Nasir said people had a right to different opinions. He was a balanced speaker and acknowledged the strong points of both the Jewish and the Arab situation. A well-read scholar, he held a master's degree in Middle East history.

He spoke to any audience that would listen; He financed his own expenses as a voice of reason on a heated subject. He never raised his voice, always maintaining calm. He accepted the reality of a permanent Jewish state. He also said that peace could only come when the Palestinians had a country of their own as well.

He believed the average Arab youth needed a justifiable hope that life could be good. This hope would end all terrorism. Nasir explained that a solution had to be found because the weapons were emerging as too powerful. He feared that a nuclear weapon would be used by some radical group with unthinkable results. None of his viewpoints were extreme or radical. Even so, Nasir had enemies.

Arab sympathisers considered him a traitor because he accepted a Jewish State. The United States government disliked him because he highlighted how much money and weapons the American taxpayer was giving to the Israeli government. The Jewish lobby hated him because he advocated a separate Palestinian State that had the rights of any other sovereign nation. This would mean the right to a formal army and the legal status to buy weapons on the international market.

Even worse, a Palestinian State would have the right to enter treaties of mutual assistance with other countries. To the current American and Jewish leadership such a situation would be intolerable.

Nasir and most of the informed world believed that a Palestinian State had to be created if Israel expected to survive. Nasir felt he had a religious duty to speak out for oppressed and helpless Palestine people. People who speak or write in support of unpopular causes live at risk. The subject of Jewish/Palestine co-existence is one of the most emotional issues existing.

Nasir had gone to speak at an international peace conference in New York City. As always, his comments were reasonable, thoughtful, but dangerous to utter.

Perhaps it was inevitable that such a moderate thoughtful man as Nasir would have a short life, inevitably to die at the hands of violent extremists. Nasir was found beaten to death in a New York alley killed in such a methodical way that almost every bone in his slim body was shattered.

He had been thirty-one years old. His only crime was trying to lessen death and suffering. Even though some evidence suggested a radical Jewish group was involved, investigators found no suspects.

Kay, her fragile stability destroyed by losing Nasir, decided for herself that Jewish agents with the political collusion of the American government must be responsible. He'd been a source of support for the weak and helpless, a big brother anyone would be proud of. The idea of her nonviolent brother being beaten to death altered her.

She resumed use of her birth name of Zaynab Bint Jahish and returned to the faith of her family and she severed ties with corrupting friends. She began an intense study of Islamic religion and history. She sought Muslim instructors who could help her cope with grieving for Nasir, making no secret of her hatred of America. She continued to blame his murder on Israeli and United States leaders.

She moved to Baghdad, Iraq, to teach English. With her parents' help she lived comfortably. Zaynab Jahish now considered the United States to be the major enemy of the Arab people, and that the path of peace had killed Nasir.

Vengeful thoughts motivated her. She spoke of them to Islamic teachers at many mosques. In a country like Iraq it does not take long for a commitment such as hers to find a murderous application. Iraqi Secret Police approached Zaynab Bint Jahsh within six months.

CHAPTER FIFTEEN

She convinced the Secret Police of her effectiveness when she fulfilled an assignment to kill an American tourist she'd lured to her room. As the amorous victim undressed Zaynab put three 45 calibre holes through his chest.

She'd killed on command and such a person fits in the dark business of intelligence. Her knowledge of English and the cultural habits of Americans made her valuable. All her kills began with the temptation of sexual pleasures. She developed a preference for knife work. Done in silence, it gave her greater satisfaction.

She made kills on several Jewish businessmen that Iraqi Secret Service believed were spies. That issue didn't matter to Zaynab. Jews had killed her brother. She'd become a Muslim extremist, obeying every command of the Koran to the smallest letter. She'd become an Arab soldier fighting for the Arab cause.

Zaynab became one of many believers who felt the United States and Islam could never coexist. She would do anything to bring the United States to ground. Her requests for more important missions were noted. Soon Saddam heard of her and sent Zaynab to Dr. Showkit.

~ ~ ~

August 1, 2004

Summer heat in Iraq is so brutal most people work at night if possible. On this morning, a visitor sought access to Showkit's office at 5:00 a.m.

He welcomed the woman into his office, noting both her beauty and self-confident American mannerisms. She appeared to be between the ages of 26 and 31. Her Arabic was flawless, but she had that American style of walking and moving. "How can I help you, young lady?" asked Dr. Showkit.

"I work for the Iraqi Secret Service. Saddam himself told me to report to you and answer any questions you ask me. I was told to inform you I might be the mentor you search for. I'm ready to answer your questions however personal."

"Then am I to understand you know nothing of this potential assignment?" asked the Doctor.

"I know nothing of any pending assignment. I hope you'll explain what you need from me," she said.

Dr. Showkit leaned back in his chair. "Your assignment would be to teach a sixteen-year-old girl to speak as if she is an American. You'd also instruct her in the arts of seduction as well as teach her a convincing level of sexual expertise.

The girl is undertaking a dangerous task. Extremely intelligent, she is yet a virgin naive in sexual matters. Your handling of her must be tactful."

"My native Arab parents raised my brother and me in the United States. I've been educated in American colleges and have instructed classes in American English. I majored in English. I teach English to

Iraqi children on a part time basis in the hopes that this will help prepare them to confront and ultimately defeat the United States."

"My brother was murdered by the Jews in New York. I have dedicated my life to avenging him. If the United States is the target of this mission, then I would be honoured to contribute in any way you prefer."

"I became sexually active at fourteen. I drifted away from Allah, and I was absorbed in worldly pleasures and the sins of intercourse before being properly wed. I went so far as to study sex manuals to increase my knowledge and to increase my own pleasure."

"I've had sexual relationships with at least twenty men, and some became extended relationships. When my brother was murdered, I returned to Allah and begged for forgiveness. I intend to continue my service to Allah and all Muslims."

"I serve to assassinate Iraq's enemies and those opposing Islam. I killed seventeen men while their minds focussed on sex. Although I killed some with a pistol, my preferred weapon is a knife. What other information do you require?"

"Are you now sexually active?" asked the Doctor.

"Not now, but I have no qualms about starting again if my country requires that of me."

"Would you be sexually active as a matter of instruction to the trainee, and would you help the trainee kill in order to perfect her skills as an assassin?"

"If I can use that learning to further the cause of Allah then I'll do so with satisfaction."

"Do you understand that if this mission fails, we all die at the hands of the State?" Showkit asked.

She smiled. "Death comes to us all. I would prefer to meet Allah in Paradise after doing my best to destroy our enemies."

Dr. Showkit reflected. His interviewee appeared competent and had the added advantage of experience teaching English. Her security arrangements being at the highest level meant little chance she'd become a security risk.

"I have a further question for you. Have you ever had any lesbian experiences? While I have no personal interest in such matters, it is important in this mission because the trainee might be influenced by such a sexual preference," asked Dr. Showkit. The lady shook her head. "No. My interests have always been in men. The youngest man that I have ever had sex with was about fourteen years of age as I was. After a time, my interests turned to older men."

Dr. Showkit felt that such an answer would be in accordance with the woman's mature ease. He suspected she was always the dominant partner. "The trainee was the sole survivor in a bomb shelter destroyed by the United States. Nearly five hundred lives were lost in that air raid including our trainee's entire family.

"She has unusual gifts. She reviles the West, is intelligent, mature, and focused on her mission. Her mental powers are difficult to understand."

"She is always hyper vigilant; her senses of sight and hearing are unusually high. She has some clairvoyance. The source of her ability is unknown, but her power is beyond question. She presents no training problems, is attentive and retains what she learns. She is beautiful, brilliant, and already dangerous," the Doctor said.

"She sounds like an interesting woman, and I'd do my best to meet your goals. I'm sure I could be effective as her trainer. Perhaps if I could speak to her, it might help both of us in our assessments,"

"Agreed. Be honest in your assessment. Give me your judgment on the girl's potential."

"Through this window you will see A'isha seated about 40 meters away leaning against the wall. It is not unusual that she remains so for all hours of the day or night. It would be interesting to know her thoughts. I am certain you will find A'isha a fascinating enigma."

Dr. Showkit accompanied by the potential mentor left his office to speak with A'isha. Tension increased as they drew closer to her. Energy radiated from the hooded figure like a burning flame. Zeynat remained on her guard. The two were within ten meters of the motionless girl when A'isha spoke.

"Do not approach any closer. Circle around to approach from the front. Death comes most often from behind."

Energy sizzled as the very air seemed to commence vibrating. When they stood before her at a safe distance, A'isha lifted her head and slid the hood from her face. Her flawless pale olive complexion and angular face were beautiful, her dark hair an almost radiant frame.

Her eyes were penetrating deep into Zeynat's who wondered if A'isha could control and compel whoever she chose, as a cobra transfixes its prey.

A'isha made her assessment. She spoke in a clear, low voice. "So, it is true that the lioness is the real killer of the pride. The male lion looks powerful, but the female pulls the prey to the ground."

"You've killed to avenge your brother, a man of peace. But peace is so seldom found on this earth. Your brother now lives with Allah. You chose war. Your path is cold steel and death in quiet settings. I too, have chosen this way. Tell me lioness, did you forget to tell the Doctor that you have killed eighteen men instead of the seventeen you mentioned?"

"Has the memory of that killing evaded your recollection? The memory of one's deeds can be painful and haunting. I know about constant nightmares. Your political masters overlooked that chosen killing as a personal matter, as fair price for other services. You were over-confident. Vanity is costly, is it not? You made a flawed judgment."

"You were not aware that casual sex can lead to love. You fell deeply although that was not your intent. A person's desire is not always what Allah grants. The victim betrayed you with another."

"Love and hate are so intertwined are they not? Your jealousy fed your pain. Do not be dismayed. A broken heart can cloud the best of minds. You could not bring yourself to use the blade. You killed him with a pistol shot as he slept."

"Allah sees into every room. You could not bear the knowledge that the man you loved cared little about you. This is a common trait of some men and a sad fact for many women. Even the Prophet could not confine his desire to one woman."

"Yet you have returned to Allah and Allah forgives all who return to Him in humility. Your lover lives today in paradise. Be at peace, your lover and Allah have forgiven you. You have much to teach me for you know the ways of a mature woman."

"You know how to lure men to their deaths by exposing a long, alluring leg, the curve of a beautiful breast, or a side glance that a man expands in his over-heated imagination. I need to learn such skills. I need to speak as my enemies do and know their culture. I do not need your deception. The world is drowning in deception."

"Teach me your skills without reservation. Allah will reward your work. You will be granted a place in the garden of paradise."

"Deceive me and I will kill you. I am a sword of Allah."

Dr. Showkit sensed the older woman's hesitation. Finally, she spoke. "What you just said is true. I regret that killing. He did not deserve death for choosing another woman. I wish I could call the bullet back. I've prayed for forgiveness. Thank you for the news you've given me."

"I'm so relieved that Allah has forgiven me. I swear to you in His presence I will train you well. I have much to teach you and there is much I'd like to learn from you. We share enemies." Zeynat's tone was firm.

In a gentle tone A'isha said, "Yes, Allah forgives your sins. I've been granted certain gifts. I welcome your training. You will never have guilty nightmares again. Your lover waits for you in the gardens of Paradise. I will meet you there. My death approaches but I have much to accomplish before I walk through that holy gate."

"You'll work with an old smuggler named Najib. Do not underestimate him. He is wise, patient, and deadly."

A'isha drew the hood back over her head. The discussion over, Zeynat and Dr. Showkit returned to his office. A'isha would remain with silence her companion.

The Doctor and Zeynat sat in their own silence before exchanging words. Finally, he picked up a pencil, rolling it in his hand to break the tension. "What did you think of our young trainee? Be truthful."

"I've known danger but nothing and no one compares to being near that girl."

"I will fulfill my commitment to train her. When her hour arrives, it will be a dark day for our enemy. She will alter the world." Zeynat spoke with dread and awe.

CHAPTER SIXTEEN

August 7, 2004

Zeynat walked toward the silent girl still resting against the wall. A'isha spoke first. "Welcome my lioness, I've been waiting for you. We can move forward with our task."

"Let's sit on the bench by the spring so our lessons can begin in privacy and comfort," Zeynat suggested.

Once there, the two listened to sounds of the spring flowing over the rocks. In the desert, water is all but worshiped. The sounds of flowing water brought ease. A'isha broke the silence, "I am ready. When do we begin?"

"Your capacity to surpass mission requirements has impressed Najib and Doctor Showkit. Today we'll discuss American culture. Once you have a firm grasp of that we'll begin language skills."

"Since I grew up in that country of infidels I can attest that their culture is alluring. Many Muslims have lost their faith to the seduction of American values. America worships money. Your value in America is measured by how wealthy you are."

"A rich man or woman in America will be respected no matter how they came by such wealth be it a stealing, criminal activity or exploiting the poor. Nevertheless, he will be admired by the vast majority in the United States solely because of his wealth. Most Americans know little about Allah."

"U.S. citizens seem to fear solitude. Silence is uncomfortable for them. Nearly every place or vehicle has a radio or a television that fills the minds of its listeners with trash that encourages consumption, violence, and casual sex. Americans want material possessions like cars and big houses to gain social status. They indulge in sex without responsibility."

"Americans pay lip service to the concept of God and final judgment. Americans tend to be self-important. Their wasted time is so often spent in idle curiosity, lust, envy, and altering their sense of reality. These infidels do not seek Allah, but pleasure."

"Americans delight in wasting. For example, we see water as Allah's most precious gift, never to be wasted. Americans pour billions of gallons of it over the ground just to grow ornamental grass to show they have wealth to consume. The grass is cut often and put in plastic bags to be thrown away in a city dump."

"It's only one of hundreds of things that Americans waste. America is a land blessed by Allah with rich soil and ample water. Yet the infidels don't acknowledge Allah and will pay for their arrogance. I thank Allah for choosing me to play a role in their destruction."

"The United States is a bloated spider whose web extends around the world intended to ensnare Allah's lands, steal our resources and our souls."

"No nation has drug problems like United States does. It sinks into a moral morass. Crime is universal, with major cities unsafe even for an armed citizen."

"Marriage there is a failing institution. Nearly half of U.S. marriages fail . . . The American family is shaky, too. Too many fathers abandon their families. There is little respect for elders."

"And women work outside the home to maintain their status. This increases strain on family units."

"The United States also violates the Prophet's commands by allowing only one wife per man. Islam permits up to four wives, therefore there is far less adultery."

"A virile Muslin man with three wives can produce at least ten children. Muslin population growth strikes fear in the hearts of the West. In time, Islam can take over the world by democratic means or with physical power. Islam is the only true religion and Allah is the only true God. Infidels are doomed."

"Pornography, even child pornography. exists in America. The infidels take a beautiful natural gift of Allah and turn it into something ugly. What culture would debase the gifts of Allah and turn lovemaking into a cesspool of perversion and sick desires?"

"A'isha, you will bring this abominable nation to ground. I am proud to help you. Now we'll focus on your language training."

~   ~   ~

August 10, 2004

Bagdad, Iraq

From outside, the rotting structure looked like just another mid-sized forgotten building. Holes in the roofing left the interior exposed to outside elements.

The building was made from shoddy materials. But this wasn't real. Within the rotting confines of the larger building sat an interior building, designed for acoustical silence.

The requirement for silence issued from one man named Sadeq. The interior contained a maze of walls, twisted hallways, and corridors. Each wall and angle had been designed to trap sound.

One man sat at a drafting table in a pool of light. The rest of the building was totally dark and silent. His long-fingered hands moved with slow, deliberate, careful grace and coordination, their poise and strength like those of a concert pianist.

Control, grace, and skill were essential for he designed and built some of the most destructive devices extant. In a world where many of the finest minds have dedicated their careers creating instruments of death, no one else had Sadeq's combined gifts.

That night he perused the written request for a weapon, one with specialized aspects. His analysis of something like this unfailingly preceded mass destruction.

A custom bed was next to the drafting table. He switched off the light and adjusted the bed to his comfort. Saddam had arranged for Sadeq to appear to have died in an airplane crash. To the world,

Sadeq was dead but to Saddam alone he existed as an ultimate human weapon.

Sadeq lived to kill Israelis and their supporters. In particular, he considered the United States to be the true power behind the Israeli State.

He'd been twelve in 1967 when Israelis killed his father, a simple, sturdy man who died defending what had been their family home in Palestine for twelve generations. These prior generations were buried in a modest cemetery on that land.

His father faced Israeli forces with only his character and his sense of justice. He'd been a faithful and peaceful Muslim all his life. He placed his unarmed body between the Israeli tank and his modest home.

The soldiers cared nothing for this man or his family's history. He was an Arab to be killed or displaced. Sadeq had been playing in a nearby ravine when he heard the tank and the infantry squad stop in front of his home. He watched with horror as the Israeli tank casually crushed his father and their home. They killed his five siblings. Sadeq could hear the solders as he lay terrified, peering over the edge of the ragged gully, his favorite place to play. Home already had grown too loud and boisterous for the reticent boy.

Sadeq would never forget the screaming and weeping of his mother as seven men raped her. After the raping ended, the squad leader put a bullet through her baby's head, then shot the mother.

Sadeq watched in frozen horror as the tank crushed every marker in the ancient cemetery, turning everything to rubble and dust.

Sadeq ran down the ravine until he found a crack in the wall where he hid from the Israeli troops until night.

The stars were clear against the dark sky when the horrified boy realized he had survived. Sadeq fell to his knees and prayed to Allah. He asked for strength and patience until he could avenge the murders of his family. Sadeq vowed that the Israeli army would live to regret his survival.

The strong forget that history has an odd way of giving the weak their turn at victory. He felt every Palestinian must decide whether to live under the yoke of domination or fight against terrible odds. Sadeq would fight.

None of these mature subjects were in the frightened boy's thoughts. Fortunately, he had relatives who would aid anyone in their family. Such is the iron law of a tribal land. The family is the only life support system that a Muslim can depend on. In deep shock, Sadeq stumbled eight miles to his uncle's home.

It took months for Sadeq to begin to recover. He used his time to plan. Although young, Sadeq knew the law of revenge rested solely on his shoulders.

As a member of his uncle's family, Sadeq worked in the fields. The small Arab community realized this boy was unusual. He had a gift for languages as well as a photographic memory.

Several elderly Arab men in the village had learned English under their former British rulers. This boy remembered every English word he heard. They tutored him until he could read, write, and speak English like any English gentleman.

Sadeq learned that powerful knowledge was found in books and devoured every one he could get his hands on. A fast reader, Sadeq comprehended and retained every shred of information in any book provided.

In three years, Sadeq could converse and read in Hebrew, English, French, and Russian. The Russians saw his genius. They had a use for Arab men who could help them gain their objectives in the Middle East. The welcome rubles persuaded the peasant family that Sadeq was destined for a larger world.

He trained in Moscow. Strong in mathematics, engineering, and electronics, he overwhelmed his instructors with raw talent. Sadeq was intoxicated by a love of weapons. For hours on end, he'd assemble and disassemble many different armaments.

At sixteen he made major design changes in Russian arms. He understood each and could point out all the strengths and weaknesses of its design in minutes. His ability to create designs of unusual simplicity and reliability impressed all his teachers.

By age seventeen the Arab boy traveled throughout the Soviet Union's weapons factories. Simple mechanical weapons such as rifles, machine guns, and artillery now bored him. He turned his mind toward the making of bombs and complex devices.

Sadeq invented the small plastic "butterfly" anti-personal mines designed to be sown from the air to be buried with a special spinning action. Designed to maim rather than kill he knew a wounded person took more enemy resources alive than dead.

This invention severed Sadeq's relationship with the Russians. To Sadeq's horror his Russia masters used this device against an Islamic country after they'd promised Sadeq his weapons and designs would only be used against the United States and Israel. In fact, Russia had sown these horrible devices by the millions in Afghanistan, crippling thousands of Muslims.

This was a hard and bitter lesson. Never again would Sadeq trust or work for non-believers. He was able to communicate his desire to defect to Iraq. Saddam Hussein's resources opened many doors. Sadeq was secreted away to Iraq in a matter of days. Even if Saddam was no true believer, the population was Muslim. He'd found a home.

Sadeq rested and concentrated. He smiled to himself with growing pleasure as he welcomed a good challenge.

Like a massive computer, his mind turned over hundreds of possibilities. The results of his thoughts changed everything.

CHAPTER SEVENTEEN

August 13, 2004

CIA Headquarters

Langley, Virginia

After months of searching, Jackson was haunted by his belief that somewhere in the Middle East, an enemy threatened the existence of the United States,

Jackson labored long days and nights in his office. He searched piles of intelligence snippets for any clue to the threat's identity.

Jackson hadn't uncovered even a scrap regarding any hidden training program or unique intelligence agent. This must be a solo operation; one agent at one place being trained by only a few people. It followed that the agent was in training for something big. An expendable agent would probably be key to an act of massive destruction.

He'd been having dreams in which he saw cities littered with bodies. At times he would see a tall, shrouded woman walk among the dead. The shroud cast her face into dark shadow. She wore dark peasant clothes that could belong to a woman of any Arab country.

He could never see her face except for her eyes which smoldered with an otherworldly hatred. They seemed to pierce his being until nothing in his entire past could be hidden from their sight.

He felt she sought to use her power to annihilate Americans in the millions. On one occasion the image in his dreams spoke in a woman's voice but one not truly human. "My power grows. Vengeance will be mine."

This was more vision than dream. Somewhere this woman existed and posed the greatest danger America had ever faced.

The problem lies in the two opposing world views contending for world domination. Western civilization believed in the separation of Church and State. To Muslims this was impossible because the Church was the state. To Muslims, only the religiously righteous had the right to lead the State.

The United States placed high value on the individual. In desert lands tribal survival as a unit overrode individual rights. Muslims had obligations not rights.

The struggle between Islam and Judeo/Christian views meant life or death. Eight million Muslims practiced their religion in the United States because of American tolerance. Jackson concluded that tolerance might mean the end of Western civilization in a remarkably short period of time.

The result would be a freedom crushing theocracy.

August 14, 2004

Najib and A'isha sat side by side on a rocky prominence in the Iraqi desert. Najib broke their silence. "You have done well, my child. You have not disappointed me or your other trainer. You've become hard physically and mentally. You will need such strength because your mission will be a terrible weight on your shoulders."

A'isha answered, "I received my task from Allah's mighty hand. I do not question or judge his will. I obey. I will not fail. I will speak for the innocent dead, for the babies destroyed by American bombs. I will avenge those with crushed limbs and shattered minds. I will speak for the mother who lost her son and the wife who lost her beloved husband. I will remember Arab men who buried their wives because of the West."

"I despise the people who sit in their safe homes in the United States watching the murder of Arabs on their televisions as if murder were a spectator sport."

"The sun is setting on the West whose aggression will soon cease, and I have the honor of striking the mortal blow. I shall be ready. I will not fail."

Najib looked deep into the desert night hearing the scratching and scurrying of its small animals hunting to survive. Never had he known such a force as this young woman. "Yes, it is your destiny, and mine to train you."

They walked back through the darkness. In the United States millions were going about their daily lives. What a mercy they did not know of A'isha.

~ ~ ~

September 11, 2004

Zeynat had never had such a talented pupil. A'isha only had to hear a word once to repeat it flawlessly. She could pass for an American in less than a year.

The girl approached her training with a cool rigor beyond Zeynat's experience. A'isha had no sense of humor. Working with the girl exhausted Zeynat. She felt as though caged with a lioness. Without frequent breaks Zeynat doubted she could take the strain.

During these breaks A'isha rested against the wall outside her room, pondering. How her life had changed. Her former expectations had been so ordinary. She'd dreamed of a simple home with a devout husband and a large, happy family. She'd hoped Allah would grant her six children: three boys and three girls.

But the bombs killed every dream of her life. She remembered the games she played with her sisters. She remembered their laughter and the joy. A'isha knew that was over for so many innocent Arab children.

She would destroy the Americans who had destroyed her world, then join her friends and family in paradise. How she longed to see her mother Mira's kind and beautiful face! She wanted to embrace her father and hear his kind voice welcome her to the fields of Paradise.

She envisioned a beautiful valley surrounded by snow covered mountains radiating golden light from the presence of Allah. Perhaps A'isha could find a man to love there.

Death was not the grim reaper that seemed to terrify the West. To A'isha, death opened the door to a world different from the cruel one she now inhabited. She believed in a peaceful world where every lawful want was provided upon simple request.

That was the world A'isha longed for and it was for that world that A'isha worked so hard.

Revenge even to personal death was something the West could never understand. Despite religious platitudes spoken from thousands of American pulpits most people wanted to continue living. Heaven was a place to go when one was forced to leave this present world. Martyrdom was just an ancient story to the West. In the East, martyrdom was a living reality.

A'isha was an uncomplicated girl turning to womanhood. Questions of duty and morality were answered for her in the Koran. One did not need to speculate; one obeyed. It is the simplicity of people like A'isha that makes them so dangerous. They have no moral doubts. They are willing to die for their religion at once if necessary.

A'isha believed she only had to be patient. The day was close at hand when the title of empire would return to the land of true believers in Allah.

~ ~ ~

September 16, 2004

Baghdad Iraq

Dr. Showkit on the other hand studied reports he received twice a week from his trainers who were expected to be objective and honest with A'isha's progress. The reports were favorable. A'isha trained hard and showed clear results. She continued to be physically and mentally strong. He was suffering his own trial, and dreaded the macabre future that A'isha would deliver.

He returned to his work. Incredible focus might be the simple clue to her powers. Most people let their minds drift aimlessly over many subjects in a day. This might prevent the brain from obtaining the focus that is needed to access its great potential powers.

The hour was still early, the temperature still bearable. He summoned a guard to tell A'isha that the doctor wished to speak with her. She arrived in moments. "Please sit-down A'isha. I would like us to have a brief conversation."

"Your instructors tell me you are progressing well in your training."

The young woman took her seat and met his gaze. "You did not call me into your presence because of my training. Perhaps it would be easier if you ask your questions."

"You are correct. I do have some general questions for you. Could you talk to me about your childhood? Were you close to your parents and your siblings?" The Doctor leaned forward with genuine interest. "Was there anything unusual in your early life?" The doctor could feel A'isha's tension rise.

"Both of my parents were wonderful people, and I loved my sisters equally. All the members of my family were murdered by the infidels as you well know," she said.

"Did you ever have periods of depression or anger that you can recall?" asked the doctor. Silence in the room lasted for many moments. The Doctor had the distinct feeling that he was being studied, that invisible eyes were searching his mind, studying the motives behind his questions. Being this close to the girl unnerved him.

"Curiosity can be a dangerous undertaking, Dr. Showkit. To invade a person's private life isn't safe. You are trying to find out the underlying causes of my behavior. In answer to your real questions, I was a normal child from a loving family. I was close to my sisters. We lived in total harmony in our home. I had no unusual gifts or any unusual education. I did not have any mental or physical problems."

"My goals in life were modest. There was nothing to distinguish me from hundreds of average Iraqi girls. Do you find it so strange that Allah has purposes of his own and that he can empower whomever he wishes?"

Showkit shuddered, reminding himself of her psychic prowess.

"I do not belong to this world any longer. I was given a destiny and a duty by Allah. I was also given certain tools to fulfill his wishes. I did not ask for these tools. It was Allah and Allah alone who selected me and chose you also. I hear his voice often and I simply obey as you must. In time, you and other physicians will speculate on my life and motives. That will come later."

"There is power here that you cannot understand. For now, I must return to my prayers." Without another word the girl rose from her chair and walked quietly out the door.

Dr. Showkit pondered on the comments of this strange spectral woman. He was aware that psychopaths were often able to function rationally. They were often cunning murderers capable of planning and carrying out heinous crimes. He felt a chill pass through him as he speculated on the damage A'isha would soon inflict upon the West.

Chapter Eighteen

October 1, 2004

A'isha was now sixteen, an undeniable beauty. She moved with a cat's predatory grace and fluidity. Regal in bearing, quiet, and self-contained, A'isha learned her lessons well from Najib.

Najib often left A'isha in the desert for several days at a time. She became a fitting part of the desert wastelands. In time, A'isha preferred solitude. The desert never lied; there was no ambiguity about the desert. Desert rules were simple if harsh.

Life was measured and diminished by the quantity of water in a living body. Water determined how long a human could live. To meet the desert on its own terms and prevail against its forces meant her growth in self-confidence. Physically and mentally, A'isha altered into a formidable weapon on that forge.

The most dangerous weapon is a person willing to focus on one act of destruction. A'isha was that weapon.

Yet at times she felt troubled. Over months she detected another mind touching hers. It belonged to an intelligent focused man who sought to kill her. A'isha often grappled with his mind and learned his unknown intellect had power. His searching intellect and intuition were relentless. A'isha sought his name. On this point Allah kept silent. She tried to accept such a mystery.

~ ~ ~

October 14, 2004

A'isha was always punctual, attentive, and mastered the material Zeynat taught her with the poise of confident woman. She'd trained a long time which drew her closer to her death. That alone gave A'isha a sense of purpose.

Zeynat decided the time to begin sexual training had arrived. How would A'isha respond? The deeply religious often had inhibitions that could stand in the way of sexual proficiency. Zeynat was considering that when A'isha appeared in the doorway like a black clad wraith.

"Please, come in and sit. Another phase of your training will begin today. It won't be as demanding as Najib's rigors."

A'isha took her seat. "Najib has his purposes and has taught me well. I need to master your skills, too."

"That's right. I've assassinated many men in the course of my duties as an agent of the State. I enticed each with sexual seduction. I'll teach you my assassins' skills as well."

"We use our bodies to lure our prey. Sex knowingly used can control a man. Once control is established we use him or kill him as we choose. Men have two areas of weakness that overshadow all the rest. One is their sexual desire to use our bodies and the other is their vanity which leads each to believe he's unique."

"Many need to feel the thrill of seduction. Yielding to his approaches in a gradual manner is the surest way to heighten a man's physical desire and the surest way to control him. Sex is a paradox. The woman who appears to be controlled holds the reins of power. Seduction is an art, a learned skill."

"Mastering such skills is critical to your mission in the United States. Some men may be in your way. Sex can blind them and make their removal easy."

"There may be a man who has access to places where you need to be. Establishing a sexual relationship or even the hint of a possible sexual relationship may be the key that you need to unlock high security places. I'm asking directly, what are your feelings on this subject?"

A'isha remained silent for what seemed a long time to Zeynat. "I've known from the beginning that Allah chose me as his weapon. Everything I have I give to the service of God. Since I am waiting to give Allah my life, would it not seem strange that I would hesitate to use the body that he gave me?"

"I am a chosen weapon, a bride of Allah. His purpose is my purpose. I have given my life, my body, and my heart to him. I am ready to use my body to become a fighter for Allah." "Does a warrior not use his body when he wields the sword? I am willing to use my body to deliver death to Allah's enemies. I have no inhibitions that stop me from learning your sexual skills."

"I am prepared to be all things to all men. To the strong I will pretend to be helplessly drawn toward his powers. To the timid I am prepared to build friendship to gently draw him into my web. If it serves my purposes I am willing to lead. If it advances my goals I am prepared to follow. Allah will strengthen me."

"Regardless of physical acts I may be required to perform I will always look upon myself as a bride of Allah. Train me well, I will not fail."

Zeynat took in these words in astonishment. Even after months of brutally intense training A'isha had not wavered in her purpose. "I expect nothing but a total effort on your part. You are remarkable."

A'isha smiled. "We are here because Allah willed it. Let us begin for I have everything to learn."

"The pace of instruction won't pressure you. You'll have time for the new to become familiar. Men are simple creatures. When sex is on their minds they become foolish. Although Allah made men and women differently it is a common mistake to believe that women are weaker than men."

"The Prophet rode into battle with women at his side. He often turned to his wives for their advice and wisdom. Their practical knowledge saved the faith on several occasions."

"Allah has chosen well when he picked you from all Iraqi girls. Men will find you irresistible. Your beauty will bring their imaginations to worlds of sensual delight. You will be able to kill or allow them to live to take advantage of who they are and what they know. I'll teach you the art of allurement and the refined skill of flirtation."

"The men themselves are unimportant. They'll be enemies of the State, their lives forfeit. We kill our victims quickly and cleanly. We give them the best of gifts. To leave this cruel and heartless world on the crest of sexual passion is a gift given to few."

"It is my honor to train you."

October 15, 2004

Sadeq the weapons designer worked steadily on the special project. He'd been told the devices were to be used against the United States. Allotted funds were unlimited. Sadeq answered Saddam Hussein through a standard cut-out system. His isolated existence was a secret to all but Saddam. Sadeq needed only information. He had no yearnings for friends or lovers. Sadeq merely needed to think alone in silence and darkness.

The device had to be reliable over a long period which required simplicity. He alone would make the devices. Each must carry a five-pound payload to a height of 200 meters. At that height, the payload had to be released in the open air.

The device could not generate heat. It could be activated by a timer, telephone, or a fail-safe acid device. If the radio signal failed, the device would fire when its own programmed timer told it to. If both radio receiver and timer failed then acid would eat its way through a disk that would activate yet another firing system.

It must not sound like an explosive device. The payload carrier had to pierce metal up to .032 of an inch and retain enough force to reach its 200 meter height.

To project a five-pound payload 200 meters into the air without making a loud noise and without generating any heat was a daunting challenge. The activating force had to be a compressed gas. However, compressed air was not without its problems. Air contains moisture and moisture corrodes most metals. Moisture was also notorious for causing problems for delicate electrical devices. Radio receivers depended on electronics and water was fatal to electronic devices.

Nitrogen was a good possibility. The moisture problems were fewer and the gas itself quite stable and readily available. It took Sadeq time to decide how to conceal the weapon. He finally decided on the everyday container known as the 55-gallon steel drum.

All countries used steel drums by the millions to convey a nearly limitless array of liquids. The actual pressure vessel hidden within the drum was made of high strength stainless steel. The vessel itself was pressurized to 50,000 pounds per square inch. That compared favorably with the force that the average rifle exerted upon a bullet when fired.

Shaped like a standard bullet but with a sharp, hard heat-treated point, this projectile would shoot a six-inch hole through .032 of steel. At a height of 200 meters a simple cable connection pulled the base of the projectile from the main body releasing the payload.

The contents were held in the container exactly like a motorist being pushed back in his seat when the car is accelerated. Likewise, exactly like a car stopping, the momentum of the payload container would throw it contents forward in a cloud.

Two hundred devices wouldn't tax his ability to meet his deadline. He had a complete manufacturing shop with the latest in computer-controlled machines. Once his automated machines were programmed he could easily turn out more than five units every fourteen days.

Upon testing, the primary firing system activated by a radio signal tested flawlessly. Sadeq believed he had designed the simplest and most reliable device to fulfill mission requirements.

Saddam approved the report.

October 17, 2004

A'isha sat before a two-way mirror in a luxurious bedroom, part of a multi-room apartment with a kitchen and well-stocked bar. A sound system played sensual music.

Zeynat wore a black miniskirt and sheer blouse with polka dots in strategic places. She'd applied American make-up: mascara, blush, powder, and bright lipstick. At ease, Zeynat moved with confidence. A man would be brought to her. She was to gradually arouse him. A'isha was to watch and learn.

Within minutes a knock sounded on the door and two men entered, one a beefy Iraqi agent, the other a well-built man in his early twenties. Bruises on his face suggested a beating.

Zeynat spoke to the Iraqi agent in Arabic, and he nodded. The agent turned toward his prisoner, patted his shoulder, smiled, and shook his hand. The young man looked bewildered as he watched the Iraqi leave.

Zeynat quietly said in American English, "I can't stand these military types. They're all the same: bullies on one hand and whiners on the other. You won't see them again. The bruised young man seemed confused. Who are you and what am I doing here?" he asked.

Zeynat smiled. "I hold dual citizenship: one from the United States and one from Iraq. I'm a high school teacher from Kansas City,

Kansas. My mother was an American. I was born in California. However, my father is Iraqi. Occasionally I come back to Iraq to teach English for a year at a time. The pay is good, but sometimes I'm not sure it's worth it. Your situation has been somewhat of a blunder by the Iraqi government."

"You were kidnapped in Paris by Iraqi agents who thought you were someone else. The animals worked you over before they realized they'd misidentified you. They brought you to me so I could explain the mix-up and get you back on a plane to Paris as soon as possible. I'm the right person to bridge the language gap."

"The authorities here can be stupid and brutal. However, they want to keep this incident quiet since the situation between America and Iraq is already bad enough. You will receive $10,000.00 for your time, your treatment, and your silence."

Zeynat opened a small box on her dresser and poured the contents onto the bed. Neatly wrapped 100-dollar bills were carefully bound in groups of 1000.00. The sight of the money astonished her guest. He'd keep his part of the bargain. A'isha recalled that Zeynat had once said the sight of enough money was all that it would take to buy the cooperation of any American.

"Does the cat have your tongue?" asked Zeynat, "You just made a lot of money for your troubles."

The American answered, "I don't know what to say. This has been a nightmare. I never thought I'd convince them I wasn't CIA."

CHAPTER NINETEEN

"The trouble with places like Iraq is that the goons who work for the government see enemies behind every bush. You're safe now. We'll fly out to the real world tomorrow, and not stay in this crazy country. I'm just as anxious to get back to the States as you are. Did they work you over very badly?" asked Zeynat, her voice sympathetic.

"Pretty bad. I played football in high school and college and took some hard tackles, but they weren't like this. It didn't matter what I said. I'm not even sure the thugs beating me could understand English," said the American.

"What were you doing in France? Were you just a tourist when they nabbed you?" asked Zeynat.

"I just got my MA in Art and my parents saved up the money for me to take a short tour of Europe. To my family in Iowa, it was a big deal that I worked my way through college. I'm grateful for their efforts, but I never expected to be kidnapped and dragged to an Iraqi prison. If I ever get back to the States I'll never leave again," he stated emphatically.

"Well, at least it's over. You'll be on your way back with me at your side. The government paid for both our tickets. You can thank your lucky stars this worked out. It's not beyond Saddam Hussein to have you shot in the head and dumped in the desert,"

"All I care about is getting out of here. If they want me to keep quiet about this mess I'll take the ten grand and call it good," the young man said.

"Sounds like a plan to me," answered Zeynat, "What do you want for a drink to seal the deal? We have beer, wine, and some of the hard stuff."

"I didn't think liquor was legal in a Muslim country."

"The upper classes of Iraqi drink plenty. Far more than the world might suspect. Are you a Muslim?" asked Zeynat.

"I really don't have any serious religious beliefs," he said.

"Well let's have a drink to celebrate your good fortune." Zeynat poured them each a glass of wine. "What would you like to hear in the way of music? I've always liked Simon and Garfunkel myself."

In moments, the music of these American troubadours played softly. "Do you have a girlfriend or a wife in the States?"

"No, I really have no one except my folks. I'm not too popular with women. I've only had two girlfriends, but they just didn't work out. Frankly, the heart break wasn't worth the trouble. Maybe someday I can meet the right person. What about you?"

"I guess my story is longer but first we should make the normal introductions. I'm Zeynat, and what is your name?"

"John Sutter, raised in Iowa. I thought I'd never miss the Midwest, but I sure wish I was there now."

Zeynat picked up the conversation, "My story is a little complicated and I've never had good luck with the opposite sex. I was married less than a year and that marriage ended three years ago. I guess high school teachers aren't too high on the desirability list of most men."

"In Iraq, no man will even look at me because I'm American. I'm not even a practicing Muslim. I go through the religious motions in Iraq because religion is such a serious issue here. Frankly, it's good to meet you because I'm lonely to talk to a fellow Yank. This year's stay in Iraq was the longest of my life. I don't think I'll come back again."

"This all seems like a bad dream, but maybe it's really true that I'll be leaving this hell hole," John mused. "I'd like to use your shower if that's OK. You'd never believe conditions in that filthy prison."

"I have no doubt the conditions are as bad as you remember. The shower is down the hall and to your left. There's a large bathrobe you can wear until we get you some clean clothes. I'll go out and buy you something decent to wear tomorrow morning," Zeynat said.

In a few minutes, the familiar sounds of a running shower could be heard. Zeynat, still a beautiful woman, slipped out of her clothes and put on a silk robe. By the time Sutter returned, Zeynat was seated, brushing her hair before the mirror. He stopped as he saw her. Zeynat wore nothing under her robe.

Zeynat smiled at him and laughed lightly. "Looks like you haven't seen a woman for a while. Am I really that ugly or is it just a matter of being strangers?"

"You're so beautiful and you've taken me by surprise."

Zeynat turned around and made no effort to cover herself. She was a work of living art, a beautiful form that flowed into the long legs of a physically fit mature woman.

Zeynat laughed. "Normally at this point you tell the woman how beautiful she is and then make every effort to flatter her into making love to you. Since you just came from such an ugly place I thought you might enjoy what I vainly think is my female beauty." said Zeynat.

The American found his voice. "You are beautiful. I've never seen a woman as beautiful as you."

"You see, you do have a talent for flattery." Zeynat rose and approached him. Let's break the ice by dancing." Zeynat swayed as she moved to the sound system and put on something slow and romantic.

"Surely they dance in Iowa. It is simple. I put my hand on your shoulder and my other hand in yours. You hold your hand at my waist." She drew his body against hers. When her hand brushed his back he shuddered.

Zeynat stopped and said, "Let me see what they did to you." Zeynat gently stood behind John and lowered his robe to his waist. The marks of the cutting whip were plain to see. The bastards really wanted to hurt you, didn't they?"

"Thankfully, I can't see my back, but it hurts like hell."

"I think I have something that might take away some of the pain." Zeynat took a jar of salve and began to slowly push the cool mixture into the ugly cuts, carefully treating every welt with the touch a mother would use.

"Drop your robe so I can get to all the welts" she said in the kindest of tones. As A'isha watched she saw the young American's tension and confusion give way to physical relaxation under Zeynat's soothing hands. Soon those hands were sliding over his buttocks and the back of his thighs. His physical response was automatic.

Zeynat whispered softly, "Do you feel better now?" A'isha was astonished to see that all the American could do was to moan.

Zeynat took his hand, guiding him to her bed. Once there, she lay down and beckoned him to join her.

A'isha could hear Zeynat telling John to go slowly and let her bring him pleasure. The American was helpless with passion as Zeynat moved her pelvis in a slow rhythmic motion. The American did slow as Zeynat had asked. A'isha clearly heard Zeynat tell the American to relax to extend the experience.

Zeynat nearly whispered when she advised the young American to close his eyes to focus on the approaching moment. The American closed his eyes and he seemed to be enjoying pleasure so intense nothing else existed.

A'isha saw Zeynat slip her hand under a fold of the blanket. Then she increased her pelvic motion whispering, "Come now and come hard." The American's body shuddered as wave after wave of orgasm passed through him. When the last pleasure was torn from his body, Zeynat slipped the blade into his heart.

It was as if the American had a second orgasm. His eyes never opened as his body shuddered with another spasm of physical sensation. Zeynat gently rolled him from her. He was dead. A'isha doubted he'd even felt the blade. His body had been so saturated with ecstasy that the blade must have pierced the narrow line between pain and pleasure. Zeynat had delivered John Sutter to eternity with a gentleness A'isha would never have suspected in her hardened mentor.

Zeynat covered his body with a sheet and took a long shower. She dressed in standard Iraqi dress and rejoined A'isha. Zeynat searched A'isha for any display of emotion. A'isha was neutral when she looked back at her trainer.

"You could have killed him at any time. Why did you not kill when you had so many opportunities?"

"It is a gift I give my victim. Few men die in the arms of passion. It is a kindness. What are a few more minutes of my life when I know that I am sending a man to eternity?"

"This dead man was my enemy. With his sort there can be no peace. Nevertheless, I respect the life Allah gave him. I am a servant of Allah. I take lives but always with respect and skill. I believe Allah would approve."

A'isha replied, "I've learned so much today, and I thank you for it."

Zeynat smiled at her student. "You'll do well, A'isha. Rest tonight. Tomorrow is another day of instruction."

~ ~ ~

November 11, 2004

Jackson kept trying to convince his higher ups to pay attention to what he perceived as a dangerous Islamic threat. To a true Muslim getting to paradise was the primary goal. Turning away from Allah would be satanic.

Muslim religion was the most important part of an Arab's life. It made no difference if the believer were rich or poor. Focus on the hereafter affected present attitudes and daily decisions.

Like all intelligence agencies the CIA depended on local turncoats for their information. However, the CIA was stretched thin. There were few resources available to find someone his skeptical superiors did not believe existed.

Yet he knew the killer hovered at some small training site out of the normal loops. If she stayed in any of the normal military or intelligence schools he would have had her pegged by now. Every morning Jackson went through all new reports and found no mention about a single woman operative. He had nothing to take to his superiors.

In his nightmares he saw the woman walking among hundreds of American bodies. Her eyes were burning coals fueled by hatred.

She posed a greater threat than the United States had known until now. To find and eliminate her, he had to keep mining the tunnels of hate in the Middle East. The person he sought was planning the deaths of millions of American lives. Never a religious man, he prayed now.

November 25, 2005

The one Jackson sought knelt on a stony outcropping 70 miles northeast of Baghdad. The outcropping emerged below the ridge line. Najib had taught her never to be visible against the sky. Never walk on ridges where Death could easily follow.

Darkness covered the desert wasteland. Only light from a sliver of moon reached the ground. A cold breeze shifting the restless sands brought a sense of timelessness as indifferent elements worked against one another.

A'isha had been here several days. The cold fingers of a desert night slipped through frayed garments that rose and fell like a tattered battle flag. Still, the woman remained motionless.

Najib's months of training had not been in vain. A'isha had become part of the desert, indifferent to its hardships. The desert taught A'isha true patience.

A'isha believed that in the end the flag of Allah would fly over all lands on earth. Jihad, time, and the fruitful wombs of Islamic women would remake the world and the world would be Muslim.

She often sought the desert to pray and meditate on Allah's will. Her trainers always granted permission. She did not fear dying. Death would bring release from her awful duty. All would be accomplished, the main enemy of Allah destroyed. She would rejoin her sisters and parents, her losses avenged. She longed to hear Allah say, "Well done my faithful servant. Your rest is well earned. Walk the fields of paradise and meet the many worthy souls awaiting you."

She'd become far stronger than that young girl pulled from the rubble of a destroyed bomb shelter. Now A'isha often heard Allah speak to her, his voice clearest in the solitude of desert wastelands.

Nothing could stand in Allah's way. Other nations would tremble seeing the mighty United States vanquished. The Americans who killed with impunity would be killed with equal indifference.

She had but to prepare and continue to be patient. In the dark of the cold Iraqi desert, she prepared for death.

CHAPTER TWENTY

November 26, 2004

Yazid the bio-weaponeer progressed well in the past months. Cultivation of "Flash Fire" dragged at first, but he finally began turning out a biological weapons grade product in steady quantities. Working alone he made a tremendous effort to produce one pound of the deadly product in a day.

Its fatality rate approached nearly 97 percent. When the disease appeared there would only be three to five days until death.

By the time the attacked country awakened to impending disaster it would be too late to stop it. The speed the virus attacked, and the speed of death would leave medical professions helpless. The hospitalized and health providers would die first. As each infected doctor or nurse went from room to room to check on their routine patients they would deliver a death sentence to each. Each nurse, each doctor, and other health aides would deliver death to already ailing patients.

As tiny particles drifted down from the sky at varying rates they would infect any human inhaling even a few of them. To breathe or touch the virus meant a ghastly death. Modern transportation would spread the disease coast to coast in hours.

The virus would be on every airplane, bus, truck, car, and every mailbox. It would be carried by air, water, inhalation, touch, and food. Everyone from the local newspaper delivery boy to the President of the United States would be infected within a matter of a few days.

Yazid believed humankind would improve without the United States and its godless culture spreading hateful distortions of Allah's will. Where children grew up without proper knowledge of the Prophet.

America had no excuse. Allah sent warnings of their folly to the infidels. America suffered venereal diseases in vast numbers, skyrocketing divorce rates, high rates of children born out of wedlock. Worst of all, the United States spread its cultural poison to Islamic lands.

They spread it by satanic means: television, radio, depraved music, and decadent art. Satan was active and alert to capture souls for hell. The Western invention of the computer and internet spread filth and misinformation day and night.

The godless materialism of Western culture led children from good Muslim families to bad ways. The myth of individualism destroyed Islamic families as it promoted disrespect and rebellion against parental Muslim values.

Americans justified their behavior touting the blessings of freedom. But their type of freedom could only destroy the international Muslim community. A proper life meant obeying the laws of the Prophet and sincerely seeking Paradise.

American power propped up corrupt Arab States. When the United States fell, justice would sweep through Islamic countries. Former puppets of America would be brought before the bar of justice. Egypt, Saudi Arabia, and Jordan would fall like rotten fruit from blighted trees. Yemen and Kuwait would be brought to heel. Israel would be destroyed.

The United States would be a memory. Allah had answered his prayers by bringing the elements of America's destruction together in his laboratory.

~ ~ ~

November 28, 2004

With no apparent qualms A'isha applied American make up. Zeynat had taught A'isha how Western women enhance their beauty. A'isha was in the special bedroom known as "the killing room." Here she'd learn the methods of sexual entrapment for assassination. The men who entered the room seemed impressed with its décor. Not one left alive to tell of it.

A'isha just saw this as another step toward her final mission in the United States. Zeynat had proved a thorough instructor. Through example and instruction, she'd taught A'isha men's erotic zones and how to arouse a man until he was beyond rational thought. At that point he became easy to kill.

Zeynat explained that even brilliant men were easy to kill when sexual desire dominated senses. Nothing blurred a man's mind more than seducing a woman. A woman's greatest talent lay in her ability to enhance his fatal misconception.

A'isha had trained long for this day. She'd employ learned skills to kill her first man. Tonight, A'isha would surrender her virginity for Allah.

Dr. Showkit and Zeynat had discussed the type of victim who would be suitable for this first step. Both agreed that the man should be repulsive and brutal, devoid of any humanity. This act would make Americans even more hateful to A'isha.

A'isha, aware of their manipulations, thought about these things as she brushed her glinting hair. It didn't matter whether the man was handsome or ugly. All she wanted was to assassinate him.

She'd eaten lightly, then waited for evening with the demeanor of a stone. The dagger felt alive in her hands. It seemed to vibrate in anticipation of killing, its blade so sharp the lightest touch drew blood.

She'd hidden it within the special fold in the sheets. She glanced at the bedroom clock. The sun dropping below the horizon meant he would arrive soon. She knew the man was an American businessman made rich through heroin trading.

He'd been promised a reward for his purchases by an evening with a beautiful woman. Beyond that A'isha had been told nothing. She realized this was in part to see how well she could function on little information.

A'isha would be watched and filmed. Zeynat had promised she would be the backup if the situation turned dangerous for her student.

A'isha placed the brush on the bed stand and studied her reflection in the full-length mirror, satisfied that she would be attractive to any man. Zeynat told A'isha to choose the clothing she deemed right for the occasion. A'isha selected a simple white sheath that complimented her black hair and struck a balance between beauty and modesty; it heightened her sensuality.

A'isha wore no lingerie under the dress. Her face was astonishing in its beauty. Her dark eyes were bewitching with their changing depths. A'isha was on the cusp of assuming her full powers as a woman. Men would find her irresistible. All speculations ended by a firm knock at the apartment door.

With grace and confidence A'isha went to the door and opened it. She faced a short, obese, white man, probably in his mid-fifties. Nearly bald he combed his remaining strands to one side.

His face was pitted. A'isha greeted him quietly with a soft smile, "Good evening. I am A'isha. I've been waiting for you. At last, you are here. By what name shall I call you?"

"Mr. Smith will do, sweetheart. A man can't be too careful in my business," the fat man responded.

"I am pleased to meet you, Mr. Smith." A'isha spoke in a low, husky tone. The day has been warm. You must need cool refreshment to recover. What would you prefer? I can offer any type of drink."

"I could drink a six pack of beer straight down. I don't know how your kind can live in this hellhole."

"I will bring you a cool beer. Would you prefer an American or a European brand?" A'isha asked.

"Bring me anything American. I wish to hell that I was back in Chicago," the large man said with conviction as he mopped his sweating face with a large handkerchief.

"Why don't you sit and relax? I'll bring you your American beer in just a few moments," said A'isha as she walked to the refrigerator with poise and perfect posture.

His eyes drifted over her body as she returned with his beer. The American didn't bother to fill the chilled glass that A'isha had placed on an elegant silver tray. He drank straight from the bottle seeming to inhale the contents in one long pull.

"Bring me a couple more. I don't know how you savages survive in this heat."

A'isha replied with a smile. "The heat does make it difficult. Perhaps if you remove your jacket you'll be more comfortable. The air conditioner should provide relief soon." A'isha walked to the refrigerator and took two beer bottles to the fat man who seemed to sweat more profusely than any human she'd ever seen.

His shirt was soaked with it. His corpulent body gave off a stale odor. As she leaned over to give the seated man his drinks she bent low enough that the man could easily see her smooth, unencumbered breasts. A'isha smiled at him as his bloodshot little eyes stared. She straightened and swiveled before sauntering across the room to a cushioned chair. Mr. Smith visibly relaxed under the effects of the beers and cooled air.

He seemed more alert after he watched A'isha sit down. "That's one hell of a body you have," stated the man, "I don't think I ever seen a sweeter piece. How long you been in this business?"

"What business?" A'isha asked quietly.

"The business of selling sex; isn't that what whores do?" he asked, irritated. A'isha looked at him for several seconds and Zeynat, watching, observed her student's eyes darken for a split second.

Then A'isha responded with a light laugh, "My business is to make your experience in Iraq memorable for us both. I understand you are a successful businessman from the United States."

"I do okay. I can hardly keep up with the demand for the shit they stick in their arms," he replied. "Let's get down to our business. How much money do you want from me to get between those long legs of yours?"

A'isha studied Smith coolly and responded in a quiet tone, "You are a guest of the State of Iraq. There is no charge for my services. I am here for your pleasure. You will not forget your evening with me," she added smoothly. "Shall I put on music and lower the lights?" A'isha could see him already swigging his third beer.

"Sure, put on some tunes. I have to say you're the classiest hooker I've ever seen," replied the man with a voice that was becoming huskier by the moment. A'isha smiled in response as she walked to the sound system and brought in some cool American jazz.

"I'm glad you appreciate me so much. I'll remember your compliment." She turned down the dimmer switch rendering the room's ambiance even more sensuous.

A'isha walked back to sit across from her chubby guest. She took several sips of ice water, crossed her legs, and stroked the top one from knee to ankle, very slowly, before addressing him again. "Do you have a family in the United States? It must be difficult traveling frequently."

The effects of the quick beers and his awakened lust were growing obvious. "Yeah, I married a bitch who does her best to make life miserable for me. I also have a couple of kids with more money than brains. Teenagers. They seem to be on the streets most of the time.

"One is a sixteen-year-old slut who seems to fuck every lowlife in town. She's not too bad looking and has a nice set of tits. I've given some thought to trying her myself." His speech was beginning to blur.

A'isha sipped from her glass, then said, "Families can be painful to consider. Perhaps it is better to just enjoy the moment."

"Yeah, you're right. Why don't you take off that dress and show me all the merchandise," his words slurred. A'isha smiled as she stood and slowly unzipped her white dress. It slipped down her nude body and pooled like liquid around her feet. She stepped away and lifted her arms above her head like a ballerina on point and turned full circle. The muted light fell on her body.

She was a work of art, every muscle toned, and each part in perfect proportion. "Is this what you wanted to see?" asked A'isha softly.

"Damn, that is one hell of a body" exclaimed Smith.

"I'm so happy I please you." A'isha said, as she moved toward him.

She held out her hand and helped him stand, saying in a lower voice, "I can pleasure you much more." She slowly kissed him, and she could see Smith becoming lost in his rising excitement. She began to unbutton his shirt. As she undid every button her eyes held his gaze. A'isha had complete control as she reached for his belt.

"Let us take our time, Mr. Smith; I want us both to remember this night." A'isha undid the belt buckle with slow deliberation. Piece by piece she removed his wardrobe until he stood unclothed and vulnerable. He seemed trapped in the dark pools of her eyes. He offered no resistance as she led him to the bedroom.

"Lay back, Mr. Smith. I will transport you to a special place," A'isha whispered. Dazed, he did exactly what this mesmerizing woman ordered.

A'isha took the female superior position. A sharp moment of pain came when he pierced her hymen. However, she continued the gentle movements of lovemaking. "Does this feel good, my American Mr. Smith?" A'isha asked in a soft voice. Trapped in his sensations, all he could do was nod.

"Close your eyes, Mr. Smith. Enjoy our moment. Tell me when you are close. I will make it ecstasy for you. Tell me when you're on the edge, won't you, Mr. Smith?"

All Smith could do was nod. With no interruption of her movements A'isha shifted her hand to her dagger. She could see all the physical signs that her victim was close.

"Tell me when you are close. I'll make the moment special." Perspiring heavily, in a wheezing tone he said, "I can't wait much longer." With a flash of her hand A'isha drove the dagger through Smith's heart. His eyes shot open with pain and surprise.

"Good-bye Mr. Smith. I enjoyed killing you." A'isha whispered. She smiled and gave the blade a quick twist to tear his heart tissue even farther. Smith died with a quivering shudder. Suddenly she felt an intense sensual warmth spread through her, encompassing her being. This exquisite feeling engulfed her in waves. She closed her eyes to enjoy the extreme sensations. She never suspected that physical pleasure could follow killing. As the feelings passed she felt sated and languid. Was this the 'little death' of orgasm that Zeynat had once spoken of? This must be a gift from Allah. She was grateful for this unexpected present.

A'isha arose from his body and wiped her blade on a bed sheet.

CHAPTER TWENTY-ONE

In a few moments Zeynat heard running water as A'isha purified herself in the shower. Zeynat marveled. A'isha had no sentimentality. Zeynat felt uneasy. Once again A'isha had shown she was abnormal. A'isha was a force.

~ ~ ~

Dr. Showkit sat across the desk from Zeynat. She'd written her analysis of A'isha's first sexually enticed kill. He'd watched the scene on video twice. A man of healing, he found watching the assassination distasteful. Yet he had to remain informed to be sure the mission stayed on track.

"Your report says A'isha's competence pleased you. You mention that her language skills were superb even though the target used many cultural expressions that would be difficult for a new American English speaker."

Zeynat paused. "I was unable to detect any errors. As I wrote, she has an unnatural ability in seduction. I never believed a virgin could have had such self-control in that situation. A'isha seemed to experience intense pleasure immediately after her assassination, then relaxed and closed her eyes. I suspect she felt an orgasm. If I am correct it can only encourage her desire to kill."

"The target was like an animal. He was arrogant, crude, and vulgar. A'isha handled all that with serenity. She established control of Smith in minutes."

Dr. Showkit placed his hands on the written report. "Your report is clear and specific. Is there anything that you would like to say to me that you did not feel comfortable putting down in a written record?"

Zeynat paused. "In simple terms, A'isha chills me to the core. She is a stone-cold killer, relentless in her studies. Her results are deadly perfection. She will kill anyone who stands in the way of her mission, including me, you, and even Najib. Any one of us."

Dr. Showkit absorbed the information, "Thank you for being frank. I will give your words serious thought. You are free to go to your quarters."

Dr. Showkit thought a long time about what Zeynat said. The possibility of A'isha having an orgasm after killing was high. Serial murderers frequently said they were driven by sexual need. Many killers couldn't have orgasms without committing murder.

Although insane, A'isha retained some remnants of humanity buried far under the overburden of hate. But the humanity existed. A'isha would probably accept orgasm as a gift from Allah. She may accept it as a reward for killing.

This would not reduce her willingness to complete the mission. If anything, it would strengthen her commitment. She was not a robot. Doctor Showkit turned back to Zeynat's report.

In general, it appeared he could not fault her opinion. A'isha was abnormal. How could a person willing to bring death to millions be otherwise? Clinically A'isha was a psychopath who could control and focus her madness. Normal human emotions in A'isha were nearly destroyed. Only thin traces of humanity remained. It was sadly true that A'isha was cynically being used as a weapon. In a proper world A'isha would be in mental treatment.

Her physical capacities went beyond fitness. Her mental control would keep a researcher busy for life. Young and beautiful, she only wanted revenge and to die for Allah. And he himself served on a team bent on showing her how.

He put the file back in his safe and spun the dial. He felt cold. What a force would soon be released in the Western world! Dr. Showkit did not sleep well that night.

~ ~ ~

December 1, 2004

Predawn in the Iraqi desert

Najib rested against the side of a wind-swept rock. Night's chill lingered on the still air. The sun would devour night's blessed cool breeze within the hour.

A'isha joined him in peaceful silence. Words were seldom necessary for them. Najib felt close affection for her. Yet no one could ever be sure about A'isha. Relentless, remorseless, and devoid of mercy, she mystified him.

~ ~ ~

December 17, 2004

At times in the desert's darkest hours, it seems the wind inhales and exhales like a living creature. It creates an uneasy ambiance that night is not benign. It delivers fear that deep in the desert wastelands there is evil. At times, the wind makes human sounds as it filters through the cracks, curves, and holes in the sandstone.

Many desert nomads have sworn upon the prophet they heard a baby crying. Others have said under oath they heard a weeping woman. Men have followed siren calls and vanished in the arid wastes.

Some have lost their minds, forever distorted by what they've seen and experienced. They speak of seeing angels of brilliant light or dark demons from the recesses of a moon- drenched wasteland. Some lost the power of speech, their minds ravaged. All who live in that solitude see and hear too many horrors to doubt. Every desert dweller knows of unnatural realities.

A'isha believed in spirits good or evil. She'd faced both entities. The evil ones encouraged her to forget her vendetta against the Western world. After all what could one peasant girl do against the mighty United States?

Nothing could pierce her conviction or the depth of hatred she carried for her family's killers, those child murderers.

She pushed such evil tempters away by invoking Allah's great reality. But they would return. Their force was persistence and that persistence ceaseless.

In the desert A'isha drew closest to her Lord Allah, the creator, and the destroyer of limitless stars. Allah made a world where every life form wages a struggle between life and death. Every second of the day the strong devoured the weak and A'isha knew no mercy exists, between living things. The Arab world would fight to survive.

A'isha gazed into the cosmos and felt humbled by the infinite mystery of everything. Not well educated, she vaguely knew the stars were suns just like the earth had its sun. Her worldview remained basic: live to please Allah and upon death experience eternal judgment. An active war between good and evil waged. Evil destroyed her father, mother, and sisters.

Her family's destroyers came halfway around the world to drop bombs on harmless human beings. The West was still engaged in killing children by the thousands. Justice demanded a response. Every grievance had to be settled, every wrong righted, and every murder avenged.

A'isha's life was forfeit to martyrdom; but like all martyrs she would be honored for eternity. At peace with herself and her purpose, she felt fortunate.

The young and foolish United States believed they alone had the right to dictate the morals, the customs, and the correct cultural values to the rest of the world. Such pride grew from ignorance.

Mesopotamia had a written history for thousands of years before the United States had been conceived. The nomads of the Middle East had preceded modern cities by eons.

The West was doomed. A'isha knew these things from childhood talks with her father. Her father was a simple man, but his simplicity gave him great insight.

The sun's first rays colored over the horizon. Islamic power was rising as well. No force in the world would stop Muslim resurgence.

She rose and began walking toward her rendezvous. Her peasant clothes were faded black with tattered edges. She moved with stately confidence over the sandy ground. The wind would pick up the edges of her garments and the frayed cloth resembled the tattered banner of a seasoned army of veterans.

To the guard waiting for her return, she looked like a specter. Step after steady step she approached.

The guard secretly made the sign against the evil eye. The woman had never spoken to him in the six months he'd been her chauffeur. He received his orders and destinations from his superiors never seeing her ever shrouded face.

He didn't doubt the rumor that she could kill with her eyes. She scared him. A'isha approached and slipped her hood down for the first time and gazed at him, her deep eyes seemed to smolder.

She spoke. "Be at peace, Abid. You will return to your wife and three children today. Never speak of me to any human until my life is ended. One word of about me before that time and you will die that very day to burn in the fires of hell forever. Do you understand Abid?"

Stunned, he could only nod. He had never been asked his name nor had he ever mentioned being married with three children. It was not permitted for anyone to ask questions or give a name. Personal questions were forbidden under threat of death. A'isha replaced her hood. "Let us return and go our separate ways."

In silence and wonder he drove her back to the villa. His duties were finished.

~ ~ ~

January 2, 2005

Saddam noted his plan was progressing well. The female commando Dr. Showkit selected was committed and capable. A'isha's proficiency reports impressed Hussein. Her talents went beyond her trainers' hopes or expectations. She killed with the ease that others inhale air.

A'isha had mastered the finer skills of seduction and Dr. Showkit acknowledged her beauty. Saddam wanted her himself. He had a strong taste for beautiful women. What could stand between him and any woman in Iraq?

~ ~ ~

January 12, 2005

Saddam's latest directive to Showkit demanded to know what date A'isha would deploy to the U. S. Showkit sighed. This day was inevitable. His trainee was ready.

A'isha had blossomed into the flower of womanhood. She could read, write, and speak like an educated American. However, Showkit, a cautious man, wanted one last check.

He decided to question each of his trainers starting with Zeynat. Soon that seductive assassin sat before him. Dr. Showkit opened with a loaded question: "Is A'isha ready for the United States?"

Zeynat cleared her throat. She, too, opted for caution. "A'isha is ready in the technical sense, but not to cope with the cultural shock of the United States." Dr. Showkit explained that A'isha would be in the hands of another trainer and that trainer would provide oversight until A'isha was ready to fulfill her mission.

She answered, "Under those conditions A'isha is ready. She'll melt into American culture after good instruction."

Showkit stood. He thanked her and sent her to her quarters.

He sighed in relief and muttered to himself, "Next, I'll hear Najib's counsel,"

Najib answered "no" to the question of A'isha's readiness with no hesitation. At such a quick response he wondered if Najib had feelings of protective affection for his student. Their relationship showed elements of parent/child.

"Are you allowing your attachment to our trainee to interfere with your assessment of her readiness? Do you feel fatherly toward her?"

CHAPTER TWENTY-TWO

The old smuggler frowned. "I am aware A'isha will not survive since she accepts Allah's will,"

"Then explain her limitation."

Najib paused. "She has yet to face death in an immediate situation where she cannot resist but must accept Allah's plan. A test of this type will show the depth of her self-control, strength of character, and absolute faith in Allah's protection."

"If she can face the horror of Death's presence without resisting she is ready. If she fails it is best we know now. And let me assure you, when A'isha dies I will mourn until the day of my own death."

The old man had never erred in A'isha's training. Dr. Showkit weighed his words. Only Saddam knew every detail of the operation. The Doctor didn't want to know any details beyond his assignment. Ignorance in a country controlled by a tyrant was a ticket to longevity. After Najib left, Dr. Showkit considered the enormity of this gamble.

Hard months had gone into A'isha's training. Neither A'isha nor Allah had failed her trainers so far. Perhaps his luck would hold. When he said his evening prayers he asked for success. Nothing but Allah could save those who trained A'isha.

January 28, 2005

Showkit waited for Najib to arrive to describe A'isha's final test. If she passed, she would be declared ready for the United States. Saddam had been patient but would ultimately demand his mission be accomplished.

Najib entered the office and nodded.

"Please, be at ease, Najib. You indicated that A'isha must pass a test during which she could not defend herself. The test will strain both her faith and self-control. What, specifically, do you intend, my friend?"

"This test's desert origins are lost in prehistory. It is a trial by ordeal imposed during serious tribal disputes. If a man or woman was accused of a heinous crime against the tribe and the evidence could neither free nor convict, the tribal elders invoked this test." Najib cleared his throat and spoke with unusual tension.

"Go on," Dr. Showkit pressed.

"They called this the 'ordeal of the pit' and its results rest in Allah's hands. As you know varieties of venomous snakes exist in Iraq. In certain rocky areas, snakes' den in large concentrations."

Showkit nodded and added, "The den is a large sunken pit usually around 25 feet in diameter and 20 feet deep. The walls consist of broken, layered rock. Snakes seek such spots for shade and to cool themselves from desert heat."

Najib nodded." During the heat of the day the pit empties as the snakes' retreat into the cool rock cracks and stone faults. During the cool of night, they reemerge from their shelters and congregate in the pit."

"Many snakes will leave the pit by serpentine routes to hunt in the countryside. Most remain in the pit until hunger forces them to leave their sanctuary. In ancient times the person under tribal charges was lowered into the pit at mid-morning when the reptiles were in their recesses."

"The absence of the snakes made it relatively safe to lower the person into the pit to be left alone there until mid-morning of the next day."

"Head men assumed an innocent person would show no fear and be protected by Allah. Most of the time there was no need to extract the person from the pit because he or she would die from snake bites during the night."

Dr. Showkit had heard of such trials in Iraqi's past. He tried to keep his voice level. "Roughly what percent of those submitted do you believe lived the twenty-four hours?"

The smuggler met his eyes and held them. "It is doubtful more than one in twenty survived."

"Are you saying that A'isha has one chance in twenty?" asked the Doctor.

"Not just of surviving. Those who live are blessed by Allah. A survivor often becomes a mighty leader or a wise counselor. Many became Allah's favored warriors."

"What species of snakes were selected?" asked the Doctor.

"Most typically the Garna viper because of its aggressive nature and deadly venom," answered the smuggler. "A quick death to the guilty was preferable to lengthy suffering."

Dr. Showkit weighed the information. All physicians in Iraq were familiar with the Garna snake. Under two feet, its common name is the Saw Scaled viper or the scientific *Echis carinatus sochurelei*. The mortality rate of those bitten was well over 98 percent. He had seen one such corpse and shuddered at the memory.

Multiple strikes brought death in minutes as the venom caused massive internal hemorrhage. A small woman or child almost never survived the bite of the Saw Scaled viper.

"I am not an educated man, but I am a man of the desert. I know the snake only by its common name of "Garna", but I have experienced many exposures to this snake and Allah be praised I was never bitten," said the old smuggler.

"If I approve this test it means life or death and not just to A'isha. Our sponsor is powerful. If she does not survive we will also die."

"Being no fool, I did not suggest the test lightly. A'isha is being groomed to inflict massive deaths on Americans. The mission's success is only possible if Allah holds her in his hands. Either we trust in A'isha and Allah, or we are not true believers," said Najib.

Showkit rubbed his eyes. "Najib, how many vipers might be in this pit during the hours of darkness?"

"In the hundreds. Survival depends on the individual's ability to maintain composure and immobility. Under these terms the snakes may not be able to tell a human from an odd rock retaining heat. The snakes won't view such a large heat source as food."

"A'isha's slightest move will invite a strike. Surviving such a test would render our trainee invincible to apprehensions and fears that might lead to mission failure. I know A'isha and love her as a daughter, but the mission must come first. She will agree,"

The Doctor mulled over these points. The entire mission rested on A'isha's faith. She must be certain she is under Allah's protecting hand. He realized, too, it was also a serious personal question. Did he himself believe and trust in Allah?

Yes. He believed Allah had the power to protect A'isha under any circumstances. Trained in modern sciences, in the end he was a faithful follower of Islam.

"I agree to the test only if A'isha is informed of the risks and consents to this ordeal. I will not subject any human to such a horror unless there is full acceptance. Najib, please find A'isha and bring her here."

In under ten minutes A'isha entered. Her presence, as so often, felt unnerving to the waiting men. She had regal poise even though her clothes were the tattered peasant garb. As always, she gave the impression of complete confidence. Finally, she broke the silence.

"So, at last I come to the last test before I go to America to die. It has been a long wait. No words are necessary. I know your thoughts."

"My father once told me of those distant days when believers were tested beyond what most could endure. Those who survived the pit were in Allah's hands because nothing else could have protected them."

"If Allah wills it I survive. If not then I die and rejoin my loved ones in paradise. I have no fear. I accept Allah's will. All life belongs to the creator of a thousand worlds. You have done well, my trainers. Because of your efforts I am ready. I ask leave to begin my prayers."

"Najib, I ask you to take me to my destiny in the morning. I will be prepared,"

"It shall be so," the old man answered. A'isha left the room with no sound. Najib followed.

Dr. Showkit went to his quarters to pray. So often he'd been torn between science and religion. Ultimately, religion carried the field.

February 1, 2005

Allison Browning, tall and self-possessed, had worked all her adult life in a tough business. At fifty-three years old, black, and strong, she'd worked for *The D.C. Daily* in the political maelstrom of international politics. It had been a long road to obtain her position as the lead writer for the prestigious old newspaper.

She became a moderate follower of Islam in 1963 when the black population in the United States struggled for Civil Rights equal to those white people enjoyed. Many blacks felt attracted to a religion that seemed opposite from Christianity as followed by hypocritical White America.

The Prophet of Islam, Mohammed, was a fighting warrior and this especially appealed to the young black community. Pacifistic Jesus couldn't compete with a fighting prophet. Many blacks abandoned Christianity.

On a fateful day May 7, 1987, she met Ali Binen, an educated Black Muslim man. He named himself Ali because he sensed that his path in life would mirror that of famous Muslim Martyr, Ali Hussein. This American Ali rose as a prominent leader, a forceful speaker, and a fearless man. He preached Jihad with no limitation.

Allison met him during an interview and fell for Ali's charisma, faith in Allah, and comfortable acceptance of his death should Allah demand his life. His extreme faith was new to Allison who felt his forceful impact through her entire being.

Ali spoke often of Holy War and prayed that Allah might give him the privilege of being a martyr. He felt his duty to Allah and spoke fearlessly even when his enemies numbered in the thousands. Men like him were not meant for long lives.

Ali was shot while speaking to a mainly black audience at the Thomas Jefferson Memorial in Washington D.C. His killer evaded capture. The day was a point of no return for Allison. She immediately became an extreme Muslim who prayed daily to Allah to use her to advance the cause of Islam.

Convinced that without Islam's control world peace would always be thwarted, she longed for the day she would see Ali in the gardens of Paradise. She hoped Allah would call her soon. She saw the United States was hostile to Islam, but not immune to Allah's laws. Allison believed Allah's promise of a Muslim world.

She became a hidden warrior of Allah. The memory of Ali's murder never left her heart. Her news articles became far too extreme for her employers, and she was finally asked to resign. She did so without regret. She felt certain Allah had a purpose for her.

She now felt Allah's light had guided her throughout her life. Her belief in a tolerant version of Islam had been swept away by Ali's martyrdom. She now believed one was either a believer bound toward paradise, or an unbeliever consigned to hell.

Like all fanatics Allison liked the clarity of her religious vision. She read the Koran daily and the violent words of the fighting Prophet pierced her heart and mind with crystalline clarity. Her days of moderation became a distant memory.

She became a warrior of Allah. The memory of Ali's murder never left her heart. She prayed for the day they would rejoin in the gardens of Paradise.

Like many dreamers Allison was prepared to fight a holy war for everlasting peace to follow. A true believer, she would kill so that killing could finally end.

Finally, she read a short note slipped into her hand during a ride on an elevator to her room. She read it carefully and burned it in an ash tray. She then crushed the ashes and flushed them down the toilet. The peace of Allah passed over her. She'd been selected for a great task.

Ali would be avenged, and Allah served. Allison Browning felt the hand of Allah during her prayers of gratitude.

She had been given a mission.

CHAPTER TWENTY-THREE

February 4, 2004

Before dawn Najib, A'isha, and their driver were on route to low mountains, part of a mountain range south of Baghdad. Najib was familiar with the area, well used by smugglers. He knew where to find viper dens.

The roads became trails narrowing until the driver had to stop and turn off the engine. Najib and A'isha hiked up the trails for another hour.

Najib advised slowing as they approached the den. The terrain felt foreboding with an aura of danger upon ground not meant for them.

Najib led in silence. The two kept their attention on the rocks and crevasses around them. Every step meant danger. It took the utmost concentration to avoid a fatal tread. Four times Najib froze as he detected a viper and waited for it to move on.

The sound of rubbing scales became unnerving. At last, they reached a singular boulder overlooking the chosen pit.

The sun's rising made it possible to make out details on the pit floor. The two could see the vipers congregating upon the floor of this foreboding depression.

There were hundreds of them. In places snakes formed a mat of intertwined bodies. Najib looked at this and surmised the depths of hell couldn't present a more horrible vision. Najib murmured, "We must wait for them to recede into the cracks in the walls at midmorning."

"Heat and light cause their retreat. Night's cold darkness will bring them back. My child, it is not too late to abandon the mission. I can hide you in the mountains where you will never be found. I will gladly sell my life to deliver you to safe haven,"

"My old friend, my destiny is to destroy the United States. My life belongs to Allah. He will take it at his will. I am only a tool in his hands. I accept his decision."

Activity in the pit increased as the sun rose higher. By the third hour of light the deadly vipers had retreated into the cool cracks of the walls. A'isha had been silent.

"It is now time. It should be possible to lower you without incident. Are you ready, my child? It is not too late for you to decide against this." Najib said.

"My dear friend, lower me down so my test can begin."

"As Allah wills," replied Najib. He eased A'isha down into the pit. She passed recesses in the wall. The snakes made irritated sounds as her shadow and her form passed their resting spots. Finally, A'isha reached the pit's floor and removed herself from the rope. Najib raised it. They gazed at each other, then A'isha smiled at Najib as if he were a beloved grandfather she would rejoin soon.

She found a smooth spot in the pit and made herself as comfortable as possible. "If Allah wills, I will see you in the morning," said A'isha.

"If Allah wills," said the old man as he disappeared from her sight.

Thus began the ordeal of the pit.

Mental control and an absolute absence of movement were her sole means of survival. If fear conquered her she would begin to sweat evoking any number of fatal strikes. She could feel the presence of vipers surrounding her, hundreds within twelve feet. The temperature itself turned hot, but water and food were out of the question. Vipers would strike at any movement.

Alone, A'isha found that each passing second seemed a day and each hour an eternity. Sitting motionless, she struggled to maintain perfect serenity.

~   ~   ~

Hours dragged on, bringing increased pressure on mind and body. She closed her eyes and made every effort to ease any physical tension. The vipers must not sense her living form. Her only hope meant being as still as the earth.

The next few hours would bring the horror of darkness and the vipers would become active, slithering from their recesses to seek open spaces on the pit floor.

Her senses had never been so clear. Her hearing reached a sharpened level. She focused on maintaining composure. For hours on end she heard the slightest movement any reptile made, infrequent and muted within the walls. Silence followed each movement.

Slowly sounds of motion increased until the noise grew constant. Vipers were on the move. She heard the soft impact as one after another dropped to the floor. Sounds surrounded her arriving within inches.

Finally, she felt the first reptilian brush against her body. A viper's tongue tested this odd source of heat. A'isha did not move. She felt other snakes as they, too, explored this oddity.

The floor hosted constant movement. She heard them emerging by the hundreds, crawling over her body with tongues in constant motion. Tongues touched her legs, her arms, and finally her torso. Some of the snakes were more aggressive. They tapped firmly with their heads apparently in the effort to test for life. Each mock strike felt like a death sentence. She felt their collective weight as they layered over her.

The boulder she leaned against was taller than her and vipers draped around her head and shoulders.

A'isha forced her conscious thoughts to retreat. The gap between mind and body widened. She felt and accepted the serpents' weight and remained still. She focused on nothingness as the snakes on her body pushed and shoved each other for more comfortable positions.

She felt the tongues of snakes touch her lips and particularly her closed eyes. Even the tresses of her hair were entangled with them, and she could feel snakes crawling across her pubic mound.

Her fears tried to draw her mind from its sanctuary of nothingness. Each time her power of concentration restrained them.

She sought to lock any fear behind the doors of her will. To A'isha time became meaningless. It seemed she'd been with these snakes for eons flowing into eternity.

Too often she heard sawing sounds as an irritated viper showed its displeasure with another snake. Her soul was nearly torn apart by that eerie noise alone. With her eyes closed, A'isha had no way of measuring time. She had no way of watching the progress of the stars or sun. A'isha could only allow the concept of the moment. She reduced her thinking to one single point of light that hovered against the endless darkness of her fear. If she concentrated on that point there was a chance that she could live another second.

Gradually it became harder, much harder, to concentrate on that singular spot of light. Again and again, she mustered her mental forces on it. Yet the spot expanded.

All was lost unless she could keep that light. Without it, how would she know how to survive? It grew harder to maintain focus. Eternity passed. Gradually she could sense a new sound. Activity increased. A viper slid off her shoulder. Several minutes later another left her body. A'isha realized the inner light of her concentration was being overcome by the physical light of the outside world. The reptiles were disengaging themselves from A'isha and each other. She could hear the slight sounds as they reentered the cracks.

A'isha remained motionless as she strained her senses of sound and feeling to decide whether any vipers remained on or under her garments. Mentally she went over her every body part. One mistake meant death.

At last A'isha heard Najib sounding like an angel of deliverance. "Do not move my child. We must be certain the snakes have retreated."

Najib studied every visible inch of her, and every inch of the pit floor. "Open your eyes slowly. Allow them to adjust to daylight. You are still in mortal danger until we extract you from this satanic pit."

A'isha obeyed him. The light seared her.

"A'isha can you speak to me and follow my commands?" asked Najib.

"I can speak but am not sure I can move. I feel weak," A'isha murmured.

"Slowly raise your arms. It will be painful, but you must make the effort."

A'isha started to lift her arms, but the pain felt so severe she paused. "Hurry child, the snakes are aggressive and may respond to movement."

With great effort A'isha raised her hands overhead, palms together like a diver. "A'isha, watch the rope descend. Let it slip over your hands until it reaches your chest. Next, lower your arms. This slip knot will tighten on your chest. Breathing will be difficult but no strength on your part is necessary." Najib spoke with urgency in his tone.

A'isha did exactly as commanded. She felt the rope go taut and the sensation of being raised. Najib's strong arms lifted her from the edge of the pit as though she were a child.

"May Allah be praised," said the old man as he hugged her to his chest.

"Yes, Allah is great," whispered A'isha. She smiled before losing consciousness. Najib carried her for two miles until he met his driver. The ordeal of the vipers was over.

~ ~ ~

In the United States, citizens of that great country went about their daily affairs. Perhaps it was a blessing. They were ignorant of the coming danger. Now nothing stood in the way of A'isha's arrival in the United States.

~ ~ ~

February 8, 2005

Dr. Showkit considered Najib's report. By the grace of Allah A'isha had survived. After two days of food, drink, and sleep, she made a full recovery. He'd written his own report to Saddam Hussein listing all the skills she'd learned as well as the tests survived. He explained the ordeal of the vipers and its necessity. In hours, the report would be delivered. All that remained necessary for Showkit was to await Saddam's reply.

~ ~ ~

February 9, 2005

The dictator sat behind an ornate desk in one of his palaces. Moving from place-to-place ensured safety; therefore, a longer life.

This commando, A'isha, had mastered the English language. Her flawless physical and mental training was complete.

Her self-control in the viper pit showed incredible concentration and courage. She'd killed and showed no remorse. She displayed eagerness to fulfill her mission. He noted she'd mastered her sexual training.

Dr. Showkit described her as extraordinarily dangerous with powers science could not explain. Saddam's eyes narrowed. He believed himself to be the sole power that mattered in Iraq.

This intriguing woman would conform to his will or die. He planned on testing her bedroom skills for himself. *Why not? Was he not the ruler of this entire land?* His money trained her. His mind created this mission. No woman in Iraq withheld sexual favors from him. Any who tried were raped and murdered.

If this commando fulfilled her mission her life would be lost. It seemed a shame that such a beautiful woman could not be enjoyed before she went to Paradise; a paradise that he personally did not believe in. He smiled as he looked forward to enjoying her charms. He drafted a short note and handed it to an aide. Within two days this woman, A'isha, would have the privilege of making love to the President of Iraq.

February 13, 2005

A subdued gathering met in Dr. Showkit's office. Besides the Doctor, Zeynat, Najib, and A'isha were included. For months they'd labored for this day now upon them. There was sadness in the hour. Only A'isha seemed composed. Dr. Showkit had received a command to send A'isha to Baghdad for one final consultation.

Powerless to prevent this meeting, Dr. Showkit had emphasized the threat of her unusual powers. Saddam could not resist taking A'isha as he had so many other women. Such foolish behavior could jeopardize the mission. If A'isha declined Saddam's advances he might kill her in a fit of rage. If she submitted to this humiliation it could compromise her fervor in the mission.

The outcome was in the hands of Allah.

The good-byes were painful for everyone except their trainee. To Dr. Showkit she remained the mysterious girl he'd found in the orphanage. She'd changed little from those early days. Her aloof self-confidence hadn't altered.

CHAPTER TWENTY-FOUR

The years had made A'isha even more beautiful. Her complexion was flawless. Her eyes could be inviting. She had perfect proportions, every physical feature in balance with the rest. Her level of physical fitness extended from her skin to the marrow of her bones.

She remained an enigma. Where did she get her control and obvious abilities?

Zeynat continued in awe of A'isha and regretted her own present relief. A'isha wore a new set of the modest dark clothes worn by the working poor. Zeynat told A'isha a small suitcase of western clothes awaited her at the safe house. She would wear them to Paris where her contact would meet her.

Najib gave A'isha a tiny locket containing a bit of Iraqi sand. A'isha took Najib's weathered hand and said, "I will see you in paradise, my old friend."

"As Allah wills," the smuggler replied. Dr. Showkit would ponder their relationship for a long time.

A'isha addressed the others. "Because of the training you have given me, I am ready to fulfill my duty. Allah is with me. The Arab world is under assault from infidels. Our main enemy is the United States and her lust for power and oil. With Allah's help and your training, I am ready to destroy that arrogant nation."

"I know of my meeting with Saddam Hussein and of his plans. I'll thwart the lion in his den. No harm shall come to me, and Allah has assured me that no harm shall come to any of you. Saddam is no fool. He'll understand that my true master has always and only been Allah."

"Saddam is but one tool in his hands. I've learned Allah often uses unlikely instruments to accomplish his goals. I am one of those imperfect tools and Saddam is another. Allah will remind him who the real ruler of Iraq is. Saddam will never forget this lesson."

"Do not mourn my death. There is much to be said for dying young. I will never know the pain of lost loves and unrealized dreams. I will not feel the pains of advancing years. I will never endure the fading of physical beauty. I will never know future betrayals and growing loneliness. The drudgery of day-to-day survival will not be my fate. I will never know the pain of ungrateful children or a wandering husband."

"I will be spared seeing friends lowered into their graves while all I can do is mourn their passing. Above all, I will die for a great cause. I will die as a martyr and that is a blessing given to few. I will avenge our people the Americans murdered. I look forward to balancing the scales of justice."

"It is my prayer that my death will advance Islam. I look forward to meeting my loved ones in paradise. I will see all of you again. Allah has promised his followers that his world does not know cruelty, pain, or death. Paradise is a world where children are not slaughtered by the powerful merely to demonstrate their power."

"I will remember each of you with gratitude." A'isha looked at each person for one last moment, then turned and walked to the car waiting to take her to Saddam. She did not look back as the car drove away.

The United States slumbered.

February 13, 2005

The Alpha Romeo advanced through Baghdad's streets. The driver had driven dozens of women to assignations with Saddam Hussein, never to see most again. His instructions were to put his passengers at ease. Saddam preferred his victims to have a spark of hope before they were trapped within his clutches.

Most chattered constantly to relieve their fear, but not this one, so silent and composed. She unnerved him. She wore the black hooded garb so common with the Iraqi poor, her head and face in deep shadow.

He could not wait for her to get out of his vehicle. His standing orders were to blindfold his passengers but when he attempted to blindfold this woman she merely said the single word "No." The command presence in the voice startled him and he instantly obeyed her.

His skin crawled. It was like having a lioness in his car. Contrary to orders he took the most direct route to Saddam's location. The quicker this creature exited the quicker he could relax.

He pulled up to the steel gates of the palace grounds. A single guard admitted them. The silent woman left the car, and its driver felt as if a Cobra had just removed itself.

The heavily armed guard had a powerful build. He ordered the woman to follow him through the opulent building's interior hallway. Instead, she walked slightly ahead of him. Most visitors paused in awe at the magnificence of the palaces but not this woman. Apparently gold fixtures and silver mounted furnishings meant nothing to her.

The burnished paneled walls of the rarest ebony and dark walnut did not warrant so much as a glance. She walked across the marble floors as if they were dirt on a market street. For the first time in many years the burly guard felt a frisson of fear.

He reached for the flap on his holster. Before his hand touched the leather he heard her murmur, "You will not need your pistol. No one will be harmed today." Her voice was so calm and commanding that he obeyed.

A'isha led the way down a large corridor lined with art masterpieces without glancing at them. She stopped at a large door, indiscernible from any of the others.

The guard found his tongue and said, "You must allow me to search your person before you go into the President's presence." For the first time A'isha slid the hood from her head and looked directly at him.

She said in her low voice, "You shall stand by this door as you always do."

She opened the door and entered without invitation.

The main room contained a large desk and behind it sat Saddam Hussein, appearing relaxed. His voice, when he spoke, seemed a little too friendly. A door to the side of the desk opened onto a large bedroom.

"Please, sit down. We have much to discuss."

A'isha chose a chair. Saddam, a man with a tuned antenna felt the air hum with tension. "I trust my guard treated you with courtesy."

"Yes, he was most helpful and presented no difficulties." Saddam sensed something in their meeting had gone awry.

Everyone showed varying levels of fear in his company. Not this woman. He felt a touch of uncertainty but brushed it away like a fly. He could and would control this situation.

"I've been told your training was successful and you are prepared to enter the United States. You will meet your handler in Paris. She will take you to Washington D.C. where she will assist you in adapting to that culture."

A'isha looked at Saddam steadily. "Yes, I am aware. I am to meet a tall black woman by the name of Allison Browning, a capable and accomplished Muslim."

Saddam paused for a long second. No one except himself knew Allison Browning's name or history. "How did you come into this knowledge? Only I know this."

A'isha looked at Saddam who detected a change in her eye color. They darkened. "Allah gives me information. Allah knows all things and I am a servant in his hands." A'isha's voice had a cool edge.

Her serious demeanor unsettled Saddam. There was something dangerous here, but he mistrusted his instincts. "Tell me what you know about me." Saddam spoke with a lighter tone. He always loved these sessions. It was amusing to hear people sing his praises to ever higher levels.

"As you wish," said A'isha. "You are the man who is responsible for financing my training. For that I and the Muslim world are grateful."

"Surely you must know more about me personally, I would welcome your insight," said Saddam. These were always the glowing moments where his actions and leadership were touted to the high heavens.

"As you wish," said A'isha. "You are a nonbeliever although you will change your views in time. Perhaps today you will gain spiritual food for your mind and your endangered soul. You are a tyrant; a dictator who rules the Iraqi people with an iron fist. You have killed many times when there was no necessity."

"You are a sadist who tortures people regardless of their age or sex. You allowed your sons to perform unspeakable crimes. You have coerced many women sexually and raped those who refused to give up their honor. I know that I am here because you wish to have sex with me. You will die the death of a dog. There are many other factors that could be discussed but I believe this should cover the larger points."

Rage built in Saddam. No one had ever talked to him in this manner. He controlled his anger, "Much of what you said is true. Remove your clothes and let the ruler of Iraq inspect your body."

A'isha smiled and said, "Allah is the true ruler of Iraq, and he has seen me nude many times. However, I will let you see my body."

A'isha stood up and removed her garb in a smooth motion. She wore nothing under her outer clothing.

Saddam looked upon this beautiful woman. The French sculptor Rodin in his finest hour could never have created a statue with a more perfect form.

A'isha's muscle tone was hard and taut from the endless miles she'd walked in the desert. Her breasts were firm and as smooth as alabaster. Her nipples responded to the conditioned air in the palace and were hard and erect. The lines of her body were an enchanting balance of curves and angles.

Her legs were long, and she'd already adopted the American habit of shaving her legs. The long hair upon her head was black with a sheen that seemed to glow as the light struck her hair at different angles. However, the face captured him. It had both a perfect olive complexion and angular planes that seemed to give her an alluring power.

A'isha's eyes were her most amazing feature. They seemed able to change colors, to evoke a bewitching power. Sensuous and inviting, they were the eyes of a woman who waited with eagerness, perhaps for her lover to return from a long absence.

Saddam forgot his rage. Lust ruled the ruler. A'isha walked to the side of the desk and extended her hand. He grasped it.

A'isha spoke in a husky voice. "Life is brief; let us retire to your bedroom. Let us enjoy a hint of paradise in this world."

Saddam led the way. A'isha reclined upon the silk sheets. Her long dark hair framed her face. She elevated one knee and slightly spread her long legs. Her eyes turned soft, sensuous, and beckoning.

"It seems strange to be the only one unclothed. I am unaccustomed to men slow in undressing when the feast of love is so prepared," whispered A'isha.

She smiled at Saddam as she slowly licked her index finger with the delicate tip of her tongue and then traced the damp finger down across one nipple and slowly down to her navel. Saddam was entranced with the movement of her finger slowly tracing its way to her pubic mound.

A'isha smiled as he, now nude, was clearly aroused. "Join me," she whispered, "and let us leave the world of care for an hour."

"Recline on your back," said A'isha, "I have much to give you." Saddam closed his eyes so he could concentrate on sensations. He'd never looked forward to having a woman more than he did A'isha.

Then in a split second he felt a sharp pain at his throat. His eyes flashed open and what he saw froze him. A'isha held a dagger into the skin of his throat. A slender short assassin's knife had been taped to the sole of her foot. Gone was her voice of seduction, in its place a murderous growl.

Her eyes burned with anger and Saddam knew this monster could kill him in a moment. A'isha spoke in a hard voice. "You would treat the 'Sword of Allah' like a common whore?" she hissed. Sweat rolled down Saddam's face like drops of blood.

He tried to speak. He tried to move. He could do neither. Her eyes projected utter disdain. "My every instinct is to kill you as you have killed so many others for your amusement."

"Did you not read the report that the good Doctor sent you yesterday? Every word that he wrote in secret was revealed to my mind. I may spare you because it was your funds and your political power that paid for my training. As you can see I learned my lessons well. Where is that voice you are so proud of?"

Saddam strained to speak but made no sound. A'isha extended a chilling smile, "Perhaps your power is not as great as you thought."

Finally, he did speak, "Spare me! I can give you anything you want. Just let me live!"

"Even now you are a great fool. Do you think the Sword of Allah is interested in such superficial things? I live only to serve and die for Allah." In his terror Saddam fell silent again.

"You will do two things to absolute perfection, or your punishment will be beyond imagining. You will not harm the team that trained me in any way, and you will support this mission of Islam totally. Do you agree?"

"I agree. I will obey." His voice conveyed fear.

"That is good. Your sons will die in their own blood. You will lose your power and your kingdom. As to your personal fate, I leave you to ponder. Send me on my way."

CHAPTER TWENTY-FIVE

A'isha slipped into her robe. She stood in the corner as Saddam hastened to put on his clothes. All thoughts of sex had vanished. He only wanted to be rid of this witch. He felt the slow seeping of blood down his neck. She could have killed him.

Saddam called for his guard. "Do not harm my guest in any manner. Call for a driver and tell him to grant her requests. See to it she is protected and comfortable. At her discretion put her on a flight to Paris regardless of the bookings."

Saddam turned to A'isha and said in tones that conveyed respect, "Your contact will meet you in Paris with the material you will require."

"Thank you, Mr. President. I will not disappoint you," A'isha said as she turned and walked away. The guard fell into step behind her.

Saddam Hussein closed his door and collapsed with exhaustion. He mopped the sweat from his pallor. He felt weak. He'd never been so relieved to get a woman out of his sight! The image of A'isha with her hard eyes and the tip of a dagger pressed into his throat would haunt his nightmares for a long time. He shuddered. Thank Allah her target was the United States! Saddam had much to ponder for many months.

March 1, 2005

Content, Yazid, the warrior/biological scientist, finished his evening prayers. He'd manufactured 200 pounds of his genetically engineered pathogen, enough to fulfill the mission against the West. The new invincible biological killer called "Flash Fire" had a complex genetic code that even the most highly skilled scientists would require months to crack. They lacked time. They would be dead within five to seven days.

As planned, Yazid received the prototype of the pathogen launcher. A simple 55-gallon drum with a removable band that allowed its top to be easily removed. All such drums were painted in ubiquitous gray.

Yazid studied instructions on how to install the payload into this work of genius. The drum's inner lid had been machined so that there was only .020 of an inch for the preloaded hardened projectile to pierce. All internal parts were made of stainless steel. Hence the device was impervious to moisture. The propulsion force was compressed nitrogen. The phone signal would be received by a computer which in turn automated four redundant powerful secret transmitters located in four important cities: Washington D.C., Dallas Texas, Los Angles, California, and New York City. The transmitters projected a powerful burst of energy. With the launchers' firing, the United States would begin to die.

The launcher was designed to pierce the thin tin roof of a standard rental storage unit. Thousands of such storage units spread across the United States. Yazid was to load each device within the hot zone. The pathogen was contained in a stainless-steel container which in turn attached to the base of the hardened tip. The seam was tight, internally sealed with a special Teflon "O" ring. Teflon is resistant to moisture or chemical erosion.

The seam itself was sealed with a thin seal of high strength epoxy. When the payload went aloft the "O" ring would compress tightly so that nothing would leak until it reached the proper height. This force of compression would break the epoxy seal. A trailing wire would then pull the base containing the pathogen from the bottom of the projectile and spill the deadly virus into the air stream 200 meters aloft.

Once released, the extremely small spores would gradually fall to earth and do their job: infecting every person. The pattern of dispersion would depend on the prevailing winds, but a cloud of death 10 miles wide and 50 miles long per launcher wasn't unreasonable. The operational plan would put four launchers around each targeted city. The launchers would be located to the north, the south, the east, and the west of each assigned city. No matter which way the wind moved targeted city dwellers would be infected. The targeted cities were doomed.

Two to three days were needed for any symptoms to be visible. Modern travel would carry the virus everywhere. In addition, the parcel service moved millions of parcels a day and "Flash Fire" could live several days without a human host.

Each parcel would be contaminated by handlers. Yazid's work was just beginning. It would take time to load Flash Fire into the launchers.

All that delicate work must be performed within the most lethal part of Yazid's manufacturing facility. Loading several launchers a day would be the best he could hope for given the constraints of his protective clothing and the time it would take to go through each protective ring of the manufacturing plant.

However, Yazid was patient. He was certain things would go well. He had prepared for this task his entire life and with Allah's help the containers would be loaded on schedule. Yazid, like many good Muslims, ended his thoughts with "As Allah wills."

A'isha instructed the driver to take her to one of Saddam's safe houses. Saddam had dozens of these hiding places. She'd been thoroughly briefed by Zeynat on these matters. A'isha couldn't take the chance of changing her appearance in one of the many modern Baghdad hotels. A Muslim woman in peasant clothing would never be found in such a place.

The driver took her to a villa in Baghdad's suburbs. The government car's darkened windows assured privacy. Once within the walled villa no one on the outside could see who exited the car.

The caretaker asked no questions as he escorted her to a room where she changed into the American clothes Zeynat had selected. She discarded her peasant clothes in the trash.

She'd been given $20,000.00 in American currency to tide her over until she left France for the States. Once in the United States she'd draw on a large account placed in a major international bank in Washington D.C. Every aspect of her attire gave off the signals of wealth. Zeynat had been particularly meticulous when it came to jewelry.

Her choices were stunning in beauty and value. A hundred thousand dollars was displayed with just a few classic pieces. A'isha's goal was to be flawlessly beautiful in the American/Franco style. When she returned to the chauffeured car her transformation from an Iraqi peasant to a sophisticated member of the international elite was complete.

Her carriage and mannerisms were those of one used to deference, power, and wealth. A'isha instructed the driver to take her to the Baghdad International Airport.

She had no problem navigating it. She'd memorized her passport. Her new name was Mary Morden of New York, New York. Mary's physical description fit A'isha well. There really was a Mary Morden from New York, the only child of a successful man who'd developed a vast import business. Her father and mother had emigrated from Saudi Arabia before Mary's birth. The Arab couple changed their names to fit within the American culture more easily.

The Morden family did well in the United States, amassing a fortune. Sadly, both parents died in an automobile accident two years ago. Mary had been a quiet girl who'd formed no close relationships. An only child, after the will was settled she decided to move to Paris.

She had no living relatives in the United States and knew nothing about her family background in Saudi Arabia. Her profile fit Saddam Hussein's requirements: a close approximation of A'isha.

She met a handsome Iraqi who seemed to be everything a woman might desire. He was handsome, wealthy, and talented in the bedroom. Her new love interest encouraged her to visit Iraq. Unknown to her, he was an agent for Iraqi Intelligence. She was professionally murdered. Every trace of Mary disappeared from the world.

A'isha held a current passport showing the aimless wanderings of a rich young woman. A'isha spoke English from the moment her driver dropped her off at the airport. She would never speak Arabic again. Once she settled quietly in her first-class seat she spoke to no one.

March 3, 2005

Allison Browning followed her instructions. She'd spent four months vacationing in Europe. She visited all the tourist sites as ordered and took photographs with her Leica camera. She gave every impression of being comfortably retired. She mixed tourism with visits to close friends but refrained from political discussions. She gave the appearance of not wanting to talk shop. United States intelligence gave Allison only routine coverage. There was nothing concerning her travels to raise red flags. She visited no Muslim countries and seldom worshipped. Her religion had never been a secret, and Allison always gave the impression of being moderate.

Allison made Paris her hub, renting an upscale flat. She walked to the most popular cafes. Allison had been told to be receptive to a drink of a special year and vintage.

That fall in Paris a distinguished white man had a waiter take that specific drink to her table. Allison told the waiter she'd be most pleased to thank her admirer. The gentleman came to her table and spent an hour discussing general topics of interest. When they ended the discussion he gave her his card.

To a casual observer it would appear to be nothing more than a man seeking to spend more time with an attractive woman. The card gave the flight number and the plane's estimated time of arrival. Several identifying features were listed. The passenger's name: Mary Morden.

The meeting would be complete if the passenger replied using her complete name. Allison retired to the lady's room a few minutes after the gentleman left. She tore his card into small bits and flushed them down the toilet. The flight was due within two hours.

~ ~ ~

March 3, 2005

A'isha felt the plane begin its approach to Charles de Gaul airport. Zeynat had explained urban sprawl, but the visual impact of seeing tens of miles of suburbs hit A'isha. She'd been warned that the number of infidels in Western nations was vast.

A'isha would be under her handler's guidance until the exact details of her mission were made clear. When the plane touched down on the runway A'isha considered how Allah had brought her a long way from the trapped peasant girl in the destroyed rubble of the Al Mariah bomb shelter.

As A'isha walked down the exit corridor of the disembarking tunnel she saw the tall woman already described to her. A'isha approached and extended her hand. The black woman took her hand and asked, "The name is Mary is it not?"

A'isha smiled softly and said, "Yes, Mary Morden. I am very pleased to meet you." Allison looked at this beautiful young woman, impressed by the other's regal bearing. However, more than her beauty struck Allison who could feel the force within this gift from Allah.

Allison brushed any fear aside. "You must be tired from your travels. Let's go to my apartment where you can refresh yourself." Thus, A'isha began the next phase of her complex mission.

March 6, 2005

Saddam Hussein was pleased that commando A'isha had made a successful connection with her handler in Paris. The general plan was for A'isha to travel with Allison as her unobtrusive friend. France was an ideal county to train an agent for operations in America. The relaxed poise of the French would help when she had to negotiate the United States.

CHAPTER TWENTY-SIX

March 8, 2005

T he rain came in gusts and bluster that day. Sammie Lock, a wiry Hispanic man, looked over the vast unloading Seattle harbor and shivered. Container ships from all over the world used this harbor to unload goods of every description for U.S. consumption. Every few minutes a squall line of cold rain passed over the rippled bay.

His working name was Sammie Lock. He came from a hard background. On the street he was known as Frankie the talker because he almost never conversed with anyone.

A loner of 46 years, he'd worked these yards for nearly 20 years. Sammie's main duty was to spot check containers to be sure they held what was on the bill of lading. It was impossible to check every container. The standard procedure was to use a handheld radiation detector to scan for a nuclear device. Sammie knew if a nuclear bomb made it to the Seattle harbor it was already too late, but he did his job.

The containers were checked randomly, the inspections cursory. Time was money and it was impossible to keep the docks cleared unless inspections remained brief.

Sammie was small but tough. His blocky hands were covered with scars. The docks were a hard place; the veteran of many fights, Sammie inflicted violence or had been on the receiving end. He looked back on those days as the stuff of bad dreams. He'd used booze, drugs, and fighting to offset what he saw as his meaningless life.

He shook his head in amazement to realize that at the time he did not even know what a sin was. He would have been the first man to admit it would take a miracle to change his life. Yet Sammie did receive a miracle that changed him.

He would never forget that stormy day. Sammie could remember looking across the unloading areas and seeing nearly every worker was a man of color. Every plush job was held by white men permitted to run for shelter. He hated racism. It poisoned his life.

He'd seriously considered suicide or mass homicide. He had no family after his hard-working mother died at the youthful age of 42. After that Sammie became a loner. He had no friends. Occasionally he would buy a whore in the SeaTac area. Such sexual encounters left him lonelier than before.

However, on that harsh day Sammie noticed a tall black man dressed in an expensive suit walking with dignity across the docks as if the day was warm and clear. The stranger had to be soaked, but that didn't affect his slow stroll across the unloading area. The tall fellow often stopped and spoke to blue collar workers.

He handed out literature to each of the workers and spoke with sincerity. Sammie was in awe that a man dressed in expensive clothing would be out in this weather to talk to simple laborers. When the man reached Sammie he introduced himself as Dr. Abel Raman, a Muslim cleric. Sammie took the offered literature but told the tall man he couldn't read well. That didn't disturb the cleric.

He gave Sammie a card with the address of a Muslim Mosque and assured Sammie that Allah the creator of a million worlds had the power to teach Sammie to read the words of the Holy Koran.

Sammie didn't know what to make of this man. Sammie only attended grade school for six years before the white teacher told him to leave because he was stupid. Sammie had always felt out of place in school. It was hard to study when hunger distracted him so fiercely and so often.

Sammie often skipped school so he could help the local fruit man unload his stock from the trucks. About the best Sammie could get from this labor was a few dollars and a dozen apples for an afternoon.

Nevertheless, Sammie stayed at it. He had to provide for his mother from one day to the next. His mother was dead from cancer before Sammie finally found a job in the harbor unloading and eventually inspecting the large shipping containers. He minded his own business and worked hard.

Sammie had absolutely nothing to live for. He missed his mother and felt nothing but rage that society would allow such poverty. He was making plans to end his life when he remembered the card from the religious man.

The address was not far away. He thought visiting a church before suicide might be a good idea. He walked two miles to the mosque, a modest but sturdy structure.

A kindly old black man stopped him at the door saying Sammie must remove his shoes to enter the house of Allah. It seemed a simple thing and Sammie knew he wouldn't be there long. On entering the building, he found its simple beauty striking. The floor and many of the walls were covered with rich geometrical patterns of color and shape. There were several people each kneeling on a small rug praying in a strange cadence.

Sammie, too bewildered, turned to leave when the religious man he'd seen handing out literature on the docks approached him.

"Greeting my friend, perhaps you would be so kind as to come and talk to me in my office. I feel concern for you and perhaps a visit would help us both."

Sammie was about to protest this kind offer but had a sudden conviction that he should stay. The cleric and Sammie talked for hours. Sammie learned the basics of the Muslim faith and that this mosque offered free language classes in both English and Arabic. His host invited him to attend and over the coming weeks Sammie's language skills in English improved tremendously.

He could soon read most English literature that the mosque distributed to the public. The mosque also had a reading room and eventually Sammie was able to read more advanced literature. Gradually ideas of suicide faded. He found meaning in the Muslim faith.

After English classes Sammie started classes in Arabic which proved difficult, but his teachers were patient. Over time Sammie read parts of The Koran in Arabic. Its poetry and cadence in original Arabic enthralled him. His vices drifted away as he became a follower.

Sammie became a different person as he immersed himself in Islam. He became one of the 8 million Muslims living in America. While Sammie was immersed in his studies he in turn was being studied by his instructors. They were watching for single men like Sammie who had fervor to do more for Islam than merely worship. Islam has many paths for believers to contribute to the cause. Some gave money, others time, and others worked in the many charitable works for which Islam is noted.

Nevertheless, the Muslim Church was always looking for likely soldiers of Allah. Islam has enemies and without soldiers willing to fight, the words of the Prophet would be lost, unthinkable to a Muslim. With the energy so common in religious converts Sammie wanted to do more for Allah.

He dreamed of martyrdom. To be in paradise with the Prophet was far better than marking time on earth. He could not do much for Islam financially, but he could give his life for Allah.

Sammie, like thousands of suicidal people, felt drawn toward the violent fringes of Islam. Sammie believed his faith to be under attack by Western nations. America and Europe had shown deep seated fear and hatred for Muslims for centuries.

Sammie offered himself as a fighter for Islam. The Mosque's leaders responded saying Allah had a vital purpose for his life and would use him when the correct time arrived.

Sammie knew Islam had made strong inroads among minority races in western nations. Quite often becoming a Muslim was a strong political statement against the ruling white class. Its strong patriarchal structure and belief in justified violence was a good fit for many poor people who felt they had endured enough from white America. Leaders of World Islam were receptive to building a strong manpower reserve within the heart of their greatest enemy: the United States.

Most Muslims were nonviolent solid citizens, but a great deal of their charity money made its way to Muslims who were anything but tolerant. Sammie became knowledgeable about the Arab situation in Palestine, and the plight of the displaced Palestinian Arabs looked like the racism minorities endured in America. Sammie became one of the hundreds of American Muslims who would do whatever they could to advance the cause of Allah even to the point of death.

A'isha and Allison spent another month in Europe seeing the tourist sites and becoming acquainted. Allison tried to draw A'isha out but found her self-contained, polite, and attentive, but no waster of words. She impressed Allison with her ability to be charming and engaging in conversation when it was called for. Allison guessed this part of A'isha's personality to be learned behavior.

Allison sensed there was a secret flame controlled by an iron will. A'isha never spoke of her past or her training. A'isha flirted with men who sought her company and encouraged them with light laughter. At other times she could be distant.

Allison finally asked, "A'isha, are you really attracted to any of these men who are obviously drawn to you?"

"Men have their uses," came the terse response.

"Have you ever had a boyfriend or a husband?" Allison prodded.

After a few quiet moments A'isha replied, "My heart, my soul, and my being belong to Allah. I have no time for such activities."

Allison replied, "I too have never had a true amour or a husband. I did love a man once, but he was murdered."

"I understand. Your Ali Binen was a good man who served Allah. Ali Binen spoke out publicly against the oppressors, an action courageous but fatal."

"He waits for you to join him in the Gardens of Paradise. Love in all facets will be yours for eternity."

"He made himself visible to the enemy. To speak truth in the light of day can only result in a bullet from the darkness. I am not like your Ali. I prepare in darkness. When all is ready I will step into the light."

"Then our enemy will know my name. However, it will be too late for them. The ground will open under the feet of the infidels and death will reap a harvest which has never occurred on earth."

"I must die. But our enemy will be destroyed. I will plunge the sword of Allah to the hilt into the heart of the beast. The beast will fall into the chasm of hell. I live for that day."

~ ~ ~

Our enemy uses money and violence to enslave Muslims. Allah will use the power of faith and faith is a force that no weapon can overcome. Their time is overdue," A'isha's voice sounded cold and flat.

Allison had stopped. "How could you know of Ali? Did you receive this knowledge from some Iraqi source?" she asked.

"Please refrain from personal questions. Many I cannot answer without compromising the mission and others are un- necessary. My knowledge comes directly from Allah whom I live to serve. I will also die serving him."

CHAPTER TWENTY-SEVEN

Allison began to understand A'isha's power and focus. A'isha had no fear or doubt or indecision. She was a dangerous force. There was a distance between her and the others. That is the power and mystery of religious certitude.

Finally, Allison's instructions were passed to her by hand in an elevator. No words were spoken and the European gentleman who conveyed them got out on the next floor and walked away.

The instructions were clear and succinct. Within a week Allison and A'isha were to fly to Washington D.C. and A'isha was to learn how to live in America. In time she would be given the tools for her attack.

A'isha kept calm. She knew the tools, the time, and her person would be in the right place as needed. The forces of Islam were gathering on American horizons. The citizens of that great country continued to live in ignorant ease.

~ ~ ~

March 15, 2005

Allison and A'isha were seated in the waiting room during the cool of the morning. The transition to Mary Morton was complete. Allison seemed animated and ready to return to the States. She spoke to A'isha as she would to a daughter. "Mary, I can't wait to show you around Washington D.C. It's a beautiful city."

"Yes, I look forward to the grand tour."

Mary Morden's passport worked. The French inspector only glanced over her documents. Allison and A'isha joined the line of people who filed onto the aircraft. A'isha showed no emotion as she took her place in first class. Deep within her hardened heart she rejoiced that she would soon be in the capital city of the enemy.

The hours in flight passed on swift wings of destiny. A'isha felt growing power as she neared the enemy. The blood of Muslim innocents would be avenged thousands to one. The infidels could expect no mercy from her.

A'isha heard their pilot announce that they were approaching Dulles International Airport and would be landing in approximately 15 minutes. A'isha could feel the aircraft's gradual descent. She woke Allison and talked in a soft voice to prepare her for the paperwork inspection.

A'isha sensed the older woman's tension. "You must relax and accept the will of Allah," A'isha murmured. Her words had a steadying effect on Allison. A'isha realized that she would take the dominant role when they walked through inspections.

A'isha approached the custom officials first. She chatted cheerfully about how good it felt to be home. She was friendly to the official but only in the manner of a clear superior to a menial. The paperwork was perfect. Mary Morden had not died in vain.

Allison had gathered her wits by the time she needed them most. They picked up their luggage at the baggage carousel and Allison selected a cab.

Once in the cab A'isha gave Allison's hand a soft squeeze as a signal that she'd done well under pressure. Allison, back on familiar ground, pointed out many familiar sights of the capital city. A'isha listened but her eyes were perusing the security.

A'isha smiled. Americans were lax and overconfident. The few policemen seemed to be merely putting in their hours. There was an impression that no one had the power to harm Americans on their own soil. Such smugness would be fatal soon.

The next few weeks flowed by without incident. Allison took A'isha on social rounds and introduced her as Mary. Mary was a friend that she'd met in Paris. Allison's friend attracted interest. Gossip flew on the wings of falcons and there were a thousand ears that hungered for details.

Society women of the leisured classes noted her. A'isha was modest and somewhat aloof, with a delicate balance. Her obvious affluence didn't impress those who'd never known want. However, her beauty and charm became the subject of much discussion in the elite classes.

A'isha and Allison explained their close friendship was based on a mutual love of writing. A'isha claimed she was writing a modest book on the current President Mr. Reston. She became a frequent visitor to the Library of Congress, spending many hours studying books that referred to President John Reston. Gradually she learned more about his past.

She mentally made notes as to character traits, mannerisms, and habits. She looked for events and places that President Reston seemed to repeat on a schedule. Habit could be a doorway to death.

A'isha also studied the history and construction of the White House. She read that it had been built over decades. Some passageways had been closed off by later construction. The White House had a vast array of underground tunnels that serviced the requirements of a large building.

Heating and cooling ducts existed, their size and location known to only a few maintenance men. Some spaces held electrical, water, and sewage networks. In truth, the building had ample points of possible entry.

She only kept maps in her apartment of the type available to tourists. Any search of her home would reveal a modest outline of the President's life and his rather dry biography. There was nothing to reveal the vast amount of information she filed mentally.

A'isha decided to have her own apartment in the affluent NW quadrant of the city. The apartment was to encourage the idea that a man could visit her there, and to counter thoughts that she might be lesbian.

Allison was often invited to bring her friend to social functions. On these occasions A'isha was friendly and she was careful to praise her host in many ways. She let it be known that she sincerely enjoyed the company of the men and women in top Washington society.

She became friendly with any man she met, even hinting of potential *rendezvous*. This encouraged their interest and pursuit. Although A'isha conversed with many men she never actually bestowed sexual gifts.

Such leverage had to be used with the correct man or her body would be devalued. Powerful men were easily offended if the object of their desire even flirted with others. Her having sex with the wrong man would be an insult to their self-esteem.

It was a warm summer morning and Allison called to say that they were invited to a special gathering that evening. Allison was clear that she could say nothing more over the telephone. A'isha knew instantly that the President would be there.

A'isha carefully selected clothes to wear that evening. She chose a form fitting sheath of light blue and wore simple jewelry. She wore little make-up because she knew the President disliked what he called "painted" women. She'd learned President Reston liked blue and preferred his women to be modest as the result of Reston's conversion to Christianity.

After years of lackluster achievements Reston had converted to the fundamental branch of the Christian faith. After years of depressions and alcoholism he accepted Jesus Christ into his heart. Thus, reborn he felt he had immediate contact with God.

With his father's fame and wealth Reston Jr. was able to make strong inroads in politics. Finally, he won the Presidential election by promising oil men he would protect their interests.

This gathering featured glittering women on the arms of entrenched men in posts of authority, the political masters of the nation. Beneath these men were the military generals and high officers, the blunt club of international power and extortion.

A'isha instantly noticed a group of security guards. She knew they must be the security team for the President. Moments later the President himself entered the room. He quickly broke the silence by telling everyone he enjoyed being among so many of his friends. This appeal caused the room to be abuzz with talk and light laughter. As the President and Mary Reston moved through the gathering he attracted people like a magnet. Everyone seemed to want to touch him or greet him.

A'isha sipped her water and remained on the edge of the crowd. Several times she saw the President glance in her direction and then he looked directly at her for several moments. She smiled modestly at this direct eye contact but made no effort to meet him.

A'isha thought to herself this was the butcher who ordered the deaths of thousands of her fellow Iraqis, the man responsible for the deaths of her family.

She willed the President to approach her. At first he seemed puzzled and then he gradually moved through the crowd in her general direction. He nodded in greetings to others but continued to move toward A'isha. He paused for a moment. He waited for her to come to him as did all the rest of the partygoers.

A'isha did not close the gap. She merely smiled at the President and her warm eyes cast invisible nets across his mind. The President thought to himself, "What a stunning beautiful woman!" She seemed so modest yet so self-assured.

Her long black hair shimmered, complimenting the beautiful dress she wore. He could feel his attraction to this woman and felt compelled to speak to her. She was so beautiful in her blue sheath. Mary had drifted to another room.

The President spoke to a guard. Then he approached A'isha and extended his hand. A'isha took his hand and said how honored she felt to meet him. "I understand you are Mary Morden, a writer. Is it true you have an interest in working on a book about me?"

"That is true Mr. President. You and your life have always been of great interest to me," said A'isha, "I hope you are not offended?"

"Not at all," answered the President, "Perhaps there will be an opportunity for you to interview me." A'isha noted the President was issuing a veiled invitation for them to meet again.

"It would be an honor, Mr. President. I think of you and your decisions of State often. The decisions you have made must be a burden at times," commented A'isha.

"Yes, at times being Commander in Chief can be very difficult. Now please excuse me. I must meet guests who just arrived," said the President with clear reluctance.

"Not at all Mr. President every life has its duties," commented A'isha. She watched the President make his way through the adoring crowd. Her eyes darkened as she sipped water again. She watched until the President left the room.

She felt a warm anticipation in her hardened heart. One of her duties was to kill this President with her own hand. The thought of killing the murderer of so many innocents presented her great satisfaction.

~ ~ ~

March 26, 2005

Jackson had been staying at his office nearly round the clock for two months, ISIS activity had been increasing even though there were no clear signs of where they intended to strike. Most of the CIA group believed that ISIS would continue to hit softer targets in lands adjacent to Arab countries.

He felt ISIS was using these foreign blows as a cover for something much larger. The ultimate attack had to be on United States soil. This would be seen as a strike that would encourage the entire Arab world. This would make the recruiting of members and money easier. Success breeds success.

The United States was a vast and venerable country. The infrastructure of nearly every American city was totally unguarded. A team of trained Arab Muslim soldiers could cripple a major city without much effort. The average citizen felt the United States was immune to events happening to other countries on a frequent basis.

The average American politician seemed to feel the same way. This attitude was bewildering to Jackson because the intelligence community issued warnings to everyone of danger signals everywhere.

Despite a crushing workload Jackson was still convinced the ultimate danger was yet to be found. He felt an even greater danger than ISIS hid somewhere. Someone evil continued growing stronger daily.

It was maddening to Jackson to be so sure of this danger and yet not be able to find one shred of evidence of the person's existence. In frightful dreams he saw images of horrible clarity. Complete cities without a single living survivor. Bodies lying everywhere in the terrible disarray of random death.

He did his best to write down every detail of his dreams. The killer was plainly a young Arab woman. The woman was always dressed in tattered black garments of the Arab poor. Her face was hidden in a deep shroud. He imagined the face of a beautiful young woman.

Her eyes, when he imagined them, made him afraid. They burned with hatred that belied description. In one of his nightmares, she described herself as "The Sword of Allah," and on another occasion the voice said she would kill millions.

He felt her growing stronger . . . felt her closer than before. Yet he still had no solid proof of her existence. He found himself praying for divine help to find this monster before she killed so many. So far his prayers met with total silence.

CHAPTER TWENTY-EIGHT

April 8, 2005

Sadeq the arms designer took pride in his unique launcher weapon. It met all Saddam Hussein's requirements. He'd been told by a human cut out that the other part of the operational team expressed satisfaction. Sadeq had been able to furnish the 200 units on his automated machinery in six months. Under cover of darkness the launchers had been delivered to the final user in lots of 6 using a common utility van.

All transport happened within days and Sadeq felt confident no one would suspect anything. Without knowledge of the rest of the operation, he only knew the capacities of his weapon and biological nature of the ultimate payload. The quantity of required weapons launchers seemed high for biological delivery. The country to be attacked must be large. He grew convinced that their target had to be the United States.

His conviction pleased him. Perhaps the damage would be so massive that the world of Islam could finally taste success. If the United States could be so weakened, the day of Jewish destruction hovered near.

This would make his life worthwhile. His morning prayers to Allah began, "Allah grant that the day of destruction against the infidels be soon."

~ ~ ~

Washington, D.C.

The weeks moved ahead smoothly. A'isha continued in her role as an affluent woman intent on writing a Reston biography. She became known as a graceful addition to any elite gathering.

Embers from her lessons in the desert still burned in her soul. A'isha often touched the tiny locket Najib had given her before she departed the training camp. The Iraqi sand was a constant reminder of her homeland. Memories of dead orphan children, victims of American savagery, never eased. Old images of watching them buried in common trenches fed her fury. As she had told many of the dying children, "Neither Allah nor I will forget you."

She had spoken to President Reston twice more since their first meeting. Each time he approached her. Her aloof demeanor seemed to intrigue him. She made no demands on him or his time. Such behavior was unheard of in his or Mary's political experience.

The President enjoyed talking to this self-assured young woman who seemed so sincerely interested in his life. He found himself talking about his earlier life, flattered when A'isha knew and reminded him of other days of personal success.

The intelligence community took little interest in Mary Morden. Nothing on her records indicated any more than a young woman of independent means attempting to rebuild her life after losing her parents. She appeared to be just another social butterfly among many who lived in and beyond the Washington Beltway.

Regardless of the rumor of their infallibility intelligence branches were stretched thin. Agents gave passing glances over Mary and found nothing of interest. Mary was one of thousands deemed unimportant to U.S. security.

Her room had not been searched. As taught, she left small strands of hair in locations that revealed the slightest human activity. She checked these signs daily, but never found evidence of movement.

It was a cold day in March when she felt the touch of a cold object against her hand as she rode in a Washington elevator. As she had been taught she quickly closed her hand on the object without drawing any attention. She noted it was handed to her by a black man who exited on the next floor. She'd never seen him before.

In the privacy of a restroom stall she saw that the object was a key to a safety deposit box in a Washington D.C. International Bank. She waited to find if it were a trap. On the fourth day she visited the bank, showing the key's number to the clerk. Mary Morden's paperwork was in order.

She took her box into a small room to inspect its contents. Before she opened the box she searched the room for secret cameras.

Inside was the dagger Najib had given her in Iraq. She picked it up with cool familiarity and prayed in gratitude to Allah for its return. She opened a small box. Clothing. It was the familiar Arab black garb.

A brief note on the clothes read, "If possible wear this before you return to Allah," signed with a single letter "N." She smiled and sent a silent reply to her ancient mentor, "Retire in peace and plenty my old friend. I will see you in paradise."

The last item was a small box which contained another key, this one to a storage unit near Georgetown University.

The tag on the key told her to go to this box only upon command. Further instructions will be there. A'isha returned the safety deposit box. She left the bank, her faith in Allah justified.

The day of reckoning was coming like a storm on the horizon.

~ ~ ~

Yazid the biological expert had just finished his day's work. Day by day he'd carefully loaded 1 to 3 launchers, the work had been painstaking. One moment of carelessness would bring death to him and failure to the mission. On days when he had the impression his powers of concentration weren't strong, he wouldn't permit himself to enter the hot room.

Day by agonizing day he loaded the launchers. The total necessary reached 200. At first this seemed impossible. But with time and the grace of Allah the needed number was reduced little by little as each week passed.

As he readied himself for his final prayer of the day he had a special reason to be grateful. He had loaded and banded his last launcher. The labor of a lifetime was rewarded by the Creator of the universe. All that remained was for the drums to be picked up and shipped. Such details were in the hands of Saddam.

Yazid believed Islam would achieve peace to the earth. War would be a thing of the past on a planet cleansed of infidels. He knew how high the price was. Deaths in the United States could be more than 275 million. The 8 million Muslims in the United States would die, too. Their sacrifice would be rewarded with pleasures in paradise. Yazid regretted this price, but the world could not continue its present course of blasphemy.

Because of Flash Fire, future generations would be raised under the watchful eye of Islam. Heresy would be discovered and destroyed before it spread through the social body.

The current costs had to be balanced by the future gains. Children would be raised by faithful Islamic parents, each role in the family ordained by Allah Himself. The shameful excesses of Western women would come to an end. The believers would have a life of sanctity on earth followed by the joys of paradise after death. Who could argue with such noble goals?

Yazid was grateful to Allah for the many blessings that Allah had bestowed on him. Of course, he'd made many personal sacrifices. He would not have a son to say the prayers for the dead when he passed on. Such things were painful, but he was certain of Allah's justice.

The people of the United States slept on.

April 21, 2005

Saddam read his agents' reports. The great attack was coming together. Only he knew the total picture. Gradually under the cover of darkness single trucks delivered the drums to a big, covered warehouse to be loaded into standard international shipping containers.

The shipping containers were to be loaded on the ship of an independent Belgian owner. The bill of lading was from a front company in India. The drums' contents were listed as industrial paint which is manufactured in many countries in big numbers.

In addition to the illegal freight the Belgian's cargo ship would make several legitimate stops in South Korea and Japan. At each location he picked up enough containers to fill his ship to capacity. The legitimate drums would be off-loaded at San Francisco, California. The final port was Seattle, Washington. It would take several weeks for his slow vessel to cross the Pacific. The captain was an experienced man who often delivered illegal goods. His cash for this job was substantial, more than enough to retire on a remote island in warm waters.

The captain's legal exposure was low. If the paperwork proved good it would be impossible to tie the owner of the ship to the cargo's contents. Like taxis of the sea the drivers were not responsible for the character of their random customers. The name of the cargo ship, *Destiny,* was ironic.

~ ~ ~

Washington D.C.

A'isha began to receive social invitations without Allison. A'isha was young, beautiful, sensual, and added energy to any party. She spoke well of everyone and never indulged in gossip.

Yet, she was working on a difficult challenge. Specifically, she needed access to the Oval Office when the President was making a public address.

It would be impossible to move her weapons through the numerous checkpoints that insulate the President from physical danger. On top of these limitations was always the constant presence of Secret Service guards at the President's and Mrs. Reston's sides. These guards were alert and well trained. However, the day-to-day sameness of their lives could dull their normally razor-sharp edge of concentration.

The assassin always has the advantage of deciding when and how to attack. A'isha still did not know the exact means for the mass attack.

A'isha wanted to destroy the President when he was on national television. That, combined with her major assault against the entire nation would illustrate beyond doubt the power of Allah.

The seed of inspiration came in a most quiet way. A'isha was studying yet another book on President Reston when the light bulb in her reading lamp burned out. The darkness was instant. Reading ceased. The power of darkness occurred to her in that same split second.

Western technology was impressive but often underlying support proved fragile. Nearly every system in the White House ran on electricity; and electricity is delicate. Entire systems depended on a single wire or a single fuse. Destroy either and none of the protection systems could perform their jobs.

Backup generators would kick in, but these systems often took several minutes to activate, and such seconds might put her in the right place undetected. It might be possible to gain entry to the Oval

Office. Her dream of destroying the President and the United States itself could be possible.

The success of such a mission would reaffirm the faith of millions of Muslims in the rightness of their faith.

CHAPTER TWENTY-NINE

April 22, 2005

The older black man moved with dignity and confidence as he worked on the day shift at the White House. He was Ellis Proctor, 76 years old. He'd worked in the maintenance department of the White House for 60 years. During that time, he had advanced from sweeping floors to being licensed as a certified building superintendent.

He supervised all physical functions in the White House. Self-trained in all his duties, he passed all necessary state tests. If it had to do with a maintenance problem he was the man who could fix it. As the systems modernized Ellis trained himself in the new computer controls.

He had many workers under his supervision. He was a quiet competent man and he had seen many Presidents come and go. Some things he'd seen and heard seemed shameful to him.

Ellis had heard various politicians having sex with staff members behind closed doors. Some partners were other men. All this was offensive to Ellis, but he had to keep his faith secret to maintain his job. He'd been Muslim all his adult life. Being a Muslim of any variety in a Judeo/Christian nation was difficult. To be Muslim meant being distrusted.

~ ~ ~

He was growing old and regretted never having been able to do anything to advance the cause of Allah. To return to Allah with empty hands shamed him. He'd heard discussions in the Oval Office that involved the life or death of tens of thousands in the Arab countries. It was as if they were not human.

Today he had other matters to ponder. A young black man had come to his apartment last evening and left a sealed envelope. The local Imam wanted to speak to him tomorrow evening.

The Imam spoke of a matter of gravest importance when they met. To defy a lawful Imam was to lose your soul. Therefore, the Imam's instructions were infallible. Their evening meeting was scheduled for 8:00 p.m.

~ ~ ~

Precisely at 8:00 p.m. Ellis knocked lightly on the Imam's door. The Imam was slight with a gentle voice and quiet demeanor. He knew much about Ellis and the details of his working life. He instructed Ellis to meet with a Muslim woman in a modest café in two days at 8:00 p.m. It was a matter of the highest urgency for the cause of Allah.

Ellis realized this summons was an answer to his lifetime prayer. When Ellis asked how he would identify the woman, the Imam smiled slightly. "You will know this woman because she has the power of Allah in her hands."

His day's work passed quickly for Ellis. Calm, he had complete faith in Allah. At the appointed time he walked through the door of the small café which had small dark booths illuminated by candles. For a moment he felt concerned that he would be unable to find his person in this unfamiliar place.

He felt the strangest emotion, a type of silent summons and he walked farther in as if drawn by an invisible cord. As he neared a corner booth he heard a kind voice address him by his name. "It is a pleasure to meet you Mr. Ellis Proctor," said the voice. "Would you join me at this table? We have much to discuss."

Ellis sat down at the table and took in the beautiful woman with bewitching eyes. "Would you join me with a glass of ice water? Only Islam knows the holiness of cool water," she said. Ellis knew he was in the presence of a powerful woman, a servant of Allah.

"You are astute, Mr. Proctor. I am a servant of Allah, the creator of all life. Allah has called me to find strong Muslims who will help bring the peace of Islam to the world. I apologize for the slight disturbance. Occasionally Allah gives me the thoughts of others. Do not be alarmed. I did not ask for this ability. It is a gift from Allah."

"Allah has told me many things about you. You are a Shiite as am I. We have both learned the wisdom of silence. You desire to serve Allah. I have come from a distant land to assure that the peace of Islam rules over the whole earth."

"You have also seen with your eyes and heard with your ears the disgusting sexual license of the Western Nations. Allah has sent me to put an end to these abominations," said A'isha.

"You are a well-read man and know the United States is attempting to destroy Islam. You have heard with your own ears how casually the followers of Satan have ordered the deaths of so many innocents."

"You are aware that Muslims are barely tolerated in much of this land. The United States wants to control the lands of Allah. They desire to destroy Islam. You are an intelligent man, and you know that what I say is true."

"Allah has prepared you for a lifetime to call upon your service. Your hour has arrived, and your decision will determine the freedom of Muslims for thousands of years. It will also determine the destiny of your soul."

The large black man answered in the affirmative, but with concern, "I am willing to serve, but how can I help? I am neither soldier nor prophet. Nor am I a man with money. Everything you've said about this nation of infidels is true. I know of the murders that have been committed against Muslims in many nations. I know of my own bondage because of my religion."

"If my religion were known I would lose my employment. I know the extent Satan has controlled this nation, and that this nation plans to control the world. I've heard of these plans of conquest and control with my own ears."

"I pray daily for a miracle. The march of Satan cannot continue without resistance. However, I am helpless. I am old and my strength is weakened. Without guidance I can't see how to resist."

"Ellis, I can tell you Allah already has a plan to destroy the United States. All he seeks is the truly faithful. These followers cannot be talkers only. They must be men and women who are willing to lay down their lives for Allah so that future generations can live in righteousness and peace."

"Before good can flourish, evil must be exterminated. This country is beyond redemption. This land must be put to the torch so that Muslims can claim dominance."

"It grieves me to tell you that the hour of your death swiftly approaches. You are 76 years old, and your health has been good. However, Allah tells me you have an inoperable brain tumor. You will die within three months. Your death is certain, but Allah offers you martyrdom. Allah has instructed me to give you this envelope containing a large amount of cash. Use it to get a brain scan from any hospital that you want."

"Tell them you have been having bad headaches and insist that you want the scan. They may want to turn you away because you are black and wear none of the symbols of wealth. Tell them you have cash and greed will alter their attitudes. Meet me here at this café in a week. This should give you time to evaluate your spiritual heart and to judge my authority from Allah."

Ellis took the money from A'isha and placed it in his shirt pocket. "I shall seek the medical test as you have instructed me. I neither doubt your words nor fear death. I'll see you here in a week."

A'isha watched with sadness as the big man left. Yet she knew Ellis had found his miracle.

April 29, 2005

Ellis went to the same booth but spotted no beautiful woman. Then he heard a quiet voice behind him say, "I am in this booth."

He turned and made her out in deep shadows. She added, "One should never form any type of pattern or habit. They are dangerous."

A'isha sipped ice water at her ease. Ellis sat down in the dark booth and spoke. "Everything is as you predicted. I have a brain tumor so twisted into my cerebral matter that there's no hope of treatment. The Doctor told me that it would be only a few months before my death."

"I've led an active life and don't want a slow death. I've always yearned to serve Allah, and this is my opportunity. I'll do anything to advance Islam."

"Until the United States is destroyed, it will continue to subjugate Muslims. I've been granted a privilege in knowing how I will die. I am ready to be a martyr for Allah. His cause is greater than my life. What do you want me to do?"

A'isha's eyes glowed like embers in a low fire. "With the power of Allah, you and I are going to destroy the United States as a world power. Our exact method of attack has not been revealed to me, but Allah has promised that the tools will be in my hands at the correct moment."

"Your task is to get me into the Oval Office while the President is speaking on national television. At that time, I will take the President hostage and use that forum to speak to the world. Allah has promised he will put the words in my mouth at the proper time."

"You and I won't survive the attack, but the entire world will hear why the Great Satan must perish."

A'isha continued quietly, "I know there are old passageways built in the White House, later sealed off for various reasons. Are you aware of such passageways?"

"There are at least nine in the White House. I'm one of the few who remember," answered Ellis.

"Is there any such passageway to the Oval Office itself?"

"Yes, there is a hidden hallway directly to the Oval Office. It starts in what used to be a ladies' restroom. One stall for handicapped has a concealed button that opens a narrow door. The hall is about 60 feet long ending at the Oval Office."

"I maintain the restroom, and the button still operates the secret door. During World War II the passageway was used by Roosevelt's mistress for many years. Later, he had the doorway sealed at the demand of his wife."

"However, the President seemed to have doubts about giving up his mistress. He had the maintenance crew build a door with a knob on the inside of the passageway. On the Oval Office side the workers put a glaze of plaster across the door. It appears to be a solid wall that matches the rest of the room."

"The plaster is only about 1/8th of an inch thick. The slightest push would open the door. Roosevelt showed his wife the sealed wall. This placated her. Roosevelt died by an aneurysm, a week after its completion. I doubt Vice-President Truman ever knew of it. The exit from the secret hallway is located to the right of the President's desk. Roosevelt disliked Truman and kept him in the dark on many important subjects."

A'isha took this information in. Allah had provided her with a door to exact her revenge.

Ellis continued, "There's a guard station in the hallway to that restroom. The bathroom itself is off limits to all but approved people. The Secret Service does not guard this section of the White House. That job was farmed out to the Marines. I hate going past the Marines to check the cleanliness."

"Why are you reluctant?"

"They are young, prideful men and often arrogant."

Ellis was silent for a few moments and his eyes were downcast. A'isha gently touched the black man's large work-hardened hand, "They mocked you and one of them called you Melon is that not the cruel fact?"

"One of the men said to me that there was no one better than a nigger to fix a shitter and I was the best shitter fixer in the White House."

A'isha squeezed his hand a little harder. "Look at me Ellis." He did. Her eyes glowed with rage. "I swear by the hand of Allah that man will die."

"He insulted a servant of Allah. He lacked the decency to respect an older man. We will wipe this race of heretics from the face of the earth. Tell me more about this Marine."

Ellis thought for a moment. "He's tall, about six feet two inches. He's white and has a strawberry birthmark on his left cheek. The mark is narrow and about 2 inches long."

"How do the military people exit the White House after their duties are done," asked A'isha.

"They leave by a side entrance located on Pennsylvania Ave. All the Marines like to go to a common bar when they get off their shifts. They talk about the place often in my presence. It is called Frankie's Bar. It's only a short bus ride and the two Marines guards arrive around 3:00 p.m. each day."

A'isha seemed satisfied with the descriptions and said, "This matter will be corrected shortly. Is it true that only two guards stand between us and the doorway to the Oval Office? Is that correct?"

CHAPTER THIRTY

There are always two secret service guards in the Oval Office unless the president dismisses them. It is rare for the guards to be dismissed. There are a total of four men before one could get to the President."

A'isha smiled, "it is a small thing for Allah. Do you think they'd be alarmed if you brought an assistant with you to help with repairs?"

"No, I often do that. I am the head of White House maintenance," answered Ellis.

A'isha thought for a few moments. "What type of identification do your employees have to have to enter the White House?"

Ellis answered quickly; "Maintenance staff enters the White house to do their shifts in one group. It is my responsibility to check the cards of all the workers who come on duty. All you'd need is an approved identity card. I issue the cards for my staff. In addition to the card each person gets a fingerprint scan."

"The finger scan is loaded to a different security system. It notes whether someone is missing, or the total count is wrong. I don't have control of that sector since it's in another building. The White House has little interest in the people who clean and maintain the building itself."

"Does the service personnel include Arabs?"

"No, most employees are Afro-American or Hispanic."

A'isha filed this information without a sign of its importance. "Tell me about your control of the electrical circuits in the White House."

Ellis answered with confidence. "I can program any electrical circuit from my office on my main computer. I can shut off and turn on any circuit."

"Is this true with circuits in the Oval Office?"

"Yes, any circuit in the White House can be controlled from my desk."

A'isha shifted her subject, "What about a cart holding repairs or linens? Do guards search the cart?"

"No, they have never inspected anything, and I often have a large pushcart full of cleaning supplies, linens, and that sort of thing."

A'isha leaned back. "Let me think about this for a week. Allah will provide a way. What type of fire suppression system does the White House have?"

"The fire system is surprisingly outdated. It's difficult to install a modern system without major construction."

"No President has wanted to impact the structure of the White House. Although the main hallways have an overhead sprinkler system, most of the rooms don't. Most rooms even lack fire extinguishers."

A'isha asked another question, "There must be a pump and a holding tank that supply the water for the sprinklers."

"That is true. There is a 10,000-gallon tank in the basement driven by a large motor. Frankly, the tank is far too small for a structure as large as the White House. I have repeatedly told the White House officials that a much larger tank is required, and the system needs to have a back-up if the first pump fails."

"Who maintains this system?" she asked.

"I am responsible for keeping the system in good working condition," Ellis replied.

"Ellis, tell me how the White House is heated."

"The White House heating system is modern. It was easy to convert the old ductwork that used raw coal to a modern oil burning system. I was a young man when that conversion was made."

"Where is the oil stored that heats the White House?"

"The oil is stored in the basement. It is my responsibility to make sure that the oil tank is filled as needed."

"Who delivers your cleaning supplies?" A'isha asked. Then she had a flash of insight.

"Ellis, tell me more about your cleaning supplies delivery for the White House."

"All the custodial supplies come from one local distributor. The quantities are large. It's my responsibility to mark off the items from an invoice list."

"Is the truck inspected before you take on those duties?"

"Yes, the grounds security inspects the truck before it enters the underground storage area of the White House."

"How good is the inspection?"

"That seems to vary with the load. If the load consists of drums of cleaning liquids or heavy crates it's difficult to inspect. The men would have to unload and open each drum or crate to insure validity. Ground security does not have the equipment to do this. It's mainly a visual inspection, but they always check the load for radiation to protect the White House against a nuclear bomb."

"Ground security always makes sure no crate is damaged or appears to have been opened. Aside from these precautions, they seem to use the same lading list I do. We have been using one supplier for decades and the load is considered safe if under supplier supervision from his dock to the dock of the White House."

"Does the truck have different drivers or does the same man deliver the load?"

"Usually, an older black man by the name of Joey drives the truck. I have known him for many years."

"How would one find this Joey in order to talk to him?"

"I don't know his exact address, but I know he lives in a poor, crime-ridden part of downtown D.C. He drinks at a bar called "The Pretty Lady.""

"What does he look like?" A'isha asked. The candle's fire at their table waved shadows against her face.

"He's short with a wiry build. His two front teeth are silver, and his hair is white. It might be risky to look for him in his area."

A'isha smiled, "All is in the hands of Allah. I will seek his will in prayer. Let's meet in four days in Georgetown."

After Ellis left, A'isha remained in the booth for another hour. Everything was coming together well. She still had two tasks to complete.

~ ~ ~

Evening

April 30, 2005

Pretty Lady Bar

Washington, D.C.

A'isha left the cab early in the evening in front of the Pretty Lady Bar. The first cab she flagged had a white driver who refused to go into the rough neighborhood. The second cab agreed to take her for a large tip. She wore dark sunglasses, dark clothes with a loose fit and she put her hair in a bun. She covered her head with a dark scarf so her face would be difficult to see. She'd taped her dagger to the inside of her arm.

The filthy street was strewn with broken glass, vomit stains, and hundreds of cigarette butts. The walk-up doorways next to the bar had discarded needles. Young black men gathered on every corner. She felt their eyes follow her as she walked toward the bar.

The door to the bar was steel plated and the two windows facing the street were covered with wire mesh. She stepped through the door and entered a dim room filled with stale air and smoke. As usual, A'isha slid into a dark corner. In minutes, a man with bad breath came from around the bar and addressed her.

"I haven't seen you around. You must be a new working girl. I might be able to get you some action. What will you have?" The bartender strained to see her face. His eyes couldn't penetrate the shadows. She might be an easy target for robbery. He often split the take with two hitters who would watch for his nod.

A'isha smiled and spoke softly, "I am new. I need to speak to a man I've never met. We have a small business matter to discuss. If you can control your tongue perhaps you can help me. This should be enough for a glass of ice water." A'isha handed the man a folded 100.00 bill.

He glanced at the bill then slipped it into his pocket. This woman made him uneasy.

"Who is the man?"

A'isha laughed. "You do know how to brief. He is older, black, and goes by the name Joey. He has two silver front teeth."

She watched him take in the information. He showed the signs of greed which were so common to westerners.

"If I send you the man what do I get?'

A'isha looked at him for a several moments. "Send me the man and I will match what I gave you. The bartender felt uncomfortable. This woman sounded too confident. This was no ordinary hooker. Yet she had money.

"He should be in within the hour."

A'isha ordered ice water and studied the room while she sipped. The smell of urine, vomit, and sweat was strong. She saw several men openly exchange drugs for cash. She watched a prostitute approach each man and offer her services. She laughed as men fondled her breasts.

A'isha knew she was in the realm of Satan. This was the danger Islam faced. This was the fruit of unbelief, sinful humans who destroyed others. She felt nothing but disdain for such filth. The gates of hell awaited drug sellers. Soon she would destroy them all.

A'isha watched as more and more men filtered in the bar. Most were dressed in poor working clothes, but some men wore expensive flashy garb. She knew the latter men were dealers in drugs and sex. She saw the bartender speak to a small man and A'isha watched him walk to her booth. He paused before her table without speaking.

She looked him over. What she sought was here. A'isha addressed him. "Please join me, Mr. Joey Blake. You drive for the Washington Custodial Company. May I buy you something to drink?" The small man strained to see the face of the woman, but the light was too weak.

"I don't know you, but I'll take a drink." He quickly waved to the bartender.

A'isha paid for the drink and the bartender nodded silently as he collected his second large tip.

"You've worked for the Washington Custodial Company for over 25 years. They don't pay well or respect you. Are you satisfied with this situation, Mr. Blake?"

The small man nursed his beer for five minutes before answering. "Not many jobs for a black man when I got out of the Marine Corps. I looked everywhere, and I needed work. I took what I found."

"You're being modest, Mr. Blake. You served your country well as a Marine in Vietnam. You lost friends. You were exposed to many chemicals." "Yes, I was exposed to Agent Orange. Tens of thousands of Marines were exposed."

"Again, you are a man of few words. Isn't it true you have permanent liver damage and a doctor told you your kidneys are failing? Is it not true the United States turned down your claim for disability because they refuse to admit the toxic nature of the herbicide?"

"Where did you get your information? This isn't common knowledge."

"Mr. Blake, I share your hate of the white man's government. You have been lied to and exploited all your life. Your friends in Vietnam died for nothing. You suffered for nothing. You were poisoned for nothing. Your life means nothing to the white masters. You were expendable cannon fodder to the white politicians."

"Your mother lived in poverty, and she had few means of survival. You stayed with her. You barely earned enough money to keep each of you alive. She died of cancer because the white system was stacked against poor blacks. She died waiting for the surgery. This is a deep sorrow for you."

"Allow me to speak of your health. You are ill and often feel terrible. You went to a doctor recently and learned that your kidneys will not last more than a few years. You are bravely facing a painful death. I am here to help you because I need you to help me."

"I'm listening," the small man said quietly.

"I need a package delivered to White House maintenance. The size is approximately two cubic feet, and it weighs about thirty pounds. The package must not be discovered by White House security. Is such a thing possible, and what would be a fair return for your time?"

"Most things are possible with enough money. Security always looks good on paper. In reality things get slack. Still, I don't plan to spend my last years not just sick, but in prison."

A'isha said, "You are intelligent. You're making little more than subsistence. I can give you one half million dollars in cash. Your payment would be two hundred and fifty thousand up front and the balance on successful delivery."

A'isha could sense she was on the cusp of success. The man was bitter as well as intrigued by the money. She remembered Zeynat telling her Americans would do anything for money. It was a matter of the right price.

CHAPTER THIRTY-ONE

The driver spoke in a tone of wonder. "That's a hell of a lot. What's going to be in the box?"

"The items are weapons: short range to be used on key White House staff. These leaders deserve what will happen to them for underpaying you so long."

"How can I be sure of the money?"

A'isha knew the deal was closed. Only a few details remained.

"I'll give you the name of a top bank. If you go there the day after tomorrow you'll find an account in your name. The account will hold 250,000.00. Withdraw any portion you want."

"Where would I pick-up the load?"

"If we have a deal, I'll give you a key to a storage box. The items will be in a backpack. The firm you work for will receive a large order tomorrow. I hope the cargo could be on the next White House delivery?"

The little man with his slightly jaundiced look knew his risk was low. He himself packed the White House deliveries in large crates held together with special tamper-proof screws. The driving heads sheared off once they compressed the wood. Then the crates could only be opened by destroying the boards. This was why the loads were considered secure from dock to dock.

A glance could tell if the crates had been opened or tampered with after being sealed on company grounds. He'd never enjoyed his life. He'd lived in poverty. Before he could answer the quiet woman addressed him.

"Mr. Blake, I know your risk is low. Nevertheless, I need your services, and for the first time in your life you have met someone willing to pay you serious money. I have no interest in deceiving you. You help me and I help you. Get a passport picture tomorrow and leave it in an envelope at the locker where you pick up the cargo. When you fulfill the job you will have a valid passport with your picture but the name will be false."

"You will also receive the balance of your payment at your new account. There will be airplane tickets using your new name to an obscure South Pacific Island. Your flight is two days after tomorrow. Take it and get out immediately or you will die."

"From that island I encourage you to charter a boat to take you to an uninhabited place. Remain there for six weeks. Then it will be safe for you to resume your life. I tell you these things because I believe we can do business together and I appreciate your services."

Joey Blake thought about his options and his decision became clear. "I'm on board."

"So be it," the woman said, extending her hand. Within minutes they went their separate ways. A'isha asked the bartender to call a cab and said she'd wait outside.

Two rough looking men looked at the bartender to watch for his nod. He watched the woman walk to the door. She had money worth any risk. He nodded.

A'isha heard the steps of two men behind her. She stepped into a shadowed doorway. She'd have preferred they walk by, but they stepped after her. One of the men demanded she give him her purse. She dropped it instead. He reached down to beat his companion to the money.

Her kick crushed his testicles. He fell to the ground in agony. The second man froze for one second too long. Her dagger penetrated his throat. He crumpled in his own spurting blood. She seized the hair of the first assailant, quickly slashing his throat and letting him drop. He died trying to speak.

She left their bodies in the doorway. She again felt intense physical pleasure after the killings. Wave after wave of exquisite feeling engulfed her body. She had to lean against the door until this pleasure ebbed away. She was sure Allah was rewarding her for the deaths of these infidels. A'isha mentally gave thanks to Allah. She stepped to the curb as she heard a cab stop. The investigation came hours later. No one saw or heard anything. As all understood, silence is the language of survival.

The next day was bright and clear. She enjoyed the warmer weather and clear skies because it reminded her of Iraq. She knew she had to stay on task. Now she must avenge Ellis the White House maintenance man before she could go further.

The next day A'isha positioned herself near Frankie's Bar. It was a typical hangout of people with low and sinful tastes. She looked over the scene and it was apparent there were too many men inside the bar. She needed to kill only one man. She knew this killing would take some thinking. Killing a man in the middle of the city during the day was more challenging. She would work it out.

A'isha had dressed to attract the right man but not put him off with the appearance of being someone from a higher social class. She dressed in mass produced clothes purchased at J.C. Penney's. The clothes were new and tight enough to reveal her curves. She wore sunglasses and dark leather gloves. She held some ubiquitous tourist maps given away by dozens of government facilities.

She had circled the location of the White House with a black marker as if to remind herself of a sight she wanted to see. She sat on the bus bench next to the bar and gave the appearance of being unsure of her directions.

At that moment she saw the two Marines disembark from the city bus that seemed to bemoan its age. A'isha hated the noxious fumes it emitted. She so missed the desert's clear air. She waited a moment before standing and searching in several directions as if unsure of her exact location.

As the two Marines approached she stepped in front of them and said, "Excuse me, but I guess I'm lost. I could use some help." The two Marines stopped, and their eyes took in the sight of this attractive woman apparently from the sticks. The older Marine with the birth mark took over the situation.

He outranked his fellow Marine and was taller and more muscular. The senior Marine said to his companion, "Go on in, I'll help this lovely lady with her directions." The junior Marine did as he was told.

The older man with the birth mark couldn't help but wonder what had fallen into his hands. "Where is the place you're trying to find?" he asked sounding almost refined.

"I'm looking for this place on my map." He glanced at the map and saw she had circled was The White House. "Well, that's probably the most famous building in town, the White House. You're not far away, go eight blocks in that direction on this street and you'll be there."

"Oh, that's wonderful. I've been waiting to take the White House tour, and I only have one more day of vacation."

"I am sorry to disappoint you, but the last tour started at 1:30 p.m. and there won't be another until 10:00 a.m. tomorrow," said the Marine in a tone that suggested he shared her disappointment. He was evaluating his chances of scoring with this inexperienced country mouse.

"Thank you, but now I'm disappointed. I saved up for a year to come here, but it's been one problem after another."

"Where are you from?" asked the Marine.

She sighed. "My name is Barbara Tyler and I'm from Sandy Hook, Nebraska. I was going crazy in that dump. I hoped this vacation would be full of adventures. Instead, I've been lost nearly all the time and even worse I haven't met a friendly person. Everyone is in such a hurry and can't spare one minute to talk."

For a moment, the Marine thought that the beautiful woman in front of him was going to burst into tears.

Thinking fast, he replied in his most concerned voice, "Really Barbara, it just takes time to know the place and learn where to meet friendly folks. Tell you what, let's get something to eat at that hot dog stand and maybe we can come up with some better things for you to do. The tab is on me, and we can get to know each other."

"Barbara" beamed. "That's the first kind remark I've heard since I arrived in D.C. It really is a beautiful city but it's hard to enjoy it when I'm alone. I don't want to go back to Sandy Hook like a whipped dog."

"Just leave it to me. My name is Johnnie Branford from White Falls, Texas. I know this city well. I'm sure we can get your vacation back on track. Let's grab that hot dog."

Seated on street benches as they ate the hotdogs Barbara seemed like a totally different person now that she was in the company of a new friend. With the slightest bit of prodding the Marine was able to read this beautiful woman like a well-worn book. She said she was 20 years old and had been a star athlete in her small town as well as head cheer leader for the boy's teams.

She wanted to do a great deal more with her life. Her mother had been against this vacation, but she was of age and could do as she pleased.

"How did you do in school, and what do you plan now?" asked the Marine with feinted interest.

"Barbara" brightened. "I was an excellent student. I must decide soon whether to attend college. I come from a poor family. I think I can get some scholarships. I really need to explore the bigger world. That's why I'm here."

The Marine took all this in. Her seduction seemed possible if he played his cards right. He followed up with a light question.

"What's with the dark glasses and the gloves?"

She laughed, "I've always been a fan of James Bond movies. I thought they made me look cooler and more mysterious. I don't think I'm too hard to look at." She removed her sunglasses.

Johnnie Branford had never seen such a face. Her soft, seductive eyes were unlike any he'd seen before. She projected an image of innocence combined with alluring invitation.

He barely heard her whisper, "I am really not that bad looking am I?"

"You have nothing to worry about in the beauty department," replied the awed Texan.

She slipped her sunglasses back on and started to bubble about her high school life. A'isha calmly calculated, "*the correct approach to this fool is childlike innocence.*"

"In some ways things were not all bad about high school and Nebraska. I had a steady boyfriend from my sophomore year on. I was in such a hurry to get on with life that I turned into a bad girl with him. It was totally crazy but totally fun. I don't know why I'm telling you this. Probably because I'll never see you again."

She laughed as she looked at the dumbfounded Marine, "Is this a little too much and a little too fast?" She laughed again as she talked about those past days. "I finally had to break off with the guy in my senior year. He was a nice guy, but I felt restless. A variety of boyfriends helped get me though my senior year. Have I scared you off yet?"

Johnnie grinned. "Marines don't scare easily. I came from a small town myself." This was becoming his lucky day.

"Johnnie would you take me to a movie? I'd be happy to pay. I'm bored out of my mind, and I must go home tomorrow. You can be my adventure. Let's do something fun together."

Johnnie knew that this woman was for real. He had no doubt he'd be sharing a bed with her before midnight.

"Let's go," he said as he offered his hand which she accepted with eagerness. She was laughing as Johnnie flagged down a cab. He took her to a movie house that was showing a tasteful but steamy movie. There was hardly anyone in the theater.

It was one of the older movie houses, the interior so dark it was hardly possible to see three feet . . . the perfect place for beginning intimacy.

In the darkness of the cinema A'isha gently held the Marine's hand. She could tell he was falling under her power. She softly took his hand and placed it on her thigh. He began to run his fingers over the new cotton material.

She responded by resting her head on his shoulder.

"How simple these infidels are," she thought to herself. "How wise are the ways of Allah," she reflected. "A Muslim man this age would normally have several wives to satisfy his sexual needs. He would not be as desperate as this idiot who seeks sex which would be readily available in any Muslim home."

She slowly removed her sunglasses and kissed the Marine's cheek. He then kissed her, but she quickly turned away and resisted further kissing.

Then she slowly withdrew his hand from her thigh and turned back to the movie. Johnnie took the clue and drew his hand back. He turned to her and asked whether he had done something wrong. She suddenly seemed tense. She reached over and squeezed his hand again. "No, God no. I like you. I don't want to go too fast. I barely know you."

Could we make this a romantic early evening date? I would like to watch the movie and go out to eat in a nice restaurant. I want to remember this evening for the rest of my life. I have never been with such a handsome man."

A'isha coldly gauged his response. *Then it came to her. She knew where she wanted to do the killing. The Potamic River.*

"Despite my bravo, I am a small-town girl, but I want to know you so much better. I was hoping we could go to my room together after our evening out. I want to make love to you, but I am scared. My first time was horrible. Could you be gentle and take your time?"

Johnnie tried to feint true concern. "Don't worry Barbara. I want to make this a great trip for you. I haven't eaten in a nice restaurant for months. Let's have a good time in a restaurant, have a great meal and talk."

A'isha quickly spoke up brightly. "After the restaurant could we walk by the river?"

Johnnie replied with eagerness. "Of course, we can just walk and enjoy ourselves next to the river. The stars should be great. I would love to see them."

Let's just follow the evening and see what happens." She was beaming as she took his face in her hands and kissed him twice.

A'isha thought to herself. *This moron will be too easy.*

"You're a great guy Johnnie, I knew you would understand. I want you to make love to me but please be gentle and slow. Just bear with me. I think it will be fine."

Barbara then smiled. "Let's pretend we are in a fairytale and see where it goes. But for now, let's get some popcorn and soft drinks and enjoy the movie!"

Which is exactly what they did. They held hands and watched the movie. They whispered to each other as they followed the plot of the show. During the sad parts "Barbara" squeezed his hand while resting her head on his shoulder. During the intimate scenes they lightly kissed several times.

After the movie Johnnie took her to an upscale restaurant. The restaurant was beautiful and expensive. Barbara insisted on paying the tab because she knew he was in the service on low wages.

Johnnie was intoxicated with this woman. He talked about his childhood and the difficulty of growing up poor in Texas. She talked about losing her father and her mother's needs. She talked about her hopes for the future. They laughed about the days of awkward adolescence. The fumbled advances and the strained silences. The conversation flowed with no effort throughout their meal.

They enjoyed themselves and touched hands often. Johnnie talked about Marine boot camp and how terrified he had been of his Drill Instructor Sargent Writner. A'isha listened seriously when the conversation called for it. She laughed at his jokes and held his hand often.

After the leisure pace and the sensual meal, Johnnie called a cab, and they went to the Potomac River. They held hands and walked along the shore until they found a grassy quiet spot. They sat down and rested under a shade tree. Time passed as they talked to each other about everything that interested them. They bought ice cream from a roving vender and enjoyed the simple pleasure of eating such a luxury. She promised to exchange addresses and phone numbers when they got back to her room. It was dusk now and they quietly watched the final rays of the setting sun.

Together they reclined on the riverbank and held each other gently. The kissing and touching seemed unhurried and natural. They watched the stars appear one by one. Johnnie was amazed that Barbara could name each bright star as it rose. She also pointed out the constellations as they appeared in the darkening sky.

"Johnnie have you ever been in the desert? Before my mom and I moved to Nebraska I was a child who grew up in the desert of New Mexico. It was beautiful. I loved the silence and I learned to be by myself."

"No, I've never been in a true desert."

A'isha pondered the timing. She had been patient and waited to be sure the darkness was thick enough. There was no moon in the sky. Her eyes and ears told her there was no-one around.

It was time to kill this unbeliever.

"Johnnie have you ever thought of God and life after death?"

"Not really, I guess I am too young to face those big questions." he replied.

A'isha thought to herself. "*How easily Satan steals the souls of fools.*"

She kissed him. She lightly caressed his chest, and she could feel his beating heart against her ear.

She thought to herself, *"Allah be served. Soon this heart will stop forever."*

"Johnnie, death is always near us, and one must be ready." He did not reply. She moved her body higher on his reclined chest.

"Johnnie, kiss me as if it was the last kiss of your life."

He responded with passion. A'isha reached for her concealed dagger from the back of her thigh. His eyes were closed when she plunged the blade into his heart. His eyes flashed open in pain and surprise.

A'isha's eyes were smoldering as she spit on his startled face. She spoke to him softly, "You pig, don't you remember insulting the black man at the White House? He is Muslim and you will never insult a Muslim again. Johnnie, you really are going to hell." Johnnie tried to move but was unable. He was pinned to the earth. The shock overwhelmed him. A'isha smiled at him as he tried to talk. His lips moved slowly but he uttered no sound. He was a strong young man and he bled out slowly. She had not twisted the blade to end his pain.

She again felt sensual warmth spread though her body. She closed her eyes. The exquisite pleasure washed over her in waves. It was many seconds before the ecstasy ebbed away. Allah again had blessed her killing. She opened her eyes and watched the light fade in Johnnie's frightened eyes with great satisfaction. Finally, his gaze became fixed, and his eyes began to film over. He shuttered a last convulsion and then his body went slack. A'isha carefully wiped her blade on infidel's shirt. She stood and thought. *This was another kill in America and I enjoyed them all. Soon there will be millions more.*

She was content, Ellis Procter was avenged as she promised. This killing would convince Ellis that she had authority and power. She felt nothing but sated joy as she walked away in the humid darkness.

CHAPTER THIRTY-TWO

May 8, 2005

S ammie Lock looked over the unloading harbor in Seattle. The weather was sunny and pleasant, but his daily unload list was large. There would be tremendous pressure to inspect and unload the shipping containers. Time was money and the ship owners and captain did not get paid until offloaded.

Sammie had been waiting for this day for a long time. He knew Allah would be pleased with his work. Sammie ran his finger down the list. His finger stopped on a ship called *Destiny*.

Sammie had been told the name of the ship two days ago by a cleric at his mosque.

The ship now held a total of 202 drums. All of them were listed as industrial paint. Sammie knew that two drums weren't paint. He did not know what the 202 containers held but he'd been assured that the cause of Islam would be greatly advanced.

It was a simple matter for Sammie to inspect the ship with another dock helper. The drums were numbered on the side. Sammie's instructions had been to check drums six and eleven which held industrial paint. The lids were removable. Most ships were inspected randomly and if those items were "clean" then the rest of the cargo was deemed legitimate.

All shipping containers of *Destiny* were to be loaded on one trucking firm's flatbeds. This simplified matters. The containers would be swung directly from the ship onto the trucks. Ship owners liked to see this type of arrangement.

Sammie knew clean drums were loaded in the front of the shipping containers. He swung the doors open. The selected drums were opened within seconds. Each numbered drum contained gray paint.

"Looks good to go," said the helper.

"Take the hot box and walk around each container to make sure we don't lose Seattle," said Sammie with his dry humor.

"Man, this is flat stupid," said the young worker with him. The device showed no reading for radiation.

"Okay kid, here are the five semi-trucks to carry the load: all from the same company. It doesn't get any easier. Let's see you lay the containers on those trucks. You could use the experience." Fifty-five minutes later the containers were all loaded and cinched down tight.

Sammie knew he had done his part for Islam on this day.

Death in massive numbers entered the world of America. The large trucks with the containers had a short haul of less than 150 miles east and south of Seattle. At a venerable factory dock in Ellensburg, the containers were unloaded by an old swing arm crane. Next morning new drivers came to the shipping docks in approximately two-hour intervals. Each driver drove a mid-sized U-Haul truck. These were not union drivers. None had a clue as to what they were hauling. Each driver was helped to load a set of numbered drums.

Each was an independent trucker who liked cash and kept quiet. Each had a list of storage units to which to deliver the drums. The storage units were all paid for in advance and managers were expecting the deliveries. The drums were numbered on the sides, and it was a required that the drums were to be placed into the storage units in a certain order.

From this location in Washington State U-Haul trucks fanned out across the United States. The trucks attracted no attention from authorities of each state. These types of truck were on the roads by the hundreds as families or others moved to new homes. The States had no interest in these non- commercial trucks as they crossed State lines.

Within three weeks the drums were in storage units spread around fifty major cities of distinction across America. Each received four lethal drums. These included Seattle, Los Angles, San Francisco, Phoenix, Houston, Dallas, Chicago, St. Louis, Denver, Atlanta, Cleveland, Memphis, Washington D.C., New York, and many more.

Over fifty major cities were surrounded with the rocket-like devices designed by an introverted genius in Iraq. These devices were loaded with the deadliest genetically engineered pathogen ever to exist on earth.

These were modern storage units surrounded by a chain-linked fence topped with barbed wire. A computerized remote control opened the main gate. The units had no attendant on the grounds. The driver did not notice that it always placed a certain drum precisely between two beams. The storage units had been pre-inspected, and the beam locations charted. Since the storage units were cheaply constructed the roofing beams were widely spaced.

May 9, 2005

A'isha had picked up another instructional message from a different drop point. She was told to use her second key to open her Georgetown storage unit. A'isha took care to be sure that she wasn't being followed. When two days passed, she felt confident she was safe.

A'isha retrieved a mid-sized box. At her apartment she carefully withdrew the contents: a lap-top computer and another key. Her knowledge of computers was limited, but thanks to Zeynat she was familiar with the basic operations. She'd been provided with a manual instruction sheet. She was instructed to start the computer and to read the instructions carefully.

When the computer screen came up she saw a large United States map. Following her second command she pushed a button, and red dots began to blink around fifty major cities in the United States. Over 50 renowned cities were surrounded by the blinking lights. Beneath the map of the United States was the simple word: Continue. She double clicked and began to read the next screen.

Details of the Operation "Sword of Allah."

The objective of this mission is to destroy the United States as a world power. The means to achieve this objective is a vast biological attack upon both American citizens and the government of the

United States. The biological agent is extremely effective. Each red dot around each of the cities is the location of a launcher that will propel this pathogen into the air currents above and across the city.

The launchers are arranged at the major compass points around each metropolis. This is to be certain that the pathogen will spread over the city regardless of wind direction. The pathogen is a virus which attacks primarily through inhalation. However, the pathogen is deadly and can be absorbed by eating, drinking, or touching.

~ ~ ~

Each launcher contains enough pathogens to infect one million people at minimum. One launcher under favorable conditions could infect over ten million. The newly infected human becomes a virus spreader of extreme potency within two days although no symptoms appear for three.

It should be possible to expect that 150 million people will be infected within the first two days of the biological release. After the first day the virus will spread though the population rapidly. The death rate of those infected is over 98%. Nearly all the entire health profession will be eliminated by death within several days.

The civilian and military infrastructure will collapse within days. A unique biological timer will kill the virus in approximately two weeks. Thus, the induced epidemic will burn itself out completely in two weeks. You and your agents must stay in a modified apartment for four days to ensure that you are not among the first infected.

You, A'isha, are encouraged to gain a world audience to explain why the United States deserved to be destroyed and to allow other countries to isolate their citizens immediately and close their borders.

If a national forum proves impossible, you are to initiate the launchers at your discretion.

Arab nations will be told in classified messages to close all travel at the right time. Infected cases in Muslim nations will be few and isolated. You have full authority to make the decision as to when to strike. To fire the launchers, you only must call a ten number sequence. This number will cause a redundant system of transmitters to send a burst transmission of great power. This transmission will hit the launcher receivers which will fire the launchers.

You will be aware how many launchers have fired by following your computer screen. Each red dot will turn black to show it fired. Ideally the launches will occur during the morning the when most people are active; this should infect most of the people in the target cities. All the programming has been done by using different time zones.

The launchers on the east coast will fire first at 8:00 a.m. local time from the East coast to the West coast. Within four hours all launchers will have fired. After the initial call is made all firing sequences are automatic.

CHAPTER THIRTY-THREE

A'isha smiled. This operation would destroy the United States as a world power and make certain the Islamic conquest of the earth.

Once you are assured of the successful launching of the devices remain in your sealed room for three days. Enclosed are three pills that if taken will end your lives within seconds if necessary.

There is one other task. When you are within five days of your launch time use your last key to open a locker where you will obtain certain additional items. In the end it will be as Allah wills.

A'isha accepted this information with composure. At last, she knew the details of the plan and her role within it. She was to pick the time when the sequence of destruction would begin. Her goal was to access the Oval Office. She knew President Reston was the most guarded person in the world. Yet Allah would be with her. She knew Allah would provide.

No one is beyond Allah's reach. A good plan, good weapons, and the will to follow through had destroyed many difficult targets. A'isha prayed for successful destruction of the United States.

~ ~ ~

May 13, 2005

Saddam felt satisfied with the mission's progress thus far. A'isha was in place and had met the American President.

When the Imam described Ellis Proctor, Saddam saw how such a man would be important to A'isha. The Shiites were historical experts at keeping secrecy in hostile environments.

Saddam had kept his promises to Dr. Showkit, Najib, and Zeynet. All sums of money and other requests were fulfilled. Najib and Zeynet were each given five million dollars and Dr. Showkit 10 million. Zeynet asked to continue being an Islamic agent but wished to work in France. She received a clean passport.

All funds were deposited under numbered Swiss accounts. This insured the trainers' funds rested safe out of Iraq.

Saddam prided himself on his business honesty. In financial matters he was true to his word. Also, Saddam had not forgotten the deadly voice in the bedroom that warned him to comply.

Saddam knew the Americans were planning moves against him. Only the timing lay in question. He knew A'isha would go forward with the operation and was attempting to soon be within killing range of President Reston.

If the President and the United States fell as a unit then the Muslim reaction would be one of untrammeled joy. Saddam would be remembered as the leader who brought down the largest suppressor of Islam.

May 17, 2005

Jackson had never felt closer danger than in the last few weeks. He could barely eat because of his apprehension for America. Horrifying nightmares plagued him. He could barely function sensing that his tormentor was already in the United States.

Who was she? What did she intend to do? He felt the evil woman nearing him. Yet he had not a speck of hard evidence of her existence.

He decided to take his fears all the way to the top.

That meant nothing less than going to the head of the CIA himself. This would be a professional risk to end all professional risks. Due to ISIS most of the law and military groups were already on high alert. What more could he reasonably do? He had to try.

Mental illness was not uncommon among the intelligence branches because of pressure to produce hard information. It was not unusual for the CIA to place an agent on enforced leave. The analyst could also be relieved of his position.

Jackson picked up the phone and made his call to the Head of the CIA.

~ ~ ~

May 23, 2005

Dean Hamilton was a beefy man, powerful both politically and physically. He'd had been raised as a favorite son in a successful Virginia family. He'd played line-backer for Yale and still looked like he could fill the position in his early sixties. His muscular body was merely the framework for an astute mind. He had the ability to listen carefully and make hard decisions in a short span of time.

He began as a lawyer and then a Virginia Senator before he accepted the position of Attorney General of the United States. From that high pressure job, he accepted an appointment to head the CIA.

Many threats were facing his country. Hamilton knew Islam was the main danger to the United States and other western nations. The Koran was a cookbook of oppression and conquest. There was no tolerance found in its pages. Islam did not allow anyone the freedom to disagree and reach his own thoughts and decisions. For fourteen centuries Islam had never given up its plan for world domination.

Hamilton had pointed this out to congressional committees many times with little effect. He knew Islam to be a poison slipping into the political bodies of free countries.

Muslims hoped to use the ballot to acquire a bloodless victory. By whatever means necessary the goal was a religious totalitarian state with freedom for none. Islam was an existential threat to the free world. Yet millions of believers would give up their lives for their prophet. Hamilton knew Islamic beliefs might bring about the end of Western civilization.

He looked at his appointment schedule noting that Robert Jackson had requested a private meeting. Jackson was one of the most astute assets the CIA possessed. It was unusual for Jackson to request a face-to-face meeting. However, he was a brilliant analyst and must feel strongly to request a meeting with a man who could fire him. The big man asked his secretary to call Jackson to his office. Jackson stood before his boss in minutes.

"Jackson, there are two chairs in this room for a reason. Please, sit down. I'm sure you are here for something important. Let's hear about it."

Jackson explained his concern that someone posing a serious threat to the United States had not yet been identified. He also admitted he had no evidence.

However, his insight was so strong that the protection of the President should be increased, and his activities reduced for the foreseeable time. Jackson explained his belief that the agent posing the threat was a young Arab woman. He explained that killing the President would be a terrorist dream. Jackson was certain the President was a real target within a larger plan. It was critical that the President's security and routine be changed for security purposes.

Hamilton listened to every word. He rested his chin on his clasped hands as he pondered what this intelligent agent was about.

"What you are telling me is that you have no evidence except your nightmares, anxiety, and intuition. Am I correct?" asked the Director.

"At the moment I have nothing more to offer," answered Jackson.

"Do you fully appreciate how strongly the Secret Service will feel about the CIA telling them to change their security plan?" asked the Director.

"I fully realize they'll go through the roof. But I can't believe I'm doing my duty unless I pass on to you something that I am certain exists very near us today," said Jackson.

"You realize that I could request you to take leave because you're not acting like a logical analyst. I could just fire you for coming to me with no evidence at all," said the director.

Jackson bristled. "Mr. Director, do what you feel is right. I could not continue my job unless I told you about this situation. I'm not crazy. I am a good analyst and am right on this one."

"Slow down Jackson. I know your record. You wouldn't be here unless you felt it worth risking your job. That takes courage and the CIA needs analysts with courage. I'll take it from here. Perhaps I can come up with some rational reason for the secret service to change their operational tactics. Go back to work. Keep tracking ISIS but keep your ear to the ground about this unidentified threat."

"This will ruffle some feathers, but I doubt if anyone is going to risk their career by refusing to work with us. Thanks for coming in today. Keep doing a good job." The director showed him to the door.

After Jackson left the room the Director rubbed his eyes and tried to relax. Jackson had just reinforced some strange feelings he'd been having, too. He suspected ISIS was not the full picture. He too had been unable to explain his own intuition.

He made an appointment to see the President. Perhaps it was time to put operation "Salvation" into place. Everything this President touched had to have a biblical name. The Director called the President's office and then called the office of the Head of Secret Services.

May 24, 2005

Hamilton set the phone back onto its base. The Director of the Secret Service had been unhappy with the request for greater protection for the President. Hamilton had also been right that no one was going to place their career on the line by saying "no" to better protection of the President.

New policies were to go into effect immediately from the bottom to the top. Changing tactics was easy for the Secret Service but to limit the President's calendar was impossible. President Reston was a strong-willed man from Texas and Texans do not run scared.

The President did say they could do whatever they wanted about his security, but they would have to live with his official duties.

He did agree to put operation "Salvation" into place. Action followed without delay. Director Hamilton wished none of the world's religions had ever been formed. It all seemed a bunch of trouble–causing nonsense.

~ ~ ~

May 26, 2005

A'isha listened carefully to Ellis as he described changes that had been made in White House security. Ellis noted the Marine guard who insulted him did not return to duty as normal. White House rumor said that he'd been stabbed to death near the river the evening before. Ellis gave this information carefully.

"Allah his ways." A'isha replied softly.

Ellis thought it wise to move on. He told A'isha that changes in security had been made overnight. It appeared that the changes had been ordered by the Secret Service. Rumor had it that the change was prompted by a CIA analyst by the name of Jackson.

A'isha felt a mental and physical response to the name "Jackson." Satan had his soldiers and sometimes they were very good. She'd long felt the touch of another searching mind seeking her. Now she knew who it was. This Jackson had touched her many times since she'd been in the States. She'd also felt his mind probing her months before she left Iraq.

This Jackson wanted to destroy her. His intellectual powers were rare. She could admire a man like Jackson except that he was an infidel. Nevertheless, Allah could enlighten the most benighted of unbelievers.

A'isha had tried to turn Jackson to no avail. Allah remained silent. A'isha decided to catalog the name and examine the issue later. Ellis reported there were four guards in the Oval Office rather than only two a week ago.

A'isha thought about the situation. She could ignore the President and merely release Flash Fire. That option was unsatisfying. This man had killed her family. "The mission stays the same. We'll have to work around the greater challenge."

"Take your maintenance cart to service the restroom and let me know what their response is. I particularly need to know where the guards are located. How big is your largest cart?"

"About five feet long and four feet wide. It barely fits into the elevator," answered Ellis.

"Good. Our time is running short. We must penetrate these defenses as fast as possible. Have you been able to make the White House modifications that we need to fulfill our mission?"

"Yes, it took some effort, but I was able to fulfill your instructions. Everything is ready. I must compliment you on how well you plan. This part of the mission is ingenious."

"You also have done well, Ellis. Allah choose wisely when he chose you. Allah has given us everything we need to accomplish our task."

"Do you know of any event that will be televised from the Oval Office in the near future?" A'isha asked.

"I know that Premier Berstein is coming from Israel and there are clear signs of a televised joint statement from the Oval Office," said Ellis.

"How strange and powerful are the ways of Allah," thought A'isha. *It would be possible that Berstein and Reston could be killed simultaneously. Two of the greatest butchers of Arabs would be in the same room. This was something worth pursuing.*

CHAPTER THIRTY-FOUR

She showed Ellis the address of another quiet café. "Are you familiar this place?"

"Yes I've been there," Ellis said.

"Meet me at the appointed time. We need information. How soon is the meeting between Reston and Berstein expected to occur?"

"I would expect in less than two weeks. I'll know the exact date soon. It's impossible to keep this type of meeting secret in the White House. The grapevine is efficient. I should know at least a week in advance."

"All is well, Ellis, Allah is giving us another murderer of the Muslim people to kill."

"I'll see how the guards respond to the cart and study their location and alertness."

May 27, 2005

This café was located near Georgetown University. Ellis spoke first. "I've used the large cart twice since I talked with you. They never bothered to inspect it."

A'isha smiled with true warmth at Ellis. "In less than two weeks you'll be known as the man who helped break the back of this oppressive nation of infidels. Tell me what else have you found?"

"The guards have switched their location somewhat. Two men are at the main general corridor. Once through the corridor the remaining two carrying machine pistols on slings stand at either side of the VIP restroom."

"The number of guards in the Oval Office has remained four men. They stand behind the President and about six feet to both the right and left of the President. They carry pistols."

"I found out that the meeting of President Reston and Premier Berstein of Israel is to be televised from the Oval Office on December 11 at 2:00 p.m. this month. We won't have much time. Is the mission still a go on such short notice?"

A'isha straightened, answering with cool confidence. "We can easily meet this schedule, and we will accomplish our mission. Allah is with us and with Allah what believer can fail? Meet me in two days and I will have more to tell you."

~ ~ ~

May 29, 2005

Time grew short. A'isha used the third key. When she opened the storage unit she found a backpack of the type used by students. Heavy, it bit into her shoulders as she hoisted it all the way to her apartment on the crowded bus.

By the time she closed the apartment door she was happy to slide it to the table. She double checked the locked door then she opened the pack.

The first items she saw were six rectangular objects, each six inches wide, ten inches long and two inches thick. Written in English on top of the outer curve were the words, "This side toward enemy." An arrow pointed to the desired side.

The devices steel feet allowed them to stand alone or be pressed into soil. After reading the instructions she understood that these were Claymores, a type of anti-personal weapon. They'd been manufactured in the United States. Each device when fired would throw hundreds of steel balls at high speed. The killing arc was 30 yards deep and 30 yards wide depending on the angle,

To arm the device a detonator was screwed into the top of the Claymore connected by two thin wires to a hand operated circuit closer. A push and everyone for 30 yards in front of the deadly device would be killed.

Then A'isha found three familiar pistols known as Scorpions, manufactured in Eastern Europe. She's trained with one in Iraq. It had the highest rate of fire of any machine pistol: 900 rounds per minute. There were 1500 rounds of ammunition for each pistol. The projectiles were custom made from depleted uranium.

The extreme weight and density of the depleted uranium would pierce any bullet proof Secret Service vest.

The third item was an object that looked like a small steel muffler approximately two inches in diameter and six inches long. Its purpose was to filter the air in A'isha's apartment for several days.

The advanced special filter would take air from outside of the apartment through a meticulously cut and sealed hole in an apartment window. This would bring in enough fresh air to sustain life and pressurize the apartment. This complex filter would block the pathogen for several days. The filter would be good for three days. This would give the team three safe days while Flash Fire was fatally affecting the American cities.

The mission against the Oval Office must happen immediately after they left the apartment because they would also be infected by Flash Fire. She repacked all items except the muffler. Joey would pick up the weapons from the agreed upon locker that she mentioned with him. He would then repack the items with his standard supply delivery to the White House.

Time was running out for the United States.

~ ~ ~

June 2, 2005

Ellis carefully cut the two-inch hole in the window of A'isha's apartment using his diamond tipped glass cutter. He had also obtained the pump to draw air from the outside. A hose connected the pump to the filter. Where the filter went through the window the small clearance between filter and the pump was sealed by silicone. Ellis tested the pump, and the device worked well. A'isha and Allison sealed each window jam with silicone and duct tape. All interfaces between the inside of the apartment were carefully prepared. The pump would not allow the virus to enter the room because the pressure inside the room was now slightly greater than the outside air.

~ ~ ~

A'isha went over every step of the operation. Ellis took a few days off from accumulated vacation time. He'd promised that he would be back to test all the wiring for the joint statement between Reston and Berstein on the 19th of the month. However, Flash Fire would be released at 8:00 a.m. on the east coast on the 16th of the month.

Therefore, within four hours the pathogen would be released across the four time zones United States. This meant that the pathogen would be released at 8:00 a.m. in each time zone. This would coincide with the morning rush hour in every major city. By the 17th of the month the American citizens would be infected by Flash Fire by the tens of millions.

A'isha, Allison, and Ellis would have three days of grace before they were also affected by the virus. The few days gained would allow them to conduct their assault on the Oval Office.

A'isha and Ellis would bypass or defeat the hallway guards and then gain access to the hidden hallway. If necessary A'isha would kill the guards with the blade. A'isha was confident that she could eliminate them. The secret of this phase of the operation was a remote control hooked to the main computer in Ellis's office.

Thus, with one click of a button Ellis could turn off the lights in any spot of the White House. The light would be turned on when he clicked his remote again. During these moments of darkness A'isha would dispatch the guards.

The strategy for the Oval Office would be the same. When certain Reston and Berstein were in the office Ellis would disable the office with his remote control. Within seconds they would enter the Oval Office through the secret mistresses' corridor in the darkness. When the lights came on Ellis was to kill the two guards on the left side of the President. A'isha would kill the others.

This would leave the United States President Reston and Premier Berstein helpless in A'isha's hands. Allison was to use her social connections to be in the Oval Office to hear the joint statement from Berstein and Reston to their world audience. She was to remain near the main door wearing an ornate, heavy necklace.

Closer examination would have revealed that the metal was made from hardened tool steel. This would secure the door long enough for Ellis to secure the main room with a chain after A'isha controlled the crowd. Under the point of A'isha's gun, the cameramen would have little choice but to continue broadcasting.

Ellis was concerned about his unfamiliarity with the Scorpion weapon. A'isha assured him that the volume of fire from the Scorpion would eliminate the guards in a fraction of a second. A'isha and Allison would strap a claymore mine to the back of the President.

A strong line would be tied to A'isha's belt. The detonator was the friction type. If A'isha was shot or disabled her falling body would pull the friction fuse and blow the American President into small pieces. However, the desired goal was to tell the world why the United States had to be destroyed. Although there were many uncertainties A'isha was sure that Allah would overcome.

~ ~ ~

June 26, 2005

A'isha, Ellis, and Allison were up for morning prayers at 5:00 a.m. Today was the day of the bio-weapon attack. Then they would wait for the virus to infect by the tens of millions.

A'isha and her partners would be praying for personal strength and success. Ellis and Allison grew more nervous with each minute.

A'isha steadied and reassured them that all lay in Allah's hands. She thought of her lost loved family and her anger deepened. She would feel nothing but joy when she dialed the phone number to start the pathogen's launching sequence.

She thought back on all the hours of training she'd endured as Dr. Showkit's, Zeynat's, and Najib's student. Above all, she thought of the thousands of innocent Arabs killed by the U. S. during the so-called Gulf War, not a war where warriors met on the battlefield and Allah decided who lived or died. No. It was murder from their uncontested domination of the sky. Most deaths were innocent civilians of various ages.

She also remembered the orphanage where she accompanied so many dead children to the horrible trench that served as their mass grave. She remembered her promise to the dying children that neither Allah nor she would forget their killers. A'isha had not forgotten. Her rage consumed her. Revenge would come in time.

She double checked every part of the plan. She checked her computer. The screen showed the map of blinking red lights that ringed over 50 American cities. These lights would turn to black dots after the launcher fired. Everything seemed to be in order. The pressure on Allison and Ellis heightened as minutes and seconds of the two-hour countdown continued.

A'isha remained stalwart. This was the hour for which she'd prayed. Soon U.S. citizens would know the agony of a sudden loss of loved ones. The population and therefore the power of the United States would be vanquished. Then at last, followers of Allah would escape the yoke of Western imperialist powers. Islam would rapidly spread across the earth.

Life in the United States proceeded as normal. Parents were getting ready to go to work and children left for school. Many

American cities were in winter inversions which proved helpful for pathogens because they'd be trapped under the inversion and would not be dissipated by rising air.

Gradually the pathogen would drift down upon doomed cities. After two days all victims would be marked with infection and human to human transmission would do the rest.

By the second day people would start checking into hospitals. On the third day thousands of patients would begin dying. The hospital staff would all be infected before they understood the citizenry to be under a biological attack. It would be far too late to make it recede.

Health providers would be among the first to go. They would be infected by patients showing up for help in their offices and hospital emergency rooms.

CHAPTER THIRTY-FIVE

A'isha watched the wall clock's secondhand circle the face of the large dial like a predator. Everyone on the mission knew only five minutes remained before Flash Fire's release. The hand seemed to move with an irresistible force. Each second seemed to fall like a stricken soldier, never to rise again. Sweat ran down Ellis's face like heavy rain. Allison turned pale and trembling. A'isha was serene and steadied the others by force of will.

"All is in Allah's hands," she said quietly, "Allah decides who lives or dies." The second hand continued its silent rotation.

A'isha watched the last thirty seconds drop into eternity. When the tip of the second hand reached the 12 o'clock position A'isha picked up her phone and dialed the necessary number. After three rings an automated voice said, "The sequence will now begin."

Ellis and Allison prayed for strength. A'isha prayed for success. All eyes focused on the computer screen. Within a few seconds the flashing red dots began to turn into black pulsing markers of death. It seemed faster than the human eye could follow. Three of the four dots around New York City turned black.

A'isha prayed to Allah and the fourth red dot turned black. Within twenty seconds every dot in the Eastern Time Zone was flashing a black marker. Not one launcher failed. The solitary man in his Iraqi warehouse had designed a weapon that did exactly as expected.

Flash Fire continued blanketing each city with the invisible odorless virus. The United States began to die. New York, Washington D.C., Boston, and Philadelphia had been struck mortal blows. In just a few days nearly each member of these cities' populations would be infected.

The system was now totally automatic. Each hour would release the launchers in each time zone at the exact hour. Ellis watched the room's air pressure to be sure it was higher by two pounds than the normal atmosphere. This would not allow the virus to trespass into the protected room.

The activity seemed to steady both Ellis and Allison. The time of waiting ended. They'd helped strike the blow that would bring down the Great Satan. In exactly one hour they gathered around the computer screen. The flashing red dots were fast turning into pulsing black ones. Detroit, Chicago, St. Louis, Atlanta, Minneapolis, New Orleans, Kansas City, Fort Worth, Dallas, Omaha, and Houston joined in. A'isha remained calm. She had lived for this day of Allah's revenge.

The virus gently drifted down and millions of its spores were inhaled by tens of millions of American citizens. There was no sense of this fatal invasion. Flash Fire was penetrating countless cells of their human bodies. Soon the virus would begin to destroy each host.

~ ~ ~

The beginning of the end came quietly and unnoticed by the people who would soon begin to die their miserable deaths. In the span of four time zones every launcher had fired its payload. The great cities of Seattle, San Francisco, Los Angeles, and San Diego joined the list of stricken cities. All the continental states were dying.

The mission was successful. A'isha kept her emotions in check. A close observer might have noticed the gleam of success in her eyes. This was A'isha's time to be patient. The filter protecting them would last three days. On the fourth day the assault on the White House would begin.

June 28, 2005

Belview Hospital

Washington D.C.

7:00 a.m.

Dr. Obermeyer looked at the charts turned over to him by the night shift. He noticed that an unusual number of cases admitted in the last couple of days seemed to defy normal definition. Dozens of patients complained about a broad range of symptoms: fever, general weakness, headaches, and vomiting.

Routine tests indicated an unknown virus of undefined strength. General antibiotics only aggravated the symptoms rapidly. One older patient who'd received antibiotics had been transferred to critical status, which is not unusual. Older people often died from illnesses that didn't affect the young.

Nevertheless, he decided to ask Barbara in the Medical Records Department to send him up the older patient's file. Perhaps he could detect something that his colleagues had overlooked. After three rings a different voice answered the call. "Dr. Obermeyer, I'm Mary, filling in for Barbara today. She called in ill. How can I help you?"

Dr. Obermeyer asked for the needed patient records. It was unusual for Barbara not to be at her station. He had known her for years. She'd never missed a day of work.

He leaned back in his desk chair and reflected on the mysteries of disease and healing. There were so many things his profession knew little about. There was a knock on his office door. The volunteer aide had the patent's records in her hands. As he scanned the medical records he recognized that this was no standard elderly patient.

The male patient was 73 years of age. For a man, his age he'd been in remarkable condition. He was a non-smoker and non-drinker. He had recently completed a 10 K amateur race.

He'd checked himself in when he began to vomit up small amounts of blood. He had a fever and complained of generalized pain in his joints. He had been given a small amount of antibiotics, but his condition had declined.

Such rapid decline after receiving a low dose of common antibiotic was unusual. The administration of the antibiotic and the patients decline could be a mere coincidence. But there might be an unusual linkage between the antibiotic and the patient's condition.

What a strange set of circumstances. The symptoms covered a wide range of medical possibilities. Too, stricken patients seemed to cover the entire spectrum of age, sex, and race. Unusual. He'd keep a close eye on this situation. It might be more serious than one older patient.

Dr. Obermeyer rubbed his eyes to fight off weariness. He hadn't gotten a lot of sleep for a day or so. At 58, he was not a kid anymore. Now he was running a slight fever himself, but in his profession that was not uncommon. Doctors were exposed to sick people every day.

What he could not know was how Flash Fire was rapidly overcoming his natural immune system. Dr. Obermeyer was the first medical professional to succumb to Flash Afire. Obermeyer would be dead in four days.

June 29, 2005

Jackson sat alone in his office unable to overcome feelings of doom caused by two simple words: *Too Late*. He'd followed every lead in his search for the source of his fears. His sleep was repeatedly haunted by fleeting images of a beautiful woman with dark, mysterious eyes.

At times, her eyes held nothing but hate. At other times they were sensual and beckoning. He wondered if he could be losing his mind.

In his dreams the woman stood on a barren ridge of sandstone. The wind was blowing so hard that her black clothing snapped in the fierce wind like a tattered banner that had survived many battles.

Jackson admitted to himself she lured him toward her like a magnet. He'd begun to hear her voice. It was hearing the voice that kept driving his concern about his sanity. The voice was strangely soft and gentle. There was a sense of allurement and clarity.

"Jackson, you have been reaching out to me. I know you and I know of your hunt. It is too late for your United States."

"It is I who will find you. We shall die together in a short time. Repent. Turn to Allah. You've been a worthy adversary. Our minds have touched many times. Let us walk together in the gardens of Paradise."

"Turn from these foolish infidels who exploit you. Give your mind and heart to Allah. After my mission is over it would be good to make love to such a man as you. I have a strong desire for you. Repent Jackson. It is too late for the others, but you still have time. Repent and join me."

Then the voice would die away, and Jackson would feel a sense of despair and loneliness such as he'd never known, an emotional pull so strong he could barely resist.

Whoever this psychically acute woman was, her beliefs had been carved in granite while his were ill defined and weak. He was no match for the seductive woman who flickered on the edge of his consciousness.

The pressure to find this monster was killing him. He was physically exhausted and had begun to feel even weaker during the last two days. Perhaps he was coming down with the flu. He felt his brow. He was running a slight fever. He never felt sick. Now he felt so depleted he could hardly move.

He decided to go for a walk. His fingers seemed to tremble as he reached for his coat and hat. He could not know that the Flash-Fire virus was destroying the cells he needed to live. Jackson was dying.

~ ~ ~

June 29,2005

813 9th St.

5:00 a.m.

Washington D.C.

Maria Santoes, a single woman who lived alone, had become an American citizen, and worked in the White House for nearly a year. Her uncle had been employed in the White House for over 18 years He pulled strings to give Maria a job after her father died in Los Angeles.

A hard worker, she led a low-profile life as one of the millions of lower classes who filled menial jobs for the privileged. Her hours were long and her pay not high. Since she lived in a poor neighborhood she spent two hours a day commuting.

To the sleepy Maria this morning was like any other. She attended her grooming and when she looked in the mirror she was pleased. She was a striking woman who attracted many men. She resisted advances. She was saving herself for the right man.

She hoped to find a responsible man who'd help her raise a large family. Maria loved children, and she was a serious follower of the Catholic faith.

Maria didn't feel well but had to go to work. Poor people don't have the luxury of being ill.

Maria stepped out of her apartment and turned to lock the door. A terrible pain pierced her back. Maria couldn't make a sound as A'isha pushed her dying body back into her room. Maria's last sight on this earth was the cold eyes of a woman who looked like herself.

A'isha covered the body with blankets from the bedroom. The blankets would absorb the blood. The woman would not be missed for hours. By the time the body was discovered A'isha knew the White House assault would be over. She removed the White House identification from Maria's neck and placed it around her own.

~ ~ ~

Then A'isha carefully removed the index finger from the right hand of her victim. She squeezed out any blood and placed the cleaned finger in a tissue in her purse. Her plan of entry to the White House was on schedule.

~ ~ ~

July 2, 2005

President Reston sat at his desk in the Oval Office reading briefing reports from intelligence agencies. They were too vague and general to be helpful.

Career ambitions had a way of eliminating those willing to offer firm opinions. He did have a brief memo on his desk from the Director of the CIA. The memo was short and to the point. It said his top analyst by the name of Jackson was confident that the country faced extreme danger from an imminent attack.

Jackson emphasized that the President himself was in grave danger from an unidentified foreign agent. Agent Jackson admitted he did not have evidence, just his own intuitions. However, he'd put his career on the line to warn the President.

This was the second time President Reston had heard of this Jackson. President Reston was impressed with the candor of this man. Here was a man willing "to stand in the gap" like the biblical

Nehemiah to warn and defend his country. As a solid Christian, President Reston admired a man with strong beliefs and firm opinions. He wondered if this memo might be another sign from God.

President Reston also felt growing concern that America was facing a strong, determined individual. Like Jackson he had no firm evidence. He'd been having nightmares. He made a note to have Jackson present during tomorrow's joint statement between himself and the Israeli Premier Berstein. He would like to speak to him. That joint statement would be tomorrow at 2:00 p.m.

President Reston realized terrorism was on the increase and the military found it difficult to defeat a force not operating like a normal army. Terrorism involved small groups. Often terrorism was possible with just one determined individual. It seemed impossible to prevent attacks from such a fluid enemy.

The United States and Christianity had clever and determined enemies. The Devil's hand-controlled marionettes of his bidding.

President Reston felt confused. He was having an unusually hard time concentrating. He also had a vague sense of falling. He had to get a grip on himself. This job could be unbearable.

Perspiring heavily, he removed his jacket. His sense of being overheated also seemed unusual. The White House air conditioning was usually good.

He realized with dread that he might be coming down with a cold or a fever. Being ill was never convenient for a President. He rose from his desk and checked the wall thermometer which showed the room to be a cool 68 degrees Fahrenheit.

He then realized that he wasn't alone. A large black man seemed to be checking all of the electrical systems for the upcoming Oval Office speech. He'd seen him before, the man responsible for the White House physical plant. He even worked in the background during various meetings.

President Reston realized that he didn't know the black man's name. He knew that everyone called him "Melon" and somehow that did not seem like a good thing to call a man. Nevertheless, he had to ask the employee a question and after all he was the President of the United States. "Melon, does everything look good for the speech tomorrow?"

The black man paused for a second and replied in a slow voice, "Yes, Mr. President, everything looks fine for tomorrow."

"Is the air conditioning working? I seem to be too warm today."

"Everything is running perfectly, Mr. President. I will check the controls again. Perhaps you're catching a fever."

"Yes, thank you. Maybe it is just in my head," replied the President with forced effort.

Ellis nodded as he left the Oval Office. A'isha had called it right. The virus would strike all humans equally. Everyone from the lowest to the highest would die. Flash Fire was the only thing that he had known to be absolutely fair. He also knew that after tomorrow no one would ever call him "Melon" again.

Chapter Thirty-Six

July 9, 2005

A'isha led her two companions in the morning prayers of Islam. Today was their day of martyrdom. Each of the three accepted their duty with quiet courage as they reconfirmed their commitment to Allah.

A'isha would be careful to wear her hair in a net as Maria had. She knew she would blend in surprisingly well with the other White House laborers. She'd look Latina. She was careful to select clothes commonly worn by domestics.

A'isha had been careful to select clothing a size too large, so she had greater physical mobility. She might kill several men today, and every detail counted.

Allison had no problem pulling strings from her old friends to obtain a reporter pass for the Oval Office. For Ellis this was a satisfying day. Allah had selected him to destroy this nation of infidels. No one would ever call him Melon again.

Everyone knew they'd be exposed to Flash-Fire. The pump that bought them time was turned off. Each of them would be dead before Flash Fire symptoms began to appear.

Allison felt as light-hearted as a teenager in love. Finally, she would be able to rejoin the man she loved. Today, his murder will be avenged. The false god of Christianity would be confronted by Allah. The match would be over in a second. Allah was the true God, and the world would see that the false god of the Christians did not protect those followers. These infidels would be destroyed. They'd learn the meaning of the simple Islamic statement of faith: "I believe in the one God Allah and Mohammed is his Prophet."

She knew without United States support Israel couldn't survive. Never again could Israeli's murder Palestinian children with impunity. Never again would another Arab home be bull-dozed into dust to make room for Israeli settlements. Muslims would soon raise the flag of Islam over all the earth.

A'isha remained calm. She reviewed the simplicity of her plan of operation. She'd learned that the best plans were those simple enough to be understood by a child. A'isha prayed she would not fail. A'isha felt confident. She'd trained for this day for years.

Once inside the White House, Ellis and A'isha would time their assault by the clock, each minute strictly choreographed. Once they were in the lovers' hallway they'd know the time to enter the Oval Office. Allah would help them overcome any problems.

~ ~ ~

July 9, 2005

White House

Washington D.C.

8:00 a.m.

A'isha joined the slow-moving line that formed part of the normal workday for the White House custodial staff. It took several hundred people to keep the White House functioning properly. Each employee had to file pass Ellis while he matched the face with the face on the required identification card and scanned the card to obtain the worker's identity. A'isha used the detached finger of her victim and passed the print scanner with no problem.

She was treated like any other person in that long line. After she had passed this point she allowed herself a feeling of satisfaction. She stood in the fortress of her enemy. This very day the world would see and know the power of Allah.

Once inside of the immense building she was escorted by Ellis to his small office. He was organized and everything seemed to be in its proper place. He kept a large map of the White House on his office wall, and he gave her a brief description of the general layout of the vast building. He showed A'isha the computer station that controlled all the electrical service in the building.

Today was an unusual day because the President would be speaking to the nation concerning the relationship between the United States and the State of Israel.

Due to these circumstances Ellis felt it would be best if she stayed in his office until about 1:00 p.m. Ellis explained that by 1:00 p.m.

all the important people would be in place. This would lull possible listeners.

Ellis said that for a few days she would be his personal assistant until she was familiar with her new duties. He explained she could help him with a last-minute check of the restroom that was only used by important people. Ellis left her alone as he went about his daily routine. The last day of his life would begin with a long morning.

~   ~   ~

July 9, 2005

Oval Office

1:30 p.m.

This was the last place in the world that Jackson wanted to be. He had been told by the Director that the President wanted him to be in the Oval Office while he addressed the nation. The President wanted to speak to him for a few minutes about his concerns about National and Presidential security. This would occur after the televised event.

Jackson hated being in groups of people under any circumstances and today was even worse. He felt miserable. Whatever bug he'd picked up was really hurting his body. He had already thrown up this morning and had a throbbing headache.

He knew he needed medical attention. After the briefing he'd check into an emergency room. He'd never felt so sick in his life. Nauseated, he could vomit at any time.

Nevertheless, one did not refuse the request of the most powerful man in the world. So here he stood on the edge of the reporter group.

He sensed an overwhelming danger. He had heard her voice several times today and feared losing his mind.

The message was the same; "Repent, Jackson, before it is too late. You are dying. Soon you will not be able to accept Allah. Your soul will be lost in hell forever. Accept Allah's grace. Let us spend eternity in the gardens of Paradise. Let us have in Paradise what we did not have on earth. Very soon, you will need to decide. Very soon you will see me."

"I will soon leave this sorrowful world and recline in the gardens of bliss that are promised to the followers of the Prophet."

"We have similar minds. It will be tragic if we are not united in a heavenly world. Decide."

Jackson closed his eyes and tried to get a grip on his mind. He felt so close to this person. She was in this building. He was certain but how could he explain this danger? His world was spinning even with his eyes tightly closed. He thought, it's not unusual for people to hear voices when under great stress. A trip to the doc should set things right.

He found a chair in a corner and sat, feeling so sick he would have been delighted to be ejected from this room. He looked at his watch; nearly 1:00 p.m.

He heard a rustle through the room. Four security men came in the room and carefully checked the identifications of all present. Jackson could barely show the men his card and hold his head up. One of the security team looked at Jackson and said, "You don't look too good."

"I don't feel too good, either" Jackson replied. The guard walked on without another word.

CHAPTER THIRTY-SEVEN

White House

Washington D.C.

2:00 p.m.

Ellis returned to his office to find A'isha waiting. She looked deeply into his eyes and asked, "It's time. Is it not?" Ellis handed A'isha her preplaced dagger.

"Yes, let's get the cart and check the private restroom."

He could not remember when he'd felt so calm and happy. He'd lived long enough. The days of being "Melon" were over. Today he was a warrior of Allah.

A'isha smiled softly, "You're right. We have cleaning to do." Ellis led the way to the cleaning cart which had a flat top and a bottom shelf. Ellis spread a sheet over the top and A'isha slipped under it. The plan involved making it past the first two guards without incident. With luck it might be possible to get by the last two the same way. None of them had ever inspected his cleaning carts before. However, at the first sign of trouble Ellis stood ready.

He held a remote control in his hand that could turn off lights to any part of the White House. It was programmed for the outer hallway, the inner hallway of the restroom, and finally the Oval Office. It would take only a minute or two to be at the first guard station.

Hidden under the sheet A'isha felt the peace of Allah pass over her.

Ellis pushed the cart slowly as he had on thousands of days. It was only a short way to the first corridor. Ellis closed the gap with his normal pace. When he was abreast of the first two guards he said, "Excuse me men, I'm to make sure the VIP bathroom is still spick and span. I guess some big wigs are going to be here today."

"Melon, you're behind the information wave today. The President and the Israeli Prime Minster are both making speeches," said the older guard.

"Well, I'm not paid to know who's here. I'm paid to make sure that the restroom is clean," Ellis said.

"Go ahead and do your job. In a couple of hours, it will all be over," said the senior guard with some irritation.

The junior of the two guards opened the door for the cart and closed it when the cart went through. Ellis and A'isha were past the first two guards with no trouble. *Two guards down and two to go.*

A'isha remained like a tightly coiled spring. The guards were posted one on each side by the door. A'isha could feel tension in the air. Ellis pushed his cart right up to the door opening. "I need to check the restroom for cleanliness. I guess there are some important people expected today," said Ellis. The senior guard replied in an even tone, "Our orders are that no one enters this restroom except the VIPs in the building."

Ellis responded in a quiet tone, "I have been told by White House officials that I am to make sure everything is neat in the restroom because it's likely to be needed today."

The senior guard thought about that for a few seconds. "I know who you are. Everyone calls you Melon and you're the head of maintenance. But I have my orders."

"All I have to do is check to see if everything is all right and do some minor cleaning." said Ellis with some concern.

The senior guard seemed at a loss. If the bathroom was not in perfect working order he might get in trouble because he refused the maintenance man. On the other hand, he had orders to admit no one. This was the worst kind of decision. "What do you have on your cart Melon?" asked the guard. Ellis kept his voice level and said, "just cleaning supplies and that sort of thing; nothing that I don't have with me every day."

"Melon, I got to follow the rules and inspect your cart. I know it's stupid but them's the rules." The guard started to bend over to open the sheet when Ellis pushed the button which placed the hallway in total darkness. The guard started to say, "What the hell…" but he never got a chance to finish. A'isha pulled the guard, unable to see in the dark, toward her and her blade pierced his larynx, then ripped out the side of his neck, severing his jugular.

The second guard was trying to bring his weapon into action, but he couldn't see in the sudden loss of light. A'isha crushed his larynx with the edge of her left hand. In a split second she grabbed the back of his head and plunged her knife into his throat. With a quick ripping movement, she tore the blade out the right side of his neck leaving both guards down in three seconds.

"Quick, Ellis, help me pull these bodies into the bathroom. Then we must clean up the blood as fast as possible. That way other guards might assume that they were called from their station for another purpose."

Ellis and A'isha quickly dragged the bodies into the room. After the killings A'isha once again felt the waves of exquisite pleasure sweep over her body. She closed her eyes and rode this ecstasy until it faded away. She silently thanked Allah for the kills, and this blessing. This was a precious gift she did not deserve.

~ ~ ~

She then turned to help Ellis. Ellis wiped up the blood then used his master lock on the bathroom door from the inside. That would give them protection in the lover's hallway.

~ ~ ~

White House

Hidden Passageway

2:15 p.m.

A'isha quickly stripped her American clothes off and slipped into the pre-placed dark peasant garb that Najib sent her. She let down and brushed her hair. She wanted to die as a member of her own social class. A'isha smiled and motioned to the end of the corridor.

"It's time," she whispered. They gathered the pre-placed weapons hidden in the secret hallway. In moments A'isha and Ellis were behind the hidden door listening to the conversation inside. The President and Berstein were expected to walk in at any moment.

Ellis seemed to draw from A'isha's absolute calm. She seemed in control of her emotions. Now that the hour was upon them she maintained even more serenity.

There was a low drone of voices in the Oval Office.

There would be absolute silence when guards entered and secured the room.

After the guards were satisfied then the President and Berstein would enter. A'isha wanted to wait until the President began to speak to the nation. That would mean that the television equipment was in order and that the images were appearing all over the world.

At that point A'isha would tell Ellis to turn off the Oval Office lights. It would take only a second to break the thin plaster that covered the concealed door. Once in the darkened room Ellis would turn the lights on again. Ellis was to kill the guards to the left of the President. A'isha was assigned to kill the guards to his right.

All was in the hands of Allah. Then A'isha was expected to speak to the United States and the rest of the viewing world. Allah's would give her the words to say. A'isha accepted that assurance without question. She heard the low sounds of people speaking cease.

A'isha heard the guards' footsteps as they entered the Oval Office and walked around the room inspecting press and other passes. The guards then waited for the President and Berstein as they approached the President's desk.

There was a flurry of sounds from the television crew. A'isha could envision the head of the camera crew getting ready to give the President the signal as to when he was "on live." A'isha knew the time for action approached.

Oval Office of the White House

President Reston had suffered since dawn. He felt terrible. His body ached with exhaustion and bouts of intense perspiration. He'd vomited twice. He ran a high fever and had consulted the White House doctors.

They insisted he should be hospitalized. He agreed to go after finishing his joint speech with Premier Berstein who commented on the President's appearance and the President responded he was going to the hospital after this speech was over.

In fact, Berstein himself was not feeling well. His health had been declining with age. No longer was he the trim tank commander who helped turn the tide during the Jewish/Arab wars. Growing obesity compounded his ability to function.

Now he felt total exhaustion. Moving his ponderous mass was tiring on a normal day but for the last couple of days he'd felt a deep illness enter his aching body. His last stool was dark and he was suffering from rectal bleeding. He hadn't mentioned that to anyone. He didn't trust American doctors.

After this speech he would be talking to the Israeli physicians. The two world leaders agreed to keep their joint statements brief. This was only a repeat of the standard American/Jewish alliance.

Oval Office
Washington D.C.
2:30 p.m.

A'isha heard the President begin to speak to listeners worldwide. She concentrated on getting Ellis in position to push the hidden door open. He placed his strong left shoulder against the door and A'isha made sure the safety was off on his Scorpion. A'isha double checked her own weapon and the spare pistol for Allison. The President's guards had to be eliminated almost instantly.

A'isha whispered into his ear, "When I take my hand off your shoulder hit the lights and push the door open."

Ellis was calm. A'isha could still hear the President talking when she removed her hand. Ellis hit his remote lighting control and pushed the secret door open with little effort. When the lights went out Allison locked the main doors with her necklace and moved to the edge of the crowd. No one could part the necklace without major mechanical effort.

The President was attempting to reassure everyone in the room when the lights suddenly came on. In that moment A'isha and Ellis opened fire. The sound of the firing Scorpions sounded like cotton ripping. Ellis killed the two guards that he'd been assigned in less than a second. The speed of his weapon and his unfamiliarity with it had caused some overspray and at least a half a dozen reporters in the room were either killed or wounded.

A'isha had been even faster, and her guards lacked even time to turn around before she cut them down. Berstein the old soldier tried to escape by running into the crowd to get other people between him and the killers. A'isha calmly shot through the wall of bewildered people until all who were between her and Berstein were dead. At least six reporters died.

Berstein the old survivor had made it to the double doors only to realize they were locked. A'isha cut him down with professional short bursts from her weapon.

"So dies the mass murderer of many Arabs in Palestine," she said in a voice that carried over the entire room.

President Reston was reaching for one of the drawers of his desk. Inside it was a 45 Colt 1911 pistol that had been part of the Oval Office since the days of President Eisenhower. The former General Eisenhower had carried the pistol in World War II. The President had not even touched the drawer before A'isha pointed her Scorpion at his chest and said, "Mr. President, things will not be so easy; your life is now in the hands of Allah."

Panicking survivors in the office screamed. A'isha took control. With a strangely calm but clear voice she said, "Be silent or I will kill you one at a time." There was something in the tone of her voice that commanded obedience.

"You will all be freed after I have fulfilled my duty. Be calm and each of the unwounded will walk out of these doors unharmed."

~ ~ ~

What was once a mob was transformed into a silent, sullen group. The television cameras continued broadcasting the scene. A'isha gave the spare pistol to Allison. Since the television operations were on the sides of the crowd they escaped the deadly fire.

A'isha's voice was steady. "Ellis, secure the main doors with your chain and lock," Ellis performed this operation quickly. With the closing of that lock the world knew that the President of the United States was being held by a terrorist.

CHAPTER THIRTY-EIGHT

Oval Office

Washington D.C.

Jackson sat in shock, too weak to leave his chair. Out of twenty-five reporters at least twelve lay dead and five others wounded. He had been on the edge of the crowd of twenty-five when the shooting started, the reason he was alive.

He knew that the terrorist dressed in Muslim garb was the woman of his nightmares. She moved with calm grace through the dead and wounded. Each of the wounded were examined by the black apparition and calmly executed. The room, its floor soaked and slippery with blood, resembled a slaughterhouse.

Everything had happened so fast that it was difficult to comprehend. Jackson was unarmed. Only field agents were permitted to have weapons and he'd never been exposed to firearms. The woman occasionally stopped and spoke words of reassurance to survivors on the edge of hysteria.

Jackson knew the nation and the world would be enthralled with this life and death drama. The Arab woman then paused for a moment as if she had heard a distant voice. She turned, searching.

She paused at Jackson and looked deeply into his eyes. Jackson sensed her communicating with him.

Her probing mental fingers were gentle as a lover's hands. She smiled as if recognizing an old friend. "So, you are Jackson." He'd never seen such a beautiful woman. Her black hair nearly glowed in the light. Her eyes were dark and had a magnetism that drew him toward her.

There was a royal grace to her movements. She seemed calm. He felt helpless, trapped by her power. She quickly walked to his side and spoke softly. "Listen to me carefully Jackson, you have little time to decide. Allah has spared your life and placed you here for your decision. Your decision will determine your eternal fate."

Her eyes were gentle and seducing, "Do not die with the unbelievers. Join me in Paradise where we may have each other for eternity. All the love that we never had in this life will be replaced by endless companionship and sensual pleasures. The choice is yours." With those words she turned and walked to the President.

"Raise your arms over your head Mr. President," she said. The President hesitated and began to object, "How could you do this? You're Mary Morton, a good woman."

A'isha cut him off. "My name is A'isha and if you resist in any manner I will kill you with no hesitation. You ordered the murders of thousands of Arabs. Your own deeds brought you to this point. Study the dead lying here. Do you imagine I would hesitate to assassinate you?"

The President slowly raised his hands.

"Allison, will you come and assist?" Allison looked wan but moved to A'isha's side. "Lean forward Mr. President, this will not take long.," Carefully and methodically A'isha taped a Claymore mine to the President's back. A'isha then took her place directly behind him.

She held a small metallic device for the camera's lens. "This is a friction fuse for this Claymore mine. I am now going to screw it into the mine strapped to the President's back." She performed that task in just a few seconds. Then she showed the camera a length of light cable about 12 inches long. She snapped one end onto the fuse of the mine and the other end was snapped to a narrow strap at her wrist.

She spoke. "If I fall for any reason this will be the end of Mr. Reston. I have a few things to say to United States citizens and to the world at large. My words will be few before I meet my Creator."

Secret Service

Camp David

George Watson was the well-known and well-feared head of the United States Secret Service. He'd been ruthless in career climbing and he was so now with his underlings. Watson demanded excellence. Any mistake by an agent was immediate termination of employment. No one from the highest to the lowest was exempt. The Secret Service's mission was to protect the most important man in the world, the President of the United States. Watson did not take that charge lightly.

There had been embarrassing lapses of security before his time and Watson was adamant that nothing would go wrong under his watch. Like others, he had been watching the joint address of the two Heads of State.

When the lights came on unknown terrorists were killing people in the Oval Office. Premier Stein was cut down in a matter of only seconds.

This was when pre-training and pre-planning came in. Watson picked up the red phone on his desk and said, "Shark Attack." With those two words the entire might of the nation's forces knew the President's life was endangered. All the intelligence agencies and all the military forces knew exactly what to do. Within seconds the country was under the command of the Vice-President. All sectors communicated through a buried fiber system designed to assure communication even from a nuclear attack.

~ ~ ~

In moments, a squadron of F-16's was in the air from the nearby Marine Base at Quantico. All United States military units worldwide went on Condition Two. This meant war was imminent. Across the entire United States thousands of military personnel were scrambling to be ready to fight. The gun was cocked, and a finger was on the trigger. Hundreds of nuclear missiles were poised to hit any location in the world. Anything could happen at this point.

The Vice-President had full powers to make decisions for the United States. This was called the Vortex Decision. The "Vortex Decision" came into play if the President no longer had freedom of action. This transfer of power took only moments, and the Vice-President was picked up at his stand-by station at Camp David.

Within minutes the Vice President was flying directly to Cheyenne Mountain in southern Colorado. It was here in Cheyenne Mountain that the most advanced communication system in the world was in place. Cheyenne Mountain had been designed by experts who believed in Armageddon.

Air Force One had been designed as a flying communication system. The power of total destruction now rested in the Vice President's hands.

Vice President Thomas Sanders was the favored son of a wealthy political California family. Everything that could be bought with money had always been obtainable. He was intelligent and ambitious. He'd been accepted to Harvard University based on his own merits. His SAT scores placed him in the top one percent. He'd graduated with honors in International Affairs and Political History

He knew he was smarter than the President. His quest to become President himself might be close to becoming real. This act of terrorism could seal the President's fate. He realized instantly this attack on the White House was bold and well executed. Sanders took control of the United States government with confidence and precision.

He ordered a complete Army division from Fort Mead to surround Washington D.C. No one was to enter or to leave the metropolitan area. He ordered a regiment of battle-ready Marines from Camp Quantico to surround the White House. In addition, the top-secret Delta assault team was deployed from Fort Benning, Georgia, for an assault on the White House.

Sanders felt comfortable holding the reins of power and the feeling of absolute power grew with each second. At last, he could bend the world to his will. It felt intoxicating. The most powerful military machine in the world was warming up the engines that could carry death anywhere in the world.

He'd been chosen as the Vice-Presidential candidate because Reston needed the 55 electoral votes that California could deliver. Sanders promised to deliver those critical votes and delivered as promised.

~ ~ ~

Such a victory was shallow for a man like Sanders. He had no real function in White House power and once Reston won the Presidency he paid little attention to his Vice-President. Such treatment toward an ambitious man could be dangerous. Thomas Sanders had considered every option to assume the Presidency, but he hadn't expected this.

A mine was now strapped to President Reston's back. The mine was also attached to a self-possessed female terrorist. If she fell or pulled more than a few inches President Reston would die.

Thus only a few inches stood between him and the Presidency. Sanders lusted for that power. He wanted to own the complete fruit tree rather enjoy a succulent bite now and then.

~ ~ ~

As they flew toward Cheyenne Mountain the acting President noted that a phalanx of F-16 fighter planes surrounded his personal plane. If a missile were fired at him each pilot was ordered to fly directly into the missile as a case of self-sacrifice for the President of the United States. Such power could not be described; it had to be felt to be understood.

Sanders felt the power coursing through his veins, and he wanted to hold it. He leaned back in his leather seat and watched the deadly drama being televised to the entire world.

He ordered that everything known about the three terrorists be on his desk as soon as possible after landing. He'd find a way for the black-haired witch to pull the friction fuse. Then the Presidency would be his. All outward appearances pointed to a respectful Vice President doing everything to save the President. The internal truth was different.

Sanders intended to make sure President Reston died. Unfortunately, at this precise moment Sanders was not feeling well. He'd vomited early that morning at Camp David. Now he had a fever. He had to conceal these symptoms until his takeover of political power was complete. It would not do to show weakness.

He felt certain it was a minor bug and he'd feel better as the day progressed. The newly empowered Sanders was on the top of his world, Yet Flash Fire had begun destroying the cells that supported his life.

He was dying.

A'isha now had complete control of the Oval Office. She felt calm in the hands of Allah. Soon she would die. Like a traveler who had struggled on foot through a long, cold blizzard she could see the distant lights of home.

~ ~ ~

Oval Office

A'isha stood behind President Reston as she faced the television cameras. She slid the hood from her head and now the world could see this fighter's face. It was a beautiful face, composed and relaxed. Light seemed to give her a faint glow. Her skin was flawless and projected a soft olive hue. Her long black hair accented her face.

When she moved it was with the grace of the killing cats of Africa. Her flowing black garb could not conceal the beautiful female form hidden from human eyes. It was her eyes that commanded attention. At times, the eyes would project great mystery and a quiet dignity. At other times, the eyes would smolder like coals in a fire.

She began to speak. She wanted the entire world to catch and understand her every word. "The woman on my left is Allison Browning. She was asked to leave her journalistic job because the owners of that paper disapproved of her writing on the plight of Palestine. On my right is Ellis Proctor the man responsible for the physical plant of the White House. He could not worship Allah openly in this country and retain his employment."

"My name is A'isha. I was only a simple Arab girl when U.S. bombs murdered my entire family. My father, my mother, and all five of my siblings were murdered at the orders of the United States. The country of my birth does not matter. A multitude of simple Arabs throughout the lands of Allah have been murdered by the United States. Unfortunately, my story is nothing new."

"It is a story that could be told by thousands of children whose parents were murdered by the force of the United States Government. All three of us are Muslims who have been selected by

Allah to be here on this day. Allison, Ellis, and I are going to die today, and our deaths will only be the beginning."

CHAPTER THIRTY-NINE

"The United States as a world power is finished. In a matter of days Allah will sweep the United States from the table of international events. Never again shall this arrogant America meddle with impunity in the affairs of other nations."

"The human remnants who survive will be objects of ridicule to the strong and of pity to those of a kinder nature. The United States will be the land of the dead within days."

"Your Christian god will not save you. There is only one God and His name is Allah. The Christian abomination of a divided godhead will be shown the reality of Allah's wrath."

"The fable that God could be born of a woman and die the death of a mortal man will be shown as false. Allah is not a human who can be born and then must die. Such a thought is an abomination. Allah is forever. Never has he been born and never will he die. I have spoken directly to Allah, and he has guided my path here to this location."

"A peasant girl and two simple believers were led by Allah to this place of sin where I speak to you. Perhaps the United States should have pondered on other matters then killing the innocent in Arab lands."

Cheyenne Mountain

Central Command Station of the combined Armed Forces.

Thomas Sanders was in control.

"All right, I want some answers," Sanders, his voice already Presidential. His eyes were on the oversized television monitor that showed the actions of the Oval Office terrorists. Analysts were taping every word, and each was being studied by major Arabic scholars in the United States.

"Who is this black-haired witch and who are her associates? What is their power and whom do they serve?" Sanders pursued his questions.

The FBI Director spoke first. "Allison Browning is a well-known retired journalist and Ellis Procter is in fact the man in charge of the physical plant of the White house. Browning was a known Muslim but viewed as tolerant. Procter was never known as a Muslim. Agents are gathering what they can on all three."

"Who is the Arab woman who seems to control this operation?"

The CIA Director answered with reluctance, "We have absolutely no idea who she is or what group she associates with. No one has heard of this A'isha.

The new President to all intents and purposes took this in. "You mean no one knows the identity of a woman who penetrated the White House, strapped a bomb to the back of our President, and claimed that the United States is going to be destroyed?"

"So far that's true. We're offering millions of dollars for fast answers and so far there is nothing about an A'isha."

"Okay talk to me about their capacities," asked the Acting President.

The FBI Director gave his opinion, "The terrorists have Scorpion machine pistols and some anti-personal mines. Beyond that, no other weapons have been sighted, sir."

"What's the status of closing off the D.C. city limits?" asked Sanders.

"Units are being deployed as we speak. The Army reports that complete encirclement of Washington D.C. will be accomplished in three hours. The Marines moved fastest and are presently surrounding the White House from a radius of 250 yards."

"Workers and White House staff are attempting to escape through every door and window. Each person is searched by capital and city police and placed behind bars until we can sort out the guilty from the innocent. How long will it take to get the Delta team in place for an assault, if an assault is deemed feasible and necessary?"

~ ~ ~

"The Delta team will be in place within an hour. They're the finest two-hundred-man assault group on earth."

"It would appear we are in a holding pattern until the Delta team can get here unless you give orders for the Marines to assault the White House. The terrorists can't escape." the FBI Director said.

~ ~ ~

A'isha in the Oval Office

The Arab woman seemed to contradict her bloody attack. Hers didn't seem to be the face of a hardened killer. She was once again wearing the expression of an innocent young girl. She seemed happy, almost radiant.

She began to speak, "I was a simple peasant. There was a time I dreamed of a husband and family of my own. Like many young girls I had no idea of the evil that lives on the earth."

"I had no idea that ordinary people could be killed merely to make a political statement. My father was a street merchant and my mother a devoted homemaker. My sisters were just children when bombs made in the United States murdered them all. Through the grace of Allah, I survived. Allah elected to use a young peasant girl as His tool to destroy this bloated, arrogant empire."

"I never dreamed I would be awarded this task. I never imagined that Allah would select me to accomplish his revenge. I tried to explain to Allah that I was nothing. I was only a girl and knew nothing about war. I had neither wealth nor power. Allah explained to me that my weakness would show the world that only Allah has total power."

"The United States in their pride and foolishness believed they had the right to rule Islamic countries. Time after time the United States interfered into the business of sovereign nations. Borders mean nothing to this mad colossus, the United States."

"As an Arab woman who is going to die today I ask why your government felt they have the right to decide how another country conducts its own affairs? Would you Americans be pleased if a foreign power meddled in the affairs of your country? You would feel oppressed and outraged."

"To the United States I say your day in the sun is over. Your name will be remembered by the rest of the world with fear and horror. You thought your military machine could intimidate Muslims. Such an evil philosophy deserves an answer. Listen to the words of Allah. The wheel of destiny has turned."

"The United States will join that long list of empires that have disappeared into the sands of history. Your military will be helpless to save you. Your science and technology won't save you either. Your aggression and sins have destroyed you."

"You sealed your fate when you began to oppress, murder, and exploit the believers of Allah. Many of these decisions were made here in the Oval Office of the White House."

"You forgot that Allah can open any door. Not a single word or thought goes unrecorded. Allah watched as the Western powers divided the lands of the Arab people. This was an abomination to Allah and all true believers. True Muslims know all Muslims are one people, with one faith, and with one Prophet. There is only one God and Allah is his name."

"The United States purposely corrupted Arab leaders to gain access to resources that belong to all Muslims. Allah did not give wealth to just the opulent Arab elite who put on a pious face before they leave to seek the whores of Europe."

"I tell you such games are over. The United States will fall, and the false Arab rulers will meet their well-deserved deaths. I swear in the name of Allah that dogs will feast on their bloated bodies."

"Now it is Americans who will feel the anguish of mass death that does not spare the lowest to the highest. And yet Allah in his mercy has allowed enough time for the dying to repent and turn to Him. I encourage each of you to save your soul before you stand alone before Allah."

Cheyenne Mountain

Central Command

Acting President Sanders addressed the group gathered around the television screen. He began speaking, "What is your take on this woman? Let's narrow this down. What country is she from? What do our medical experts think of her? I'm concerned that she seems so sure of herself. It's clear she's an Islamic fanatic, but I'm not so sure she's bluffing."

"Give me facts so that we can plan our response and save President Reston." Sanders felt satisfied with this political setting. He was projecting a calm, logical, and concerned voice to the whole group. It was crucial to appear to be a team player willing to listen to the experts around him.

Of course, the Arab woman was a complete nut case. He felt it should be easy to push her over the edge. Only a few inches of slack stood between him and presidential power.

The FBI Director spoke first, "She speaks of being a victim of United States bombs. Our weapons have been used nearly everywhere in the Middle East. She could be Palestinian. We've provided Israel with plenty of bombs over the years. The United States and Israel have bombed many countries: Syria, Lebanon, Iraq, and Iran, to name just a few. Israel has a history of killing its enemies everywhere."

"She might very well be a Kurd. I doubt if she's Egyptian or a Saudi. We have controlled both Egypt and Saudi Arabia from behind the scenes for many years."

"There are many Muslim nations that she could be from. We're the largest arms seller in the world, and many of those weapons end up going to the Middle East."

The President turned to the Director of the CIA and said, "What do you think? We must respond and need to know where to do it. American citizens and the world will expect retaliation. We better get the address of the right enemy."

The CIA stated, "I must agree with the FBI position. She could be from nearly anywhere in the Arab world. My gut feeling is that she's Iraqi. We dropped over 100,000 tons of bombs there and most fell randomly. Nevertheless, we've also penetrated every known intelligence agency in the Mideast."

"My agents are coming up empty. That can only mean she is a singular student of someone with expertise in terrorism. There are many wealthy Arabs who might have provided the money and training for such a creature. She could be sponsored by any Arab government but that would be difficult. Every government is riddled with spies under many flags."

Sanders took in the information, "I want Israel on the line. It's unlikely she'll stand still after seeing her Premier cut down by terrorism. Tactfully inform them that all foreign aid to their country will cease if they go off half-cocked. We must think our way out of this one and respond against the right parties."

In the Oval Office A'isha continued to speak, "It is not hard to understand why our Arab world can't allow the United States to exist. We don't want your materialist culture, or your form of government which is for sale to the highest bidder. We do not want your false religion."

"We want to be left alone to forge our own destinies using the tools of our own culture. The United States won't allow the Arabs this right. The days of the United States threatening Muslims are finished. Through Allah's power the United States will be destroyed. Within days only feral dogs will roam the streets of every major American city. The birds of the air will fatten on the flesh of those who believed themselves invincible.

The United States will be removed from the lists of the living."

CHAPTER FORTY

Acting President Sanders
Cheyenne Mountain

Acting President Sanders watched the giant screen with close attention. The woman keeping calm and focused seemed a bad sign. This serene terrorist appeared too confident. To imagine she could destroy a country such as the United States was utter fantasy.

Yet, he sensed that tragedies of considerable magnitude were in the offing. He turned to his team of advisors and posed hard questions.

"What does she have for weaponry that makes this woman so sure of herself?"

The head of the CIA spoke first. "It's not possible that she can fulfill her threats. Maybe she imagines Allah will swoop down like an avenging angel. A nuclear bomb would be horrible, but that weapon would have only local effects, at least in the beginning. Chemical warfare is not likely because it's so difficult to control, and chemical attacks would also be local."

"Biological warfare is the wild card. Our scientists insist that biological weapons are delicate, typically weakened by sunlight and/or other effects of weather. Our own experience with biological weapons has proved inconclusive. U.S. scientists believe any biological agent would be detected quickly and most of the population saved."

The acting President turned to the FBI Director. "What are our doctors coming up with as far as the mental state of these terrorists?"

"From what we've seen the older man and woman are simply followers. However, our people are quite concerned with the Arab woman. Her absolute conviction and calm are reasons for concern. Our medical experts feel there will be no negotiating with this A'isha."

"They conclude that she's clinically insane. She's absolutely of the belief that she will destroy the United States. If what she is saying is true, we'd be facing massive losses."

The acting President listened with cool poise. He leaned back in his chair and said, "So we're facing a tricky situation. I find it difficult to believe this young woman has the power to destroy us. The United States is huge. Even a regional disaster would only affect part of the country. I'm skeptical. How is she going to achieve her threats?"

The dark Arab woman on the large television screen began to speak again. "I warn governmental authorities of the rest of the world to close your borders to all international travel immediately. Furthermore, all persons who entered your country within the last four days by air, boat, or land must be quarantined for a minimum of six weeks. They are marked for death and are infectious."

"The United States is being destroyed by a new genetically engineered virus called 'Flash Fire' and there is literally nothing able to stop this disease. The virus was released around 50 major American cities three days ago and has shown itself to be incredibly virulent. It's spreading with every human contact."

"The victim shows no discomfort for two to three days. Due to the density of people and movement of material nearly everyone hearing my voice will be dead within the next seven days. Science cannot save you. Few of my listeners will live much longer."

"Within three to four days people will be dying by the tens of millions per day. Within ten days nearly all the American population will be dead."

"The virus is genetically designed to burn itself out in approximately two to three weeks. The flame of Allah will be searing. Yet due to His mercy it will be relatively short."

"I urge all people to accept Allah's invitation to join Him in paradise. Allah in his kindness has given you an opportunity to accept Him and save your souls. To be saved before Allah is a simple matter. Merely repeat the holy words, 'There is no God but Allah, and Muhammad is his prophet' no other statement or action is required. You then have Allah's promise that you shall be saved. Allah in his great kindness does not make salvation a difficult task."

Her audience froze into silence expecting to awake from their nightmare. Jackson knew immediately that the words the young Arab woman had spoken were true. Years of study had convinced him this type of attack was inevitable. There was nothing he could do. He realized why he felt so dreadfully ill. Marked for death, he doubted he'd see next morning's light.

A'isha began to speak, "Ellis, please unlock the door so that all these people except the television crew can leave."

Ellis walked to the door and removed the locks. He opened it saying, "You may all leave and return to your families. Take the kindness of Allah and obtain your salvation." All walked out of the room in silence, stunned beyond rational thought.

A'isha hadn't moved from behind President Reston. The television crew and Jackson remained. He was too ill to move. Jackson realized that he was irrevocably attracted to this strange Arab woman. She seemed so sure in her faith and her actions. He had never seen a woman so beautiful and so committed.

He had searched for her so that she would be destroyed and now he realized he wished she could live. But, even in his feverish haze he realized she would be dead shortly.

A'isha spoke again. "There is very little left that needs to be said. This is the time of death and death waits to carry my soul." Then A'isha paused for a moment as if she had heard a distant voice. Her eyes turned cold. She seemed to be looking into unknown depths.

She began to speak in a voice laced with malice, "I see you clearly Mr. Thomas Sanders. You are the acting President of the United States. You have lusted and plotted for the death of this infidel known as President Reston so you can assume the power you feel you deserve. Your heart is hoping that I will kill this man so that you can have what you want: presidential power."

She unclipped the friction fuse from her belt. No connection remained between A'isha and President Reston. "Mr. Thomas, I can sense your anger rising because you fear your ultimate prize may evade you."

Suddenly there was a flashing movement that was nearly impossible for the eye to detect. President Reston slumped, and the world watched in horror as the Arab woman withdrew her dagger from the President's body. "Thus dies the killer of tens of thousands of Arabs including my family."

"All that remains for Allison, Ellis, and me is to show the world how the martyrs of Allah die." The now familiar physical warmth passed over her. More intense but shorter. In a few seconds she resumed control.

"Mr. Sanders, you have what you have wanted most of all. You are the President of the dying United States. Within three days you will be dead. Enjoy your time of supremacy." She turned to the television crews and said to them, "Repent and turn to Allah. Your role is finished. You may leave." The television crew fled out the door.

"It is now your move President Sanders." With professional bursts from her Scorpion pistol she destroyed the television cameras. Televisions went blank all over the world.

~ ~ ~ ~

Cheyenne Mountain

President Sanders and those with him stared at their oversized screen. Inwardly Sanders filled with joy. Finally, the Presidency was his and his alone courtesy of a fanatic swept away by dreams of religious glory. Ignoring her message of national death, he addressed the collected group, "I will never rest until these three killers face justice. She has killed President Reston. We must go forward based on that fact. How tight is Marine security around the White House?"

The FBI Director looked at his laptop and answered with assurance, "There's no chance of the terrorists escaping the White House. Marines stand shoulder to shoulder forming a 250-yard radius around the building. Over three hundred members of the Secret Service stand behind that Marine line. Nobody is left alive in the White House but the three terrorists. Your options are open."

"How long would we have to wait for Delta Force to be in position?" asked the newly installed President?

Again, the FBI Director answered, "Delta Force will be in position in twenty-five minutes or less. If you give the order they'll assault the White House using two hundred men. Our medical experts don't believe the terrorists will make any effort to escape. They are unanimous in predicting that the three killers will remain in the Oval Office. They seek martyrdom, not escape."

"That makes sense," said President Sanders, "I believe it wise to wait for the Delta Team to be in place. They're trained for this type of job. Hopefully no more American lives need be lost."

The President then turned to his political aides. "Inform the television networks that I will address the nation in twenty-five minutes to reassure everyone that there is no virus and that the American people have nothing to fear. That time schedule will also allow me to tell our nation that Special Delta Force will be assaulting the White House if the terrorists do not surrender."

The President then addressed the Director of the CIA. "Contact all our international friends and assure them that the mad claims of the terrorists are not true. Be sure to tell them that the power of the Presidency has passed smoothly according to the laws of our Constitution." *Yes, things were going very smoothly* President Sanders thought to himself. He felt he had assumed the reins of power with the right balance of firmness and decisiveness. The only problem was that he still felt ill. Worse, in fact. Bad timing.

President Sanders turned to the FBI Director. "I want a report as soon as possible from all major hospitals in the 300 largest cities of the United States. With that report we will be on solid ground so far as the claims of that insane woman. I want to know whether there have been any unusual health trends in the last few days. It's essential that we prevent the public from panicking and flooding our health centers with unfounded fears."

In like manner the new President issued several dozen directives to the political machinery of the United States. All the directives were logical, addressing all likely contingencies of the situation. All except one: that the Arab woman was telling the truth...

~ ~ ~

Oval Office

A'isha said, "We must be calm. We have thirty minutes to prepare for the attack. We must sell our lives dearly." Everyone knew what to do. First, Allison turned on a battery-operated radio. The radio broadcast news of the attack on every station.

Then Allison placed the Claymore mines and carefully connected them to manual detonators. Four mines were placed in the main hallway to the Oval Office. These were placed so that two mines could respond to an attack from either direction. One mine was placed in the secret Lovers' Lane hallway.

Ellis was pushing buttons on his programmed remote control. The first button when pushed caused a sound like rain in the hallway.

A'isha opened the doors and she saw that the anti-fire system was spraying liquid from the ceiling. She smiled at Ellis and said, "You are a genius Mr. Proctor."

The sprinkler system was now filling every hallway in the White House. However, it wasn't spraying water. The entire 10,000-gallon tank was discharging heating oil.

The flammable liquid covered the floors, walls, and ceiling with an even spray. Nearly 1000 yards of White House hallways were being coated with a thin covering of oil. The long hallways were perfect for fire. Once lit the flames would spread everywhere. Heating oil burns hot for a long time. Ellis had modified the fire system by draining all its water down a main drain in the basement.

He then filled the tank with heating oil, a simple job he completed without a hitch. The heating oil also converted part of its mass into fumes. The spinning suppresser heads transformed some oil into vapor.

Ellis figured that 5% of the oil would convert to vapor. That 5% would ignite like a bomb and the entire White House would show the effects. Every door and window would be destroyed by the explosion. The now open doors and windows would provide oxygen to the flames creating a massive updraft. The White House would be an inferno. Nothing would save it from becoming a charred shell. The heat would be so intense that even the stones would crack from the elevated temperature.

A'isha helped Ellis carry a ladder he'd placed in the hidden hallway several weeks ago. The twelve-foot ladder would allow Ellis to shoot down on the assault team as they entered the room. None of the assault team would be looking up.

CHAPTER FORTY-ONE

Allison would be shooting from left to right and A'isha would be shooting toward the open doors. In that manner each had their own field of fire and would not endanger each other. She was to push the detonators either upon A'isha's command or when the doors swung open. Oil already seeped in the room from the hallways. A'isha watched as oil slowly mixed with the blood of the dead.

Her reverie was interrupted when Allison called her attention to the radio. The voice from the radio was the newly empowered Thomas Sanders now President of the United States. His voice was the perfect mixture of command and humanity, "I am asking you to surrender. You will get a fair hearing in our legal system.

"We know your background and it is possible that the courts will take those factors into account. Join me in ending the killing. I am now going to call you on the red line. Will you answer me?"

In moments, the red phone on the large desk rang. A'isha calmly picked up the telephone and said "I am A'isha. We have little to talk about."

The new President paused for effect, and then said, "You don't have a chance. Either you surrender or I will immediately send in a

200-man assault team to eliminate you. You can trust me to treat you fairly."

A'isha calmly answered "I trust only Allah. Remember you only have three days to live, I hope that you enjoy them. Please send your best troops. I will enjoy killing them." With those words she hung up and cut the phone line.

Enraged, the new President turned to the stocky commander of Delta Force. He gave one command: "Attack immediately." The commander of Delta Force responded with an eager demeanor, "It will only take about 50 men less than 15 minutes to finish this operation."

President Sanders, white with fury over this mad Arab woman, said, "No, I want your entire force to assault en mass. I want her dead."

"Yes Sir, she will be dead and soon."

The Delta Force commander gave the command by radio and the full assault began. Dozens of men landed on the White House roof by helicopter. Many of those rappelled down to the separate floors to enter through windows. Dozens of others swarmed through the doorways on the ground floor. The trained men were familiar with the White House layout. They went room to room systematically making sure not to bypass the terrorists. All doors were left open to indicate which rooms had been cleared.

All the men became aware of the slick floors and a sweet smell growing stronger. However, their orders were to attack, and combatants are reduced to finding and killing. From every direction these trained professionals converged on the Oval Office where they expected to find the terrorists.

~ ~ ~

A'isha calmed her colleagues. "They are coming from many directions. Be at peace for Allah fights with you. This is the hour we prayed for. The infidels have sent 200 troops to fight us. Allah will kill them all."

A'isha hurried over to Jackson and helped him lie on the floor. Jackson was so ill he could barely make out her features. She spoke to him softly, "The minute of decision is now. Death is in this building and none of us will escape her embrace. Be with me in paradise."

Jackson could see her beauty and her certainty. He could hardly talk but finally the words came, "You are evil beyond words. I want nothing from you." He saw her eyes darken. He never felt the burst of bullets that tore his chest apart.

~ ~ ~

Then she heard the quick voice of Ellis, "I hear them coming in the hallway, many arriving from both directions."

In an instant A'isha returned with the mien of a goddess of war. "Allison, hit the first two detonators." Allison pressed the small levers. The following explosion was like the hammer of God. Several dozen fighting men died.

The oil did not ignite.

A'isha moved about eight feet to the right of the dead President and took cover behind a small end table. A'isha told Allison to get ready to fire the mine on the dead President's back. In that second six or eight men burst into the room.

Allison hit the detonator. The Claymore mine tore the attackers and the dead president to bits. More men were running toward the oval office from both ways on the main corridor.

A'isha calmly walked to Allison and said, "Fire when I tell you." The fire command came when the Delta Team members were within 20 feet of the door.

Again, the explosion in the narrow hallway was horrendous. A great many of their enemies were lost, but A'isha and her team members were down to one mine. A'isha placed it fifteen feet from the main door of the Oval Office. At that range, the spread of lethal pellets would be narrow.

Things were happening fast. More men were coming. She could hear their curses as they leaped over the bodies of men they'd known and trained with for years.

At least a dozen men burst through the doors and the last mine turned their bodies into shattered meat and bone. In seconds another six came in on full automatic. Ellis poured fire down upon the attackers. The rage of battle consumed him, and he shouted as he fired, "I am Mr. Proctor, you infidel bastards." The men fell before him as if they were cut down by an invisible sword.

However, one of the falling men emptied his clip at the elevated man and A'isha saw the bullets cut a diagonal line of red splotches across Ellis's chest. A'isha killed the shooter, but it was too late for Ellis who fell dead. A'isha grabbed the Scorpion pistol and reloaded it. She handed it to Allison and said, "All you must do is point and pull the trigger. Slow them down for a few seconds and I'll light the fire."

Allison ran out into the hallway and began to pour dozens of rounds in both directions. A'isha lit the oil-soaked carpet and flames exploded. A'isha saw Allison stagger as bullets struck her. She was still firing from the midst of the flames when she fell.

~ ~ ~

Allison had bought the precious seconds that enabled the fire to be lit. The open flame ignited the oil vapor, and the ensuing explosion rocked the White House on its foundation. A'isha was thrown nearly 15 feet by the pressure wave. The attacking Delta Force was consumed in seconds.

There was no escape. The wall of flames covered every hallway and the blast burst every window. The doors that were left open to every room added to the inferno.

The White House burst into unstoppable flames. President Sanders was horrified at what was happening. The White House had become a ball of fire. He could hear the screams of Delta Forces dying in it.

He turned to the Army Commander and told him to place a tank shot directly into the Oval Office. He did not want to take any chance that the Arab bitch might escape.

A'isha lay on the floor trying to breathe. Down to the last clip on her Scorpion, she was weighing her options when the thick Oval Office windows exploded into glass shards. The tank round over-penetrated and exploded 30 yards deeper into the ruined building.

A'isha had been struck unconscious for a few moments. As conscious thought returned, she felt once again as she had in the Iraqi bomb shelter where she'd lost her family. She thought, *"How strange that at the end of my life I would again be surrounded by dust and darkness."*

She shook the haze from her mind and realized where she was. The fire had grown into an inferno. Her peasant clothes clung heavy with oil and blood. She felt amazed she hadn't caught on fire. There were no soldiers to fight. All in the building were dead. No other would venture into the walls of flames.

A'isha saw that nothing remained of the heavy Oval Office windows. She could easily walk through the shattered glass and double doors onto the balcony. The main doorway of the Oval Office was blocked with bodies of Delta Force. Blood, bodies, and body parts were littered like burned and broken dolls.

A'isha glanced down at the floor and saw a large puddle of oil that was not on fire. She smiled, realizing what must be done. She stripped herself of her peasant garb, then took her clothes and soaked all of it in the pool of unlit oil. She slipped the peasant garb back on. She could feel the slick oil as her clothes clung to her.

The heat in the Oval Office became unbearable. The White House was an infernal.

A'isha knew the time had come for her to go home, home to her loved ones, and home to Allah. She had done her duty to her god. She placed her Scorpion, now useless on the floor.

A'isha walked toward the shattered doors and windows leading to the balcony. She stepped out and looked at the ring of advanced armaments that had failed to prevent the revenge of Allah.

She heard soldiers shouting as they saw her. She stood silhouetted with the fiery White House as her backdrop. With her dark clothes and the flames behind her she appeared as an angel of death. She could see the dozens of military personnel in a circle around the White House. Before any of them could act she lit her lighter touching the flame to her oil-soaked clothes.

~ ~ ~

She stood firmly with her braced legs apart and her head held high in the faces of the enemy. Her knife was held over her head with both hands. The tip of the blade pointed toward the heavens.

A'isha stood, a statue of living flame. The flames ran over her body and up the blade of her knife. From every direction bullets reached out for her. Dozens of rounds hit her as she staggered to stay erect. Then she swayed and slowly fell to the earth.

A'isha was gone. The White House was destroyed. The enormous heat consumed all that could burn and shattered all that could not.

~ ~ ~

Post Action Day One

Belview Hospital

Dr. Obermeyer had watched the entire drama unfolding at the White House from his hospital bed. A patient of the hospital where he'd worked as a doctor for so many years, he watched as the strange woman met her death on that balcony. He knew instinctively that the Arab girl's words were correct. A deadly virus had been released in the United States and he realized he would be among the first to die.

Hundreds of patients had been admitted that day. Over a third of the hospital staff were patients or missing. He had been coughing blood and passing it from his bowels. He closed his eyes to try and resist the dizziness he was enduring. His intellectual side was trying to remember what the symptoms of Ebola really were.

He felt the bed sheeting getting wet and warm. He knew he was bleeding to death. When the floor nurse came in to check on her old friend Dr. Obermeyer she found him dead. She realized she would follow his path in a few days.

Post Action Day One

Camp David

President Sanders

President Sanders sat behind his desk within his circle of advisors. Although extremely ill, he tried to fulfill his duties.

He first turned to the FBI Director, "What do you have for me in the way of hospital trends? Are we facing a major epidemic?" The FBI Director was sick and getting sicker by the minute.

He resisted his nausea and addressed the President. "People are pouring into every hospital by the tens of thousands from the east coast to the west coast. Every hospital is being swamped by the number of people who are seeking help. It looks very bad. Medical professionals are also succumbing by the hundreds. It appears that the terrorist told the truth about the virus "Flash Fire."

"That damned bitch," responded the President. "Do we have any idea as to where she came from? We will respond in force." The head of the CIA took that question; "As before, we do not have any specific idea where she was from. It's certain to be the Middle East. Most of our language experts feel she's from Baghdad because of a faint local accent on her English.

The President turned to the Director of the CIA and asked, "What has been the response of other countries on this issue?"

The CIA director had to recover from a coughing bout before he could speak. Everyone tried not to notice the blood on his handkerchief when he finally gained control.

CHAPTER FORTY-TWO

"Every country, including Canada and Mexico, have closed their borders."

President Sanders felt such fatigue he could only follow the conversation with difficulty. However, he was the President and the country needed strong leadership. He began talking, "It appears that we do not know enough about this terrorist group even to retaliate."

The CIA Director again fielded that complaint. "At present we don't know where this A'isha came from." He continued, "She must be from the hard-core Middle East. I would say Iraq or Iran. I feel Saddam's hand behind this. We could learn the answers to such vital questions if we had time. I doubt if we do. The terrorists themselves are dead and many sought after answers died with them."

"All too true," muttered President Sanders, He gave the directive that all National Guard units were to be activated for citizen protection and essential services. The leader of the Joint Chiefs of Staff accepted that responsibility. War powers had been given the president by unanimous vote of surviving members of congress.

The President pondered. Specialization of American trades reduced the ability for any group to survive alone. Few people were self-sufficient. The farmer needed fuel, seed, pesticides, and fertilizer to grow a crop. These elements came from distant specialized factories.

If crops could be grown it would take a big, complex social system to deliver foodstuffs to the cities. Once in the city it took a vast amount of organization to get the food to every neighborhood. How would anyone price food when food was priceless?

The poor would plunder the rich immediately. President Sanders asked the FBI Director, "How well is Law Enforcement holding out in the cities?'

The FBI Director responded quickly, "It appears that the enforcement arm of the Law is operating at a third of its normal agency power. They need fuel and supplies to operate. Nearly another third of the officers are dead and up to a third have failed to show up for duty."

"They may be so ill that they can't function. America is collapsing fast."

President Sanders took that information in without a word. What did the killer say? She said I had three days to live and today was day one after the holocaust. He was unsure how much longer he could perform his duties. With the social fiber torn asunder how long could any of them last?

The President asked the group, "What type of assistance can we expect from our treaty allies?" The Head of the Joint Chiefs of Staff replied, "We can expect no help from our allies. They refuse to sacrifice their medical professionals for any price."

The FBI Director added, "I have people manning the phones 24 hours per day, but communication operators are dying off fast. We've lost phone contact with over 40% of our hospitals as of this moment. Their key employees are dead or have chosen to die at home with their families. I have never seen, read, or heard of such a disaster."

"Okay, I get the picture," said the President. He turned to his aides and told them to broadcast by radio, internet, and television to the nation the need to isolate themselves from infected people. "It's critical that we save as many people as we can. Our goal is to save a percentage of citizens who can defend and rebuild the nation."

"Everyone stays in this compound and keeps monitoring the situation by telephone and radio. I will speak to citizens by national television and tell the people of our efforts to save as many Americans as possible. Everyone is to gather here tomorrow for another meeting at the same time as today." With those words each person left to perform assigned duties. President Sanders felt his own life fading by the minute.

Post Action Day Two

Camp David

President Sanders

President Sanders presided from his hospital bed. He no longer felt strong enough to sit in a chair. He could not help noting some missing faces. The President asked the group about those absent. The Head of the FBI was missing, and three political aides were gone, "Where have our usual members gone?"

The Director of the CIA spoke up "The FBI Director died last night. He's been replaced by one of his junior officers."

"I see" said the President quietly, "Give me the update on the national situation."

A young FBI officer took the question. "We've lost over 60% of our mass communication across the board. Apparently, systems have either broken down and cannot be repaired or the personnel that ran the systems are gone." The President looked at the young agent intently, "gone" as in dead or dying?"

"That is correct, Mr. President. We can only assume that the people who keep the systems running are either dead or dying."

The President took that in. He turned to his old friend the Director of the CIA, "Can you give me any idea as to the death rate occurring here in the United States?"

The CIA Director had a brief coughing bout before he could answer. "It appears that people are dying by tens of millions. People no longer seek help at hospitals. Medical professionals are also dead or dying. It appears that people are doing their best to stay with their loved ones. Many sick people seem to be walking the streets of their old neighborhoods or working areas. Apparently they simply want to be outdoors as much as possible."

"Tens of thousands are dying on the sidewalks and streets from massive hemorrhaging. A massive hemorrhage from any of the body orifices seems to be the main cause of death. Our projections indicate that 200 million people will die within the next twenty-four hours."

"Surprisingly, the crime rate is low. People have lost interest in material things."

The President seemed to shrink into his bed as he replied, "Am I to understand you correctly that 200 million of our citizens are to die today?"

"Unfortunately, that appears to be a conservative estimate. The number could be higher."

"How has our military fared in maintaining order and manning critical facilities?" asked the President. "Communication with most military forces has been good. We also have communication with our sealed missile sites and our ships at sea. Civilian communication systems are more delicate and need constant maintenance."

"As per your orders the United States is under Martial Law. All state and federal workers are to report to duty until death. All normal citizens have been ordered to stay at home and to resist with deadly force any party seeking to enter their lawful homes. All citizens have the right to defend themselves without fear of prosecution."

"Thank you," said the President, "under these circumstances all these acts are necessary."

The President never dreamed of a burden of leadership so heavy. His quest for power seemed so empty now. He turned to his gathered group and asked, "Is there anything else that we in this room can do for our country?" Silence hung in the air like a damp layer of darkness.

The President noted the silence and said, "Keep working our communication lines. Keep me abreast of what's happening. Gather tomorrow at the same time. May God have mercy on us."

Post Action Day Three

Camp David

President Sanders looked out the window from his hospital bed. *Where are the birds?"* he thought. There was no sign of life outside. The simple signs of life that each human takes for granted were gone. His life had been consumed by an obsession for political power and now it seemed such a futile race.

He expected that today would be his last. It didn't seem possible that the great freedom loving nation of the United States was being destroyed without a shot fired. Who could have imagined that the vast military machine of which he was Commander in Chief meant nothing against a murderous virus that killed so quickly? Over 250 million Americans were already dead.

He glanced at the wall clock. Now it was time for the cabinet meeting. He heard their footsteps now. He was struck by the small number left before him of this group. He would be advised by only eight people out of twenty. His oldest friend the Director of the CIA still lived.

The rest were young, probably in their twenties. The President addressed this small somber group, "Are the rest dead?"

A young man with blonde hair answered, "Yes, Mr. President. The rest have died. All of them died quickly once the massive hemorrhages bore down. Some died through nose bleeds, others from their mouth due to lung and stomach bleeds. Most died of rectal bleeding. Once they started to bleed there was nothing to stop it."

"I see." President Sanders rubbed his eyes. "They were all good people. The world will miss them and their service. Do we have any outside communication with our cities, our military, or the law enforcement agencies?"

The same young blonde-haired man answered, "We have communication with most cities. Many of these voices are home shortwave amateurs who are doing what they can."

"Communication with our military forces is good. Military discipline in our armed forces is outstanding. State and local governments are still holding against chaos. Thousands of brave men and women are dying at their posts. In the beginning we had tens of thousands of contacts. The numbers have since dropped to less than a thousand connections. One by one the voices at the end of the line go dead. Some have merely said they are bleeding. Then the line goes silent."

The President addressed this small group of survivors, "You have done well. I appreciate your dedication. Your duties are at an end. I suggest you return to your families. I will know what our next step is within the hour."

The President asked the Director of the CIA to stay with him. The young men looked at the pale, ravaged man in the hospital bed. How hard to believe this was the same energetic man who took the reins of power so smoothly after the terrorist attack. His family had died that morning.

The President turned to his CIA director and said:

"The enormity of this attack is hard to take in. Please fill me in on Operation Salvation? Our former president was not able to give me the details before he died. He never really trusted me. I deeply regret my former ambitions."

"I am sure President Reston would have understood. He was ambitious as well."

"Operation Salvation was established during World War II to deal with ultimate disaster for the United States. Ten secret bases were set up in underground caves in remote mountain areas. Each base is totally isolated and can support a thousand experts of essential fields with food, water, and weapons to survive for six years. The plan has been updated annually to reflect current dangers. As the nuclear threat increased the underground bases were hardened and sheltered from radiation."

"Life will be hard in the underground communities, but they will survive. They can emerge when it's possible to sustain life in the United States. Although there were several dire contingencies the greatest threat was deemed to be militant Islam."

CHAPTER FORTY-THREE

"Pursuant to presidential orders all designated men and women were flown to their retreats. They were to remain there until ordered to return to their homes and civilian lives. The order came into play several weeks ago when one of my agents by the name of Jackson came to me. I recommended to President Reston to give the order without delay. The President agreed. It seems he'd been having fears also."

"These people are isolated and not exposed to the disease. They await your instructions."

Thomas struggled against growing weakness. "I always felt superior to President Reston but I now realize I was wrong. He's given us a slim chance to rebuild our civilization. I feel it is time to turn to Operation Cauterize. Thankfully, President Reston felt I needed this information. We have no other choice if Western Civilization is to survive."

The director took a thin folder out of his briefcase. "I was sure this order was coming so I was prepared. It is a terrible thing and I ask you to review it before you make your decision. However, I agree. It must be done."

The President took the folder and read the terse military statements.

Appendix One

Subsection C

Operation Cauterize:

If Muslim forces are successful in destroying the freedom and power of the United States then the following steps will be taken to ensure that Western Civilization will survive.

1. All Muslim cities in the Middle East over one thousand population will be destroyed by nuclear weapons.

2. All known and suspected military bases in the Middle East will be destroyed by nuclear weapons.

3. All centers of energy production in whatever form are to be destroyed with nuclear weapons.

4. All major infrastructures that provide and distribute food stuffs not in targeted cities are to be destroyed by nuclear weapons.

5. All educational facilities in the Middle East are to be destroyed with nuclear weapons.

6. All major military targets in Muslim countries are be destroyed by nuclear weapons.

7. All Islamic mosques are to be destroyed by nuclear weapons.

8. All State and Federal offices will be notified of this order immediately after military attacks have begun.

9.   Western nations are to be informed of our actions as close to the impact time as possible. All major powers are to be warned that the United States retains enough nuclear weapons to eliminate any nation that attempts to attack the remnants of the United States of America.

The purpose of these operations is to destroy the ability of Muslim countries to challenge Western Civilization for many decades if not centuries. The reason for this action is:

A.   To avenge the murder of the United States.

B.   To allow time for the United States to rise from its ashes and again take its proper place among the world powers.

I call upon all military forces and government agencies of the United States of America to remember your duty and your families.

Signed

The President of the United States

Commander in Chief of the United States Military Forces.

The President handed the document to his friend. "So, the madness of religion has brought us to this. We have been destroyed by zealots who believe they obeyed God's will. The extremists want a government where people cannot give a dissenting thought or opinion without fear of decapitation. They want a Muslim world of extortion and the loss of rights for women. Hard to imagine anyone would follow these delusions in the 21st century."

"Yes, of course, sir. The delusions of an illiterate tribal murderer have reappeared to reverse the centuries of gains of secular knowledge.

Muhammad was a killer and a thief from the beginning. I have always detested him and all he stood for."

Although weak the President replied in a hoarse tone, "Well, we are mortally wounded but we cannot let the world be ruled by extremist powers. We cannot let enlightenment be replaced by theocracy."

"This brutal attack must be answered. No matter what the price we cannot take this blow knowing our enemies are rejoicing. Hand me the phone, please."

The next fifteen minutes changed the entire world. The proper codes were exchanged, and all formalities completed. The awesome military power of the United States strained at the leash in its yearning to attack.

One final cycle of commands was given to be sure that all sites would fire simultaneously. Then the dying United States President began to bleed from his ear just before giving the command to fire. In six seconds, missiles lifted from hundreds of United States sites. In eighteen seconds, missiles began lifting from several dozen surface ships. Nuclear armed submarines were held in reserve. Every crew fired.

All world powers were instantly given the details of the mission and the reasons for this destruction. The other nations were warned that America had large nuclear reserves that would be fired at any country who attempted to step in or retaliate. Not one moved against the United States.

In less than forty minutes over five thousand nuclear warheads struck across the Middle East. The number of dead will never be known. Certainly, the number of victims in the Middle East alone was tens of millions. As in America the innocent died alongside the guilty. Literally nothing remained of the Muslim countries.

All means of life and production were destroyed. Radiation blanketed the entire Middle East and killed with horrible efficiently. Deadly levels of radiation spread rapidly on the wind currents and jet streams of the earth. No living person could project the world deaths due to radiation from these impacts. Over the course of three years, it was possible that the death toll would be in the billions. Militant Islam had pushed the world over the edge of the cliff.

A'isha had not realized that freedom is an idea that needs no gods. She failed to understand that the United States was full of men and women who would die for their freedoms of action and belief. A'isha did not realize that nonbelievers can also be courageous. She knew nothing about the history of freedom. She knew nothing of political and religious tolerance.

She knew nothing about a world where men and women are allowed to choose their own paths and follow their own dreams. She knew nothing about the Western World where people can choose their own religious beliefs or reject all religion without personal fear.

A'isha's mythical desert god is a primitive myth from a distant time of ignorance and illiteracy. The Koran was a creation of an illiterate madman who heard delusional voices from a so-called angel within the depths of a cave.

Dr. Showkit and Najib were vaporized in Baghdad. Yazid the genius scientist and Saddam the Iraq president died agonizing deaths from intense gamma nuclear radiation. Zeynat the patient teacher of death met her end in a Baghdad suburb. Her beautiful body was burned beyond recognition from nuclear fireballs. Islam did not inherit the world but suffered its own destruction. Allah did not save the Muslim world.

In turn, the biological attack against the United States was totally successful. Nearly 310 million Americans died. Approximately 15 million Americans survived the initial strike. Most survivors were rural residents and people from small towns.

Approximately ten thousand professional elites lived thanks to the meeting between Jackson and his CIA Director. The CIA director in turn advised the President to implement Operation Salvation.

President Reston saw no reason not to follow this wise precaution. Due to "Operation Salvation" a vital remnant remained. This isolation of key human resources saved the United States. Their expertise would be used to educate tens of thousands of survivors. The infrastructure of the United States was still usable.

Teachers at all levels, medical professionals, engineers, computer experts, and scientists survived. These priceless educated citizens would rebuild a decimated nation. It would take decades or centuries for America to recover the nearly irreplaceable losses.

In addition, due to wise precautions by the United States Government nearly all known knowledge of human past and present around the world were stored on gold plated disks. This stored information was available to all who survived. Thankfully, American libraries public and private would be intact ready to reclaim when it was safe.

These were resources beyond price. The fate of the destroyed library of bereft ancient Alexandria would not be repeated. Thanks to Jackson the United States would rebuild.

The source of A'isha's powers and her religious certitude is not known. The source of her communications is also unknown. Religion has many mysteries that science has never solved or understood. Clearly the promises that A'isha received went un- fulfilled. Religion has the power to inflame believers to violence. It has always been so. Islam of the present-day floats upon a rising sea of blood. Allah did not save the world's Muslims either individually or collectively.

United States Capitol Building

Death knew these things as well. She arrived on the crest of a cool wind and gently settled in the silent corridors of the United States government. She noted that many of the bodies had been people of power in this place. Death smiled as she noted that power is only an illusion. Only Death is certain.

History has repeatedly shown that the step from an advanced civilization to a primitive one can be short. Death walked slowly down the hall to the Senate Chamber. She gazed at her surroundings. Decisions that affected millions of the world's citizens had been made in this building.

She smiled: Soon the beasts and birds that feed on flesh would be contesting for flesh of men and women who thought they were too important to die. How disheveled they looked with their limbs askew, and their expensive suits soaked in their own blood.

Did these people of power realize that an industrial nation is a fragile thing? Flash Fire put an end to the finely tuned interworking of the complex machine of human interaction.

Each component of the system broke down causing a thousand failures further down the line. Those interconnections were not a minor thing. Human survival depended on them.

Death continued until she reached the Capitol steps. Her black robe stood out in splendor against the white marble of the massive building. Death let her gaze sweep across the grounds to the distant horizon.

The dead lay everywhere.

~   ~   ~

Her eyes had seen many battlefields with limbs severed, stomachs ripped open, and skulls shattered. She had witnessed the cleaved skulls, the torn flesh and burned bodies. In her eons of existence there were few surprises left. However, this harvest surpassed them all. As she cast her vision across the entire nation there were dead bodies spread before her beyond count; all lying in pools of their blood.

Yet death pondered.

CHAPTER FORTY-FOUR

A solid remnant of Americans still lived. Perhaps ten million still lived to hope for better days. This was a powerful land. Dying men and women had struck back. A'isha had been mistaken.

Blinded by religious fire she failed to see that freedom does not die easily. The wounded eagle could still strike. The final blow from the United States had been crushing.

Death remembered the harvest of death that she had collected in the bomb shelter in Baghdad where she had first noticed A'isha. Death had been right about the young girl. Never had Death witnessed such hate in a mortal. A'isha had matured to become the most prolific killer that the world had ever known. This Muslim girl had created a vast bounty of bodies.

Yet A'isha failed. She overlooked that a wounded country is not a dead country. The wounded often take their murderers with them.

Death cast her eyes across the modern lands of Islam. A'isha knew nothing of the centuries of conflict between the East and the West. A'isha knew nothing about the battle of Tours which was a massive Muslim defeat where the West stopped the spread of Islam in Europe and saved Western Civilization. Death had walked across those battlefields of the ancient past. Both sides believed that they were fighting for God.

Death smiled. As if deities could not fight their own battles. As if any God needed the help of mortals to command an endless cosmos. She smiled. Yet this latest clash was horrific. There was movement. Death walked slowly through all the modern cities of Islam. There was no sign of life. The very stones were still smoking. The heat must have been intense beyond imagination.

She smiled as she realized how much of life ultimately ended in dust, ashes, and smoke. Death looked upon the remains of these modern cities built upon lands of great antiquity. How they loved their killer prophet! How they adored their violent god. How the men had dreamed of endless sensual pleasures in paradise. How they yearned for their imagined virgins.

She smiled. Dead men do not make love. Invented gods cannot save anyone. A'isha would be remembered for a long time. Would they remember the harvest of her hate, or would they remember the nightmare of the counterattack?

Death pondered on humanity's follies. From the beginning people invented gods to evade the certainty of death and constant human fears. In the ruthless struggle for life humans tried to gain advantage from a deity. Did people not realize that each culture had its own deity? Surely they knew that each deity reflected their fears, their hopes, and their own environment.

Where life was easy the gods tended to be gentle and sexual. Where life was a deadly struggle to exist the gods were violent, cruel, and selective. The monotheistic desert god is a rampant killer of his own creations.

Death had seen a great deal of change in the eons of her time. In the beginning man could only inflict harm for the length of his arm. Now men and women could send unthinkable destruction to any part of the world.

Humans could not survive with their imagined religions led by murdering gods. Did believers imagine they could walk through the gates of heaven with blood dripping from their hands? Couldn't believers realize there is no paradise? Paradise was a dream, a seducing dream, a monument to the human imagination.

Death cast her vision to the rubble of Baghdad. So much had started here. The dark figure of death watched the full moon rise over the ancient lands. The moon was a brilliant white as if it had been created anew and never shone before. Death smiled. The beauty of this moon reminded her that she had a great deal to do. There was an answering shimmer of moonlight and Death took her leave.

THE END

AUTHOR'S NOTES

BIOLOGICAL WARFARE

Explosion based warfare is obsolete; the competition for bigger bombs and faster planes is finished. The idea of battalions, regiments, and divisions has become as obsolete as lords and knights in the feudal system. Tanks, fighter jets, and conventional weapons have no value on a biological battlefield. No amount of armor can stop pathogens. Specially trained troops are helpless and will have no value.

The new enemy is invisible. Its toxic pathogens drift on gentle breezes. Deadly spores can drift for dozens of miles onto humans, livestock, and bodies of water. Where the pathogens meet human life there will be death. Infection will be in the food, water, air, and touch. Human mortality will follow in the hundreds of millions.

A military paradigm has shifted. Ships at sea will cruise through unseen pathogen clouds. Their crews will die. Aircraft carriers worth hundreds of millions of dollars will become floating cemeteries drifting aimlessly across the oceans.

High technology ship defense systems will never fire a shot. All the billions of dollars that are spent on explosion-based weapon systems will not be worth one American dollar.

Biological weapons are a new paradigm, but few can face this reality. The defeated countries factories, cities, and infrastructure will not be destroyed if properly attacked. In time the winning country can inherit the enemy's country intact.

Gene editing changes everything. Technologies such as CRISPR point the way to the future. The creator of this new life has nearly endless permeations of his/her creation. There will not be time to discover a vaccine or a cure. Once reaching perfection, bio-weapons will be the dominant weapon of future wars.

Currently the large powers base their ultimate politics on possession of nuclear weapons. Against nuclear weapons, mass gatherings of conventional troops cannot survive. The superpowers have a nuclear monopoly. Third world countries cannot sit at the same table with the superpowers. Smaller countries deeply resent this reality. Therefore, many small countries are turning to biological weapons. Biological weapons are the poor man's equivalent of nuclear weapons. They are cheap and easy to produce.

As noted in this novel the machinery for making biological weapons is readily available. Anyone who can make vaccines can use the same equipment to make biological weapons. The knowledge to make biological weapons is already held by tens of thousands of college science graduates. The vast resources of the Internet make such knowledge available to nearly anyone. Biological weapons do not need methods of expensive delivery. The world's civilian transportation system is perfect. Even one individual can produce a biological weapon. Edited virus will be a new creation and it will easily kill in the millions. Through bio-weapons a third world country's war chest will be enough to break the chains of the superpowers. Sadly, it is only a matter of time until the United States becomes a bio-victim. The future is known, and its name is death.